Here, for the first time, are the heroes of Star Trek, living their legend again in new stories, never seen on the screen, never published in a book.

STAR TREK: THE NEW VOYAGES

The Winged Dreamers: Shore leave turns to mutiny in a sylvan paradise.

The Enchanted Pool: Spock gazes into the magic waters and sees an exquisite wood nymph—his true love.

Mind-Sifter: Victim of the Klingons, Kirk lands in the twentieth century, his mind destroyed.

Visit to a Weird Planet Revisited: A multi-parallel space-time inversion transports the actors onto the real Enterprise—far in the future.

AND MORE!

STAR TREK:
THE NEW VOYAGES

Edited by
Sondra Marshak and Myrna Culbreath

RL 7, IL 5-up

STAR TREK: THE NEW VOYAGES

A Bantam Book | March 1976

2nd printing .... March 1976	5th printing .... November 1976
3rd printing .... April 1976	6th printing .... April 1977
4th printing .... June 1976	7th printing .... December 1977
8th printing .... February 1979			

*The story "Visit to a Weird Planet Revisited" was originally
published in Spockanalia #5, and is copyright © 1970 by
Devra Michele Langsam, Sherna C. Burley and Deborah Michel
Langsam. The cooperation of the editors of Spockanalia is
gratefully acknowledged.*

ISBN 0-553-12753-5

Published simultaneously in the United States and Canada

PRINTED IN THE UNITED STATES OF AMERICA

For Sondra's mother, Mrs. Anna Tornheim Hassan—"Mama" to us both now, and "Mama" wherever *Star Trek*'s Camelot convenes.

And for Alan Marshak, royalty with a touch of Merlin thrown in, without whose magic and magnanimity our voyages wouldn't have been possible.

Contents

...t before McCoy could react, Kirk broke in.

"Dr. McCoy, I firmly believe this is none of your job."

"Now, just a moment—" an... looked from one to other, and Kirk realized in dismay that between him he and Spock had quite effectively roused the

Foreword

Those of us who were involved in making *Star Trek* are proud of our creation. There are things we might have done differently, and certainly there are things we might have done better, but we tried always to make it the very best we could under the circumstances of the television system, budget, time, fatigue, personal talent, and other restrictions facing us.

Star Trek was not a one-man job, although it was something that was very personal to me—my own statement of who and what this species of ours really is, where we are now, and something of where we may be going. I have always been particularly grateful that *Star Trek* became an equally personal and meaningful thing to so many others. This includes those who made their own invaluable contributions to the show—from the stars and episode writers and production staff to the technicians and crew of the set. It was bone-crushing, exhausting work that often drained every drop of creative juice and plain stamina we had. And we wouldn't have missed it for the world.

There was a kind of magic on the set in those days. The *Enterprise,* its crew, and its universe became very real to us; it became our own affirmation that the human adventure is far from over and, in fact, may be only in its beginnings.

Certainly the loveliest happening of all for us was the fact that so many others began to feel the same way. Television viewers by the millions began to take *Star Trek* to heart as their own personal optimistic view of the human condition and future. They fought for the show, honored it, cherished it, wrote about it—and have continued to do their level best to make certain that it will live again.

It will.

You know, it was our old joke that, contrary to the opinion of various network executives, we thought that there must be an intelligent life form out there beyond the television tube. But we never expected anything like the outpouring of comments, interest, and affection that occurred.

We were particularly amazed when thousands, then tens of thousands of people began creating their own personal *Star Trek* adventures. Stories, and paintings, and sculptures, and cookbooks. And songs, and poems, and fashions. And more. The list is still growing. It took some time for us to fully understand and appreciate what these people were saying. Eventually we realized that there is no more profound way in which people could express what *Star Trek* has meant to them than by creating their own very personal *Star Trek* things.

Because I am a writer, it was their *Star Trek* stories that especially gratified me. I have seen these writings in dog-eared notebooks of fans who didn't look old enough to spell "cat." I have seen them in meticulously produced fanzines, complete with excellent artwork. Some of it has even been done by professional writers, and much of it has come from those clearly on their way to becoming professional writers. Best of all, all of it was plainly done with love.

It is now a source of great joy for me to see their view of *Star Trek*, their new *Star Trek* stories, reaching professional publication here. I want to thank these writers, congratulate them on their efforts, and wish them good fortune on these and further of their voyages into other times and dimensions. Good writing is always a very personal thing and comes from the writer's deepest self. *Star Trek* was that kind of writing for me, and it moves me profoundly that it has also become so much a part of the inner self of so many other people.

Viewers like this have proved that there is a warm, loving, and intelligent life form out there—and that it may even be the dominant species on this planet.

That is the highest compliment and the greatest repayment that they could give us.

GENE RODDENBERRY

Acknowledgments

Our warmest thanks go to the creators of *Star Trek* —not only for what they say here, but for their generosity in saying it, and—most of all—for *Star Trek*.

Our heartfelt thanks go to a very special friend, Carol Frisbie. Greater love hath no man—or woman—than to type for a friend. And Carol did it in uncounted late-night hours and all-night stands, producing reams of crisp, clean typescript—far more than can finally appear in this volume—meeting deadlines, and remaining cheerful and even sane. Thanks, Carol, beyond measure.

Finally, we must particularly thank all the writers of *Star Trek* fiction—not only the few who are represented here, but also the many who are not. In any one book, the choices suddenly become painfully narrow, and much that we would have liked to include simply is not here, because of such considerations as time, length, variety, and balance. We thank the many writers who sent us published and unpublished manuscripts and hope to remedy many of the omissions in the future— in many future voyages.*

*Manuscripts may be sent to us at Box 14261, Baton Rouge, La. 70808. Please send two copies. Your comments are also welcome and may find their way into future works, although we may not be able to answer them individually.

Introduction:

The Once and Future Voyages

Man's most shining legends of heroes always seem to carry the dream that the heroes will return again. King Arthur will rise—the once and future king. Camelot will live again, and does, at least in the minds of men.

Star Trek was just such a shining legend, for one brief moment, a few brief years—a living legend of heroes and high deeds, of courage, glorious quests, splendid loves found and lost.

It was the most shining legend of all—man's truest legend, seen at last: the legend not of a golden age lost, but of one yet to be found.

A golden age yet to be found, never to be forgotten, always to live again; those who saw *Star Trek* in that way could not let it die . . . and did not.

They were not content to live with the memory.

They wanted to see the legend live again, real and whole, in their own time and for years to come—with new voyages, new quests, new loves, new windows into that golden future yet to be found.

They fought for that.

And they won.

Through the efforts of people who love it, in a real-life saga rivaling any legend of a quest for the Grail, *Star Trek* does live again.

It will live again on the screen.

And it lives here.

These are the new voyages.

Here, for the first time, are the old heroes of *Star*

Trek living their legend again in new stories, never seen on the screen, never published in a book.

For seven lean years there was *no* new *Star Trek* fiction published, with the single exception of the James Blish novel *Spock Must Die*.[1]

Star Trek fiction publication was limited to the adaptations of the aired episodes[2] and later of the animation episodes.[3]

Such was the hunger for *Star Trek* that those tales of the old voyages sold in the millions of copies. But there were no new voyages.

That is, there were none that were available to the general public.

But *Star Trek* fiction, like the show itself, never did die.

It, too, was kept alive by people who loved it. That story is told in *Star Trek Lives!*[4]—which gives some reasons for that love, and undertakes the first serious analysis of the *Star Trek* fiction that was being written in those years.

It can be called "fan fiction." It is that, but it is more than that; it is simply *Star Trek* fiction.

It is fan fiction of the kind that people write for one single, simple reason: they cannot help themselves.

It was not written for money. During all those years, for legal reasons, there was no possibility of publishing *Star Trek* fiction professionally, and it seemed certain that there never would be.

Yet many professional writers and those on the way to becoming professionals wrote it as cheerfully and as passionately as those who had never written anything before, even knowing that it could never be published except in small fan magazines—"fanzines"—put out for and by fans.

That expectation would have been correct, except for another remarkable "first" for the remarkable *Star Trek*.

[1]James Blish, *Spock Must Die*. New York: Bantam Books, 1970.
[2]James Blish, *Star Trek*, Vols. 1–11. New York: Bantam Books, 1967–1975.
[3]Alan Dean Foster, *Star Trek Logs*, Vols. 1–5. New York: Ballantine Books, 1974–1975.
[4]Jacqueline Lichtenberg, Sondra Marshak, and Joan Winston, *Star Trek Lives!* New York: Bantam Books, 1975.

To our knowledge, this is the first time that the fan fiction of anything—any book, any characters, any series—has reached professional publication.

Yet it is *Star Trek*'s peculiar fate to make the impossible seem inevitable.

The quality of much of this fiction was excellent. The hunger for new *Star Trek* was profound. What, really, would make more sense than to let the millions in on the fiction that has so delighted the thousands who were able to track it down in fanzines?

We asked. And we illustrated—showing the quality of the fiction and its range from high drama to high humor.

Fortunately, we were presenting the idea to Frederik Pohl, himself a giant in the creation of science-fiction legends, winner of many Hugo awards, a creative editor, and a delightful man about whom sagas ought to be written. (And we just might try, Fred. You have been lovely to us from the very beginning, and far beyond the call of duty.)

There are editors, and editors. He is in a class by himself. We have learned that a word from him is as good as a bond. Neither *Star Trek Lives!* nor this book would have been possible without his judgment and that word.

Here, then, are a few of the stories that most delighted us. They are hardly even the barest tip of the iceberg of what we have available, but they are a beginning. (Manuscripts may be sent to us at Box 14261, Baton Rouge, Louisiana 70808.)

And they are real *Star Trek*, written with care and love, faithful to the sunlit universe in which the *Enterprise* still flies on these voyages to strange new worlds.

In another impossibility that now seems inevitable (although it must be admitted that the inevitable frequently requires careful arranging), the creators of *Star Trek* have taken this as an opportunity to express their appreciation of the people whose love has kept *Star Trek* alive and made it live again.

The creators have very generously given of their time and thoughts to return some of that love, with thanks.

Here, then, in their introductions to the present stories, you will find the current thoughts of the living men and women who helped to create a living legend —their delight in its return, their hopes for its future, their warm thanks to fans, writers, readers who have given it a future.

Here, also, you will find the creators' thoughts, not only on the legend of *Star Trek* and its future, but on the future of man, of intelligent life on this strange world and others.

That, really, was what *Star Trek* was all about; its once and future voyages ventured into the shining sea of stars, and into the inner reaches of man, where no man has gone before—and where man must go.

In these new voyages we see even more of the outer reaches, and the inner; and heroes who live again, not in some ancient legend, but in a future that may be ours—and in a real, tough universe that is nevertheless sunlit and shining.

Here are not merely bold knights and fair damsels, but flesh-and-blood men and women of courage and achievement, knowing the value of love, and of laughter. They know also tears and terrors, doubts and divisions, frailties and fears, yet they do not bemoan their fate, and they do not merely endure; they prevail.

If *Camelot* and *Man of La Mancha* are legends of glorious quests for the unattainable, then *Star Trek* is our new dream, the *possible* dream—to reach for the reachable stars.

No, we have not forgotten Camelot.

But if this be our new Camelot, even more shining— make the most of it.

SONDRA MARSHAK
MYRNA CULBREATH

Star Trek:
The New Voyages

Introduction to Ní Var

by *Leonard Nimoy*

I am reliably informed that *Ni Var* is a Vulcan term dealing with the dualities of things: two who are one, two diversities that are a unity, two halves that come together to make a whole.

Perhaps that is singularly appropriate.

I have written a book titled *I Am Not Spock*—and, indeed, I am not.

Yet I know that in the minds of millions, in some sense, I am.

Certainly Spock is a part of me, and I of him.

I have spoken elsewhere of how the experience of thinking for Spock has affected my own thinking, and my life.

Nor would Spock have been the same if I had thought for him differently or if it had been someone other than I who gave him form and voice.

We are two who are one, in that sense, and yet still two.

I have my world and my life, and he has his, and somewhere we share something of both.

In another sense, Spock himself is a curious duality, as Claire Gabriel's story graphically illustrates. He stands astride two cultures, two worlds, even two biologies—Vulcan and Human.

He is man divided, as so many of us are divided in one way or another today. And yet he creates a certain unity out of that division. He feels the stress of being pulled in different directions, but he is not torn to his roots, and he turns the tension to creative purpose.

Perhaps for some of us who must live with division, he stands as a symbol of the fact that division need not destroy.

Certainly he seems to stand as a symbol that diversity is, indeed, delightful. In a world where that thought seemed strange and new only a decade ago, where mere color of skin could divide to the point of murder, I was

1

always startled and warmed by the fact that I could walk anywhere wearing the face of an alien from a far place and be greeted only with love.

We could still use more love for different faces from closer to home, but we have made a start.

I would like to think that Spock and the vision of the *Star Trek* world where he had found home and friendship away from home made some contribution to that, and can make more.

The fact that so many people have continued to see that in Spock and in *Star Trek*—and to respond to it so warmly—still touches me.

None of us who have felt that tremendous outpouring of affection, warmth, love, devotion, can be indifferent to it. It is, at times, almost overwhelming.

I am not Spock, and I would not deny a certain— you will pardon the expression—emotion, in return.

Some of those people have told me that their response to Spock and to *Star Trek* is purely "logical."

The Vulcan in Spock would say, "One does not thank logic. But I think that his Human half—and Leonard Nimoy—might be permitted to say: "Thank you."

And I would not be surprised if the Vulcan were saying it, too.

Even a Vulcan would be hard-pressed not to be moved by the fact that there have been people all these years quietly writing letters fighting for the return of *Star Trek*, gathering in thousands and tens of thousands in conventions, reading and watching the old voyages . . . and very quietly writing these new voyages.

It is remarkable to see the depth of feeling and sensitivity of thought that have gone into that writing.

Here is yet another duality—Spock as he was seen, *Star Trek* as it was perceived and reflected to us like a mirror image.

It is a rare gift to be able to see ourselves as others see us; yet the people who have responded to *Star Trek* have even given us that.

And if this is what they see, then perhaps the response is, in fact, "logical."

But it is also a tribute to their own capacity to see, and they cannot be thanked enough for that.

Ní Var

by *Claire Gabriel*

Captain's log, Stardate 6834.5. En route to R & R on Starbase Ten, the Enterprise has been ordered to divert briefly to Fornax II in order to pick up and transport to Starbase Ten a sealed tape. The tape contains a partial record of the genetic research of Albar Exar, a native of Fornax I. Dr. Exar, one of the most renowned geneticists in the galaxy, has voluntarily isolated himself on Fornax II for six standard years. He and his wife, Shona, an Andorian biologist, have lived and worked under a pressurized dome, and their son was born there. Dr. Exar has reported that his work is not complete, but he wishes to have a sealed record tape of the incomplete data stored in the Federation archives for reasons known only to himself, to be opened only at his death. He has also requested that I and First Officer Spock beam down to get the tape, and that no other crew members accompany us.

Albar Exar was almost seven feet tall, with an almost rectangular head set directly on his shoulders. His skin was crimson, and his features prominent and finely chiseled. Jet-black hair fell to his shoulders, and his resemblance to the Native Americans in the history of Kirk's planet was enhanced by his tunic, which was a soft tan material much like buckskin.

Exar's Andorian wife was even more striking in appearance, Kirk thought. Shona was as tall as Kirk, and her antennae gave her an other-earthly aura. Antennae or no, Shona was an extremely attractive woman by any standards, and her Earth-sky-blue skin and silky white hair added to her attractiveness even as they emphasized her alienness. But when Kirk greeted her politely before addressing himself to her husband, she declined to answer, nodded briefly, and favored

3

him and Spock with a faint frown that was neither friendly nor unfriendly, but simply . . . preoccupied?

"Captain. Mr. Spock." Exar had not risen from his chair when they had materialized in what was apparently his living quarters. "Shona, perhaps the gentlemen would like a drink."

Spock seemed interested in surveying the terrain, as usual, so Kirk took it upon himself to answer for both of them. "Thank you very much, Dr. Exar, but I'm expecting a message from Star Fleet Command, and my first officer—"

"Is a Vulcan," Exar said quietly. "But only half Vulcan. Am I correct, Mr. Spock?"

Spock turned, for once obviously surprised. "Affirmative, Doctor. Is it of importance?"

"Of interest," Exar said, and stirred painfully in his chair. Ill, Kirk realized, very ill. "Together with some of your scientific papers, which have contributed to my work on a private research project."

"Indeed?" Spock said, but his attention had suddenly been caught by something outside the window.

"Is that . . . the purpose of the sealed tape?" Kirk asked, drifting toward Spock.

"It is my greatest hope," Exar said softly but fervently, "to be able to complete my research myself."

"I understood, Doctor," Spock said without turning, "that you had only one child."

Kirk could follow Spock's intent gaze into the dome-garden now. And he saw them.

The two children were purplish in hue, each with a rectangular head of silky black hair through which the Andorian antennae protruded. One of them was sitting astride the lowest limb of a tree, examining the bark, his manner more than a little suggestive of the single-minded investigativeness of his father's race. The other was worrying one of his brother's legs, obviously trying to pick a fight, and as single-minded in that pursuit as the other child was in his. The child on the tree limb ignored him. It was as though he were not there.

But in size and appearance, they were absolutely identical.

"We *had* only one child," Exar said from behind them. "Shortly after his birth, severe physiological trauma developed, trauma that was directly caused by his hybrid makeup. I also anticipated . . . problems of personality integration. I had been working for two years to perfect a mechanical means of what might be called 'hybrid twinning' in layman's terms. One of the 'twins' has the internal physiology and the personality of Andorians, the other those of the natives of my planet. This, gentlemen, is the substance of the material on the sealed tape. The research is not complete, but if ill luck should befall me before it is, you can see what importance this discovery of mine will have in Federation genetics. All hybrids are not as healthy as Mr. Spock is, as you know. If I cannot complete the research myself, someone else must go on with it."

"Now, wait a minute," Kirk said softly. "Are you trying to tell me that you've invented a *machine* that can separate a living being into two identical, functional parts that look exactly alike but . . ." And then he stopped.

After a moment Exar asked uneasily, "Captain, are you ill?"

"No." Kirk settled his shoulders. When he had been "twinned" by the Transporter into identical "wolf" and "lamb" . . . "We . . . encountered a similar phenomenon once, on Alfa 177. It was not a pleasant experience."

"Captain . . ."

Spock. Not touching him, and yet it was as though Spock had laid his hand on Kirk's shoulder from behind.

"For anyone," Kirk finished. Turning, he gave his friend what he hoped was a reassuring smile. That was . . . over. "But I suppose this is hardly the same thing." He turned to Exar.

"There are similarities, Mr. Spock. The paper that you published on the effects of Alfacite ore on the matter-energy Transporter was the starting point of my research. I and my sons are deeply indebted to you—on several counts."

Spock now favored the scientist with an expressionless stare that somehow managed to convey that he had no wish to be given credit for any part of Exar's work. But Exar was not to be discouraged.

"You are perhaps unaware, Captain," he continued, "that your first officer is a scientist with a galaxy-wide reputation. The paper under discussion is one of several. A few years ago, no scientist would have believed it possible that a mass converted to pure energy could be duplicated and rematerialized physically intact, in duplicate. Nor would anyone have believed it possible that personality could be transferred by mechanical means. But Mr. Spock's papers on the Alfacite Energy Phenomenon and on the impression of engrams on an android duplicate are magnificently lucid as well as most scholarly. As you Earthmen would say, I had only to follow his lead."

The first officer's face remained totally expressionless—a circumstance that Kirk knew often indicated profound disapproval.

At that moment, Kirk's communicator beeped. A message was coming in from Star Fleet Command that was to be received only by the captain.

Kirk made his farewells to Exar and his wife and then took Spock aside. "Get that tape and be ready to beam up in twenty minutes. Take it easy on the scientific curiosity, for once." No reason to be uneasy, Kirk thought, but . . .

"Understood, sir." Kirk nodded and left.

"I wish to know," Spock said to Exar as they headed for the laboratory where the research tape was filed, "how it is possible to factor a personality along genetic lines. My paper on the Alfacite Energy Phenomenon did not include an explanation of the factored personality of Crewman X. The data were too meager."

"Selective impression of engrams," Exar answered a bit breathlessly. "The process is incredibly complex, as you may imagine. You, perhaps, could formulate the necessary equations in days. But I am not a mathematician, and it took me many months."

"Indeed." They walked in silence for a moment, Shona trailing them like a one-woman security guard. "Is the procedure reversible?"

"Theoretically. Why?"

"The solution to a personality conflict within an individual," Spock said with iron control, "is integration, not disintegration. In 'anticipating' your son's problem, Doctor, you made it impossible for him to solve it."

"He was dying, Mr. Spock. My wife is a physician, and she could not help him. We did what we could." Exar's voice seemed to fade away. He was nearly exhausted by the short walk to the lab. "My laboratory, sir."

No lights flashed on the computer consoles, and no sound emanated from the huge three-chambered center of it all. But even quiescent, the machine seemed to emit portentiality—for hope or for destruction, depending on the viewpoint of the observer.

"Fascinating." Spock was inexorably drawn toward the machine by his overpowering desire to examine it.

"This laboratory was originally set up for analysis of tissue samples," Exar was saying. "I built and programmed the genetic duplicator myself." Still absorbed, Spock did not answer. "I am dying, Mr. Spock. But my work is unfinished," Exar went on softly as he moved toward the safe where the tape was kept. "The research I was sent here to do has claimed my life before I have completed the research I was born to do. It will not be long before the knowledge contained on this tape will be the property of the Federation. But it is not complete. I have had only one subject. I had so hoped . . ." Spock did not hear the choked emotion in the scientist's voice. "I had wanted very much to be able to continue this project before I die. Do you understand?"

"Albar!" the wife cried out. And at the same moment, Spock—inspecting the computer already programmed for the physiological and psychic factoring of a Vulcan-Human hybrid—understood.

He whirled. But a standard phaser set on stun was in Exar's trembling hand.

"Please understand!" The phaser beamed out as Spock lunged forward, cutting him down in mid-stride. The last words he heard as one entity were: "Stay back, Shona! I don't want to hurt . . . Shona!" The phaser whined again, but Spock heard no more.

The message from Star Fleet Command that had been "for the captain only" turned out to be what the captain called a Red Tape. Fuming, Kirk instructed the Transporter room to let him know immediately when Mr. Spock beamed aboard. He got the notification just before watch-change.

"Mr. Spock on board, sir."

"Acknowledged," Kirk answered, relieved. "Ask Mr. Spock to meet me in my quarters." He left the bridge, now off duty himself. No sooner had he arrived in his quarters when the wall intercom whistled at him.

"Kirk here."

"Transporter room. Mr. Spock is on board, sir. We were ordered to notify you—"

"Yes, thank you." Must be the relief, a little behind on things. "I've already been notified."

Dead silence. Then: ". . . Sir?"

"I've already been informed," Kirk said patiently, "that Mr. Spock is on board. Thank you, Lieutenant."

Another silence. Then, faintly: "Yes, sir. Very good, sir."

Kirk stretched out on his bed, making a mental note to tell the chief engineer to see to it that watch changes in his department included the relaying of all messages to the relief officer. Funny. Scotty ordinarily ran his department flawlessly.

When his door buzzer sounded, he opened his eyes but did not raise his head. "Come."

The door slid open and closed, and Kirk looked up at a stranger.

There was no way he could define it. Spock looked exactly as he always had. And yet the friend who had so recently gazed at Kirk with such understanding seemed to have vanished without a trace. It was as though there were a force field between them—a barrier of Spock's making. Yet, behind it, the Vulcan was as tense as Kirk had ever seen him.

"The tape, Captain." Spock held out the cartridge, face and voice expressionless. Yet Kirk had the fleeting impression that he did not want to let go of it. "Request permission to return to quarters, sir."

"Permission denied." Kirk sat up slowly, staring. "Are you all right?"

"Yes, sir." But it was only a whisper.

"Like hell you are." Kirk stood up and moved slowly toward his friend, studying him intently. "What happened down there?"

"Dr. Exar became ill shortly after you left," Spock informed him woodenly. "It is my opinion that he will shortly be dead. The disease from which he is suffering is incurable—a result, I believe, of the work he was doing on Fornax II. The work he was sent there to do, that is."

"You mean," Kirk said unbelievingly, "that you left that woman alone with a dying husband and two little kids?"

"It would have been illogical for me to have remained, sir. Andorian women are known for their strength of purpose and for their resilience. Dr. Exar's wife assured me that she will be able to manage without the help of the *Enterprise*. She is . . . an extraordinary woman." For a moment there was an unusual expression in Spock's eyes—respect? Gratitude? Then it was gone, before the astounded Kirk could identify it. "She did not need my help, and I had duties to perform."

"Are you out of your mind?" Kirk almost shouted. "Spock, that's not like you!"

Spock stared ahead of him, almost vacantly. "A part of me," he said softly, "wished to remain. But it has always been so. I have . . . learned to deal with it."

"A *part* of you!" Kirk exploded. "Now, look here, mister! Leaving that woman alone wasn't just inhuman. It was un-Vulcan. What is the matter with you? Have you lost contact with reality? Even a Vulcan . . ."

He stopped, horrified. In spite of his control, the Vulcan was obviously in agony. Spock—unable to tolerate a reprimand?

"Something's . . . hurt you," Kirk said quietly, scarcely aware that he was now speaking in an entirely different tone. "For God's sake, tell me. Maybe I can help."

The Vulcan's gaze dropped, and there was a long silence between them. Kirk sensed that Spock was controlling—suppressing, repressing—whatever it was that Vulcans did to keep their emotions in check. But somehow the invisible barrier that he had felt when Spock first entered his quarters was no longer there. When the Vulcan looked up again, his body was no longer rigid, and his eyes were almost expressionless. But those eyes seemed to look into Kirk's soul, perhaps finding some comfort there.

"Not yet, Captain," he said. "I am asking you to accept that."

Kirk compressed his lips, not quite biting a lip. The woman's plight or the dying scientist getting through to Spock? The very idea of the hybrid twinning making him uneasy after his long struggle for unity? Some worry that Kirk himself was too disturbed by the old memory? It seemed more than that, and Kirk longed to drag it out of the Vulcan, as he had once done against the same request. But then he had known that it was a question of life or death. This could not be. Nor could it be refused. "All right, Spock—for now." Spock nodded gratitude and left.

It was a long voyage to Starbase Ten. Kirk had checked with Shona, but she again refused help, although reporting that her husband had lapsed into a coma. The following day, she reported his death, and his last wish—that the sealed tape be given to Spock. No, no help required, because a ship from her husband's nearby world would come for her and the children. Spock received the tape without a word. Kirk restrained himself and tried to settle into routine.

Spock remained taciturn and uncommunicative, although his performance on the bridge was, if anything, more efficient than usual. Kirk felt irritable. When, about a week after their visit to Fornax II, McCoy requested somewhat peremptorily that Kirk drop into Sickbay, the captain could not but wonder if the whole ship were going to the dogs. Too much inactivity, he decided. With nothing to do but warp through space day after day, it was no wonder that Spock could get upset over some point in Exar's research that he didn't understand. If that was what was disturbing the first officer. If it was only that. . . .

"What's up, Bones?" he asked wearily as he entered Sickbay and dropped into a chair.

"Spock. He's the only one on the ship that hasn't reported for his physical, and he's giving me a runaround like you never saw."

"Well, the crew physicals don't have to be finished for another month, do they?"

"True. But everybody else is all done, and I want to get the whole project stowed away before R & R."

"Business before pleasure, huh?" Both of them grinned, anticipating, and then Kirk turned serious again. "Maybe I better put some pressure on him. He seems in the pink physically—"

"In the green," McCoy interrupted dryly, and Kirk nodded impatiently.

"Bones, I'm worried about him. This past week he's been so . . ." Kirk hesitated.

"Vulcan," McCoy said glumly. "Jim, it's a phase. We've seen this kind of behavior before."

"Not quite."

"It's a matter of degree, then. Look, he's half Human. Nobody who's even *half* Human can operate the way he does without some quirks showing up now and then. This . . . I wouldn't be at all surprised if it's what the old Freudians called 'reaction formation.' "

"You got a better name for it?" Kirk asked, grinning.

"I prefer descriptions to labels," McCoy said grumpily. "His Human half is acting up, and he has to be double-Vulcan to make up for it. I'd let him stew if it weren't for these physicals."

"Well, let him stew, then. My advice, Doctor, is—"

The doors opened, and Spock stepped into the room.

"Forget it," McCoy said before Spock could open his mouth. "The captain's on your side. You get one standard month to report for a physical. So go raise a little hell on R & R—if Vulcans can raise hell on R & R."

Spock stared at him, eyebrows on the rise. Expecting one of their familiar gambits, Kirk leaned forward in his chair and bowed his head, resigned. But when

Spock began to speak, Kirk's head came up with a snap.

"Captain," the Vulcan said frostily, "I respectfully suggest that you require your officers to observe military decorum, as befits their rank."

McCoy was speechless, and after a moment Kirk said faintly, "Wha . . . ?"

"Do you wish me to repeat . . . ?"

"Mister," Kirk exploded, "did somebody shove a poker up your—"

"Sir, is that a request for infor—"

"No, *damnit!*"

"Then I respectfully request permission to leave, sir."

"Permission granted!" Kirk shouted, and Spock turned on his heel and left, radiating a veritable halo of affronted disapproval.

After a moment, McCoy said thoughtfully, "*That* is a whole new can o' worms. I haven't really had a chance to observe him lately, he's kept to himself so much. Has he played chess with you in the last few days?"

"Once. He beat the pants off me," Kirk said dully. "He played like a freshly overhauled computer. I couldn't psych him out. Bones, he's a stranger. I don't know him anymore." Kirk rose. "I think I better go apologize."

"Leave him alone, Jim. Take your own advice. Either this'll wear off, or it'll get worse. If it wears off, forget it. If it gets worse . . ." McCoy sighed. "Well, you can't put him on report for acting like a Vulcan."

"I want to talk to him."

"Jim . . ."

But the door had closed behind the captain before the doctor could say any more.

Yet, as he approached the door to Spock's quarters, Kirk's exasperation began to wane, and with it his determination. What could he do—stalk into his first officer's quarters and demand "How dare you act like a Vulcan on my ship?" The Spock he had known this past week would admit no more personal approach, much as Kirk might wish to make it.

He slowed, and then stopped just beside the door to

Spock's quarters. The corridor was empty, and in a moment of sheer weariness he laid both hands against the bulkhead and rested his weight on his arms, feeling a sudden surge of despair. *My friend. . . .* The words of Bonner, the Orion novelist, came to his mind: *Let me help.*

The fantasy was so strong that for a moment he thought he was hallucinating visually. It seemed that he could see Spock sitting at his desk, reading. Then it seemed that Spock raised his eyes from the viewer as though he had heard a sound very close by. His face was in shadow, and he did not speak. But the words were as clear as if he had.

Not yet, my friend. Not yet.

Slowly Kirk stood erect and began to walk down the corridor. Two crewmen passed him, talking together, and he greeted them casually. Later, alone in his room, he wondered that they had not looked at him curiously, for surely the turmoil that was raging inside him was visible even to a casual observer.

But: *Not yet. . . .*

As their watch began the following day, the captain tried to keep his attention away from Spock as much as possible. He did not begin to understand what was happening, but the request had been so clear and so definite that he could not ignore it.

But there was something else he could not ignore.

Turning in his command chair just a few minutes after arriving there, he began to issue an order to Uhura. The bridge crew was still assembling, for it was not quite time for the watch to begin. As Spock approached his station, Kirk could not help watching him. The first officer moved slowly toward his console, almost as though he had not worked there for an entire shift just the day before. The relief technician had already left, and so the console was fully visible. Spock hesitated, and Kirk, watching him from behind, tried to focus his attention on what he himself was saying to the communications officer. But it was difficult, and growing more difficult by the minute. Spock stood with his hands at his sides, but not in the attitude of semirigid attention that had characterized him in the last few days. He seemed, rather, relaxed but alert. A moment longer, and then he approached the console and simply laid his hands on it, standing motionless, lost in thought. There was a kind of reverence in his attitude, and a kind of quiet joy. Almost the quiet joy of a man contemplating the home he had thought he would never see again.

Then, in an instant, the impression was gone, and Spock was expressionlessly summoning the computer to divulge whatever bit of information his duties required him to have at the moment.

It was a dull watch. Like a rainy Sunday on Earth, Kirk thought. One could almost hope for a tribble or two to make life interesting.

Sulu and Chekov were talking shop.

Kirk caught the word "piece" and glanced quickly over his shoulder at Uhura. But the lovely communications officer was a good deal more intent on her work than the navigator and the helmsman were on theirs, and Spock too appeared thoroughly absorbed. Like a kid with a new toy, Kirk thought fondly. But that was nonsense. The ship's library computer might be something of a glorious toy to the Vulcan, but it was hardly new to him. Well, better absorbed in that than counseling Sulu and Chekov about their military decorum. . . .

". . . aware of the dichotomy," Sulu was saying, and Kirk pricked up his ears.

"Dere is no dichotomy," Chekov insisted solemnly, but with a hint of a twinkle in his dark eyes. "You may *tink* you vant a vife, Sulu. But vat you really vant is a woluptuous, vanton geisha." Proud of himself, he finished with a flourish, "In every port."

Sulu muttered something that sounded both sheepish and argumentative, and Kirk caught the words, "By definition . . . not 'woluptuous,' Pavel. . . . 'Vanton' . . . a matter of viewpoint." And the captain fought to keep a straight face.

"Explain, please," Chekov countered with a certain wicked innocence.

Sulu took a deep breath and then paused, apparently becoming aware of what he was getting into. At that moment, Spock's voice drifted over Kirk's shoulder—not loud enough to attract Uhura's attention, but carrying clearly to the two young men.

"En garde, Mr. Sulu."

Kirk froze. Rainy Sunday though it might be, there were shafts of sunlight in that tone—that and warmth, amusement, even affection.

Before he could turn, Sulu did. Kirk had seen the young helmsman smile many times, but never like this. The smile broke over Sulu's face like the sun—shining, totally delighted, shyly responsive.

But responsive to what?

Yet again Kirk's attention was distracted before he could turn. As quickly as it had begun, Sulu's smile faded, and he turned back to his console, obviously totally confused. Chekov, whose attention had been summoned by a minor aberration on his board at the crucial moment, had not turned around.

By the time Kirk finally turned, he saw exactly what he expected to see: Commander Spock, first officer of the Starship *Enterprise,* very busy at his work. But a few minutes later he left on some errand, and when he returned, the face was stone. Kirk invented an errand for Sulu and left with him.

As the lift whirred into action, Kirk said casually, "Ah . . . Mr. Sulu, off the record, what . . . was that all about near the beginning of the watch?"

He knew that Sulu knew what he meant. The smile returned briefly. "Nothing, sir. Mr. Spock was . . . smiling, and I wondered if anybody else . . . well . . . had seen it. That's all."

"I see. Haven't you ever seen Mr. Spock smile before?"

"Well, yes, sir. But not like he meant to. You know how he is, Captain."

"What'd he do—grin at you?"

"No, sir." Sulu looked away, apparently at a loss for words—which, Kirk knew, was as though a fish were suddenly unable to swim. "Mr. Spock was . . . enjoying himself. You could tell." He stared helplessly at Kirk as the lift opened.

"I see. Well, carry on, Mr. Sulu."

"Yes, sir. Thank you, sir." Sulu slipped out, and the doors closed behind him.

Kirk tried to dismiss it, and it would not dismiss. He had seen Spock smile in his own person and his right mind only once, when Kirk had as good as returned from the dead. If the Vulcan was smiling, then he was *not* . . . But that was impossible. No, it was the smile and the stone face that were impossible. The other was only . . . He felt his stomach turn over. He sent the lift to deposit him near Spock's quarters.

He did not know how he could get Spock to open the door. He knew without trying that the buzzer would go unanswered; Spock was on duty on the bridge, so therefore Spock could not acknowledge his presence elsewhere.

But the Human Spock had heard him once. Right through the bulkhead.

Spock?

He stood in the daywatch-empty corridor, his hands on the door, sweating.

Spock!

The door slid open without warning, and he almost jumped back in surprise. But someone was coming along the corridor now. He slipped through the door, and it swished shut behind him.

"You heard me," he blurted out.

"Some things can be learned, Captain." Spock sat on the edge of the bed, where he had apparently been lying when Kirk approached the door. He was in uniform except for his blue shirt and his boots—a long, slim figure in black, sitting on the edge of the bed, elbows resting on his knees, hands clasped loosely between them. The reading light on the bed was behind him, and Kirk could not yet see his eyes, for there was no other light on in the room. "Even by Humans. You 'heard' me too—the last time you came here."

"I . . . Yes. Yes, I did." Kirk strained his eyes. "Spock, what's *happened* to you?"

"But you already know that, Captain. Else you would not be here, looking for me during my watch." The voice was very gentle, but without much expression. Pitched slightly higher than the Vulcan's, but a voice that Kirk had heard many times. ("Captain, are you all right . . . ?") "May I ask how you came by your information?"

"I . . . guessed, Mr. Spock. It doesn't matter now."

"Indeed it does, Captain. It is not logical to assume that, after all this time, you suddenly 'guessed' that you have two first officers."

"Logical?" Kirk repeated helplessly. "Now, wait—"

"I am what I am," Spock said gravely. "As I said, some things are learned. A way of life. . . ." His voice drifted into silence. Then he went on, still softly. "Other things are indigenous to a species." He bowed his head, and his next words were almost inaudible. "My curiosity was, quite literally, my undoing."

Kirk's first impulse was to reach out and touch his shoulder. But without knowing how, he suddenly realized that this Spock might be even harder to reach than the other, perhaps because he was so much more vulnerable.

"I did guess," Kirk said carefully. "Today, you were different. And . . . your . . . the oth . . . The Vulcan is different."

"Yes, I know."

Kirk reached for Spock's chair and sat down, straddling it. "Spock . . ."

"It was most fortuitous," Spock said softly, "that the Vulcan was so absorbed in the research today that I had to take the watch."

"Why?"

"Once freed, it was difficult for him to contemplate being reunited with me." Almost expressionless, yet with an undertone of agony that Kirk could feel tearing at his soul. "This has presented me with a complex problem in . . . tactical maneuvering."

If Spock had not smiled at that moment, Kirk did not know how he could have borne the combined weight of his own memories of an all-too-similar situation and of his friend's pain. The smile was, Kirk was sure, only a shadow of the one Sulu had responded to—wistful, fleeting, wry, one eyebrow on the rise, but so utterly unselfconscious that Kirk almost held his breath for fear Spock would realize what he had done, and regret it.

"Can you talk him into it?" he asked.

"That should not be necessary now. You see, Captain, each of . . . us has always relied on the other for certain restrictions. The Human has relied on the Vulcan for emotional control, even that minimal control that Humans ordinarily attain on their own." No condescension there. Simply a statement of fact.

"That's why you stayed in here until yesterday." And in memory Kirk seemed to hear again: *Lock me away, Captain. I do not wish to be seen.* "Did he . . . have you been a prisoner here?"

"No, no. The choice was mine." Again Spock's head was bowed. "But we have also discovered that the Vulcan has relied on the Human to . . ." He looked up, and again the wry, fleeting smile. "I believe the expression is 'keep him in touch'?"

"But Vulcans . . . Your father isn't out of touch."

Spock's gaze dropped abruptly, his face becoming rigid with his effort at control. Kirk looked away, cursing himself silently for bringing up the one subject that should not have been mentioned. "I'm sorry. I shouldn't have . . ."

Spock rose—the quick, almost uncontrolled motion of a Human male who must, at all costs, *move* or jump out of his skin. But then he seemed to regain a measure of control, pacing slowly past Kirk to the other side of the room. As he turned, Kirk saw something that he would probably never see again: Spock, of Vulcan, hand on the back of his neck, stretching to ease the tension in his neck and shoulders.

"Dependence is also learned," he said grimly. "My father is a full Vulcan, not a hybrid. He never learned to depend on a Human element within himself, but developed ties with concrete reality the way any Vulcan does—or any Human—out of the total configuration of his personality. My Vulcan half learned dependence. We both did." He laid his hand on the wall at forehead height and leaned his head against his arm, and Kirk realized that they were both near exhaustion, after having spent only a few moments together. "My

. . . The Vulcan has been spending more and more time immersed in research and deep concentration. I thought it best not to rouse him. It was a risk for me to begin the watch, as I knew. But I believe it will bring home to him the . . . illogic of protesting against our . . . nature."

After a moment, Kirk asked softly, "Do *you* want *him* back?"

"I have no more choice than you had. Nor has he."

"Spock . . ." It was only a whisper, and Kirk's head was bowed. But he knew that his friend had turned to look at him again.

"Don't come here again, Jim," Spock said softly but with great intensity. "Logically, you should be the one who can help me the most. But the situation in which we find ourselves is tragically illogical."

Kirk raised his head. He knew from experience that Spock habitually used "logically" as the antithesis of "emotionally." Yet this seemed hardly the time for such distinctions. "But *why?* Yes, damnit, I admit that I'm emotionally involved. You're my friend. How could I be anything—"

"Your . . . emotion . . . is not only for me, Jim. You have not fully settled with your Impostor, your . . . wolf yet, no more than I have settled with my . . . Vulcan. It is why we could not tell you."

Much as he wanted to, Kirk could not deny the truth of Spock's reluctant accusation. His memory of his own words was now all too vivid: "The Impostor is back where he belongs. . . ." Out of sight, out of mind. "I'm sorry, Spock. But whatever I feel, I have to see this through with you. You did with me."

Spock shook his head once. "It is not the same. I had not been there before. There is one thing that you can do for me, though. Now that you know . . . what has happened."

"Name it."

"Keep McCoy away. From both of us."

Kirk stared, understanding at last why the Vulcan Spock had been so adamant about avoiding a routine physical. "Your blood. It's red, isn't it? And his— there are no Human elements in it now."

"Affirmative. And . . . unknown, but highly probable."

Kirk returned to the bridge as though he were sleep-walking in a nightmare. But as soon as he arrived there, he realized that he must immediately face still another confrontation.

The Vulcan's eyes met his as soon as the lift doors opened, and then flicked away. But in the instant their eyes met, Kirk saw fear.

Reading him? His mind, or only his face? But even the Vulcan's logic might have expected Kirk to guess after Kirk left so abruptly for so long.

"I haven't heard a word he said," he said very softly, knowing that Spock would remember the one other time he had made that promise. "You have my word, Mr. Spock."

"I did not require you to give your word on that occasion, Captain. Nor shall I require it now."

After a moment, Kirk returned to his command chair, deeply shamed that, until now, he had believed that the only Spock who was his friend was the Human one.

It was only a few hours later that Kirk was called upon to give the only help that either Spock had asked of him, and found himself totally unable to give it.

"He just doesn't look well, Jim," McCoy was saying as they sat over dinner together, watching Spock take his tray to an isolated table. There had been just an instant of hesitation, an instant in which Spock had considered joining them. Kirk drew his conclusions as to which Spock it was as McCoy continued, "His color isn't right. If I didn't know better, I'd say that he looks what we call 'peaked.'"

"That's not a very scientific observation," Kirk said lightly. "Back off, Bones. We're all tired. Once we get to Starbase Ten . . ."

"He'll find somebody to play chess with," McCoy grumbled. "Some R & R."

"To each his own."

"Hey, Spock." McCoy raised his voice only slightly, and no one else in the room took notice. "Come on, join the family. Aren't your ears ringing?"

Spock looked up gravely. "My ears, Doctor?" But a ghost of a smile played about his eyes, and Kirk thought: *Watch it.*

"Come on over." McCoy jerked his head, grinning. He was obviously in an amiable, father-confessor mood, and Kirk sensed disaster. But Spock just as obviously did not. What impulse prompted him to rise and carry his tray to their table, Kirk could not fathom. He knew only that although Spock moved with his usual deliberate grace, he did not move reluctantly.

"I am here, Doctor," he intoned, seated himself, and resumed his meal.

"Well, you're eating anyway." McCoy's gaze fell to Spock's tray, and Kirk panicked. But there were no animal products on the tray. "Youbash," McCoy continued approvingly. "Plenty of protein, low in carbohydrates, no cholesterol to speak of—"

"Doctor," Spock interrupted mildly, "if you feel called upon to discourse on the nutritive elements of my repast, I shall be forced to return to my table. You are spoiling my appetite." He cocked an eyebrow at McCoy, obviously ready to be challenged, and Kirk felt his own tension ease.

"That's better," McCoy said inexplicably. But then Kirk realized that it was he to whom the doctor's last comment had been directed. "Relax, Jim. I'm not gonna rush Spock here. I'm gonna let him finish his dinner, an' then I'm gonna have him report to Sickbay for a quick once-over. Nothing formal. Just a blood sample. I don't remember the technical term for the Vulcan equivalent of anemia, but I can look it up quick enough. And I'd bet my tricorder he's got a touch of it. Spock, have you been experiencing any—"

"No, Doctor," Spock interrupted very quietly. "I have not been experiencing any. And I shall not report for a physical examination until after our stop at Starbase Ten. I was under the impression that we had settled that matter several days ago."

"Bones . . ."

"Captain," McCoy drawled, "this is my territory. Just let me do m' job. Spock . . ."

"Leave me alone," Spock said with controlled fury. But before McCoy could react, Kirk broke in.

"Dr. McCoy, I hardly think that harassing a patient is your 'job.' "

"Now, *wait a minute!*" McCoy looked from one to the other, and Kirk realized in despair that between them he and Spock had quite effectively aroused the doctor's diagnostic intuition. "What is this, a conspiracy? Look, I don't know what you two are up to, but I commence to smell a rat."

"Doctor," Spock broke in with a bleak imitation of his usual literalism, "you are of course aware that no rodent of that species has ever been found on a vessel of the Starship class outside of laboratory cages."

"Cut it out, Spock! Now, let's get down to business. As chief medical officer, I can order any crew member, even the captain, to report for a physical if in my judgment he may need medical or psychiatric treatment. If I have to do that to you, I will. You're jumpy as hell, and at the moment you look like . . . like a Human about to go into a dead faint. I'm not about to—"

"That'll do, Doctor." Kirk had not intended to snap the words out, but his inner tension prevailed. *Not yet,* Spock had said. But *Not yet* had somehow become *Right now.* "You're trying to win one at Spock's expense, and Star Fleet regulations are not set up to facilitate one-upmanship. As you were, Doctor. And *that's* an order."

The talk continued to buzz around them as McCoy turned slowly to face the captain. But Kirk found himself unable to meet his eyes. "Tell me, *Captain,*" he asked quietly, "are you prepared to take responsibility for your first officer's physical condition?" But although he endeavored to keep his voice flat and lifeless, the hurt in it was all too evident.

"If necessary."

"Well, I hereby overrule you, *Captain.* Mr. Spock, as chief medical officer, I order you to report to Sickbay for a complete physical at nineteen hundred hours, pursuant to Star Fleet regulations . . ." He paused in mid-sentence. "Spock, you don't believe that nonsense about one-upmanship, do you? My God, you're looking more like death warmed over every minute. Just because the captain here feels like trying to pull rank . . ."

"Bones . . ."

"What's the matter, Jim? Things too quiet for you lately?" For the first time it became obvious just how angry and hurt McCoy was—too angry and too hurt to think carefully about what he was saying. "No chance to play God with Tyree and his friends, so you'll just aim a little closer to home, eh?"

"As a psychiatrist," Kirk managed to say, "you play damn dirty pool, *Doctor*."

"Stop it," Spock said softly. "Jim, stop it, please. You're tearing each other apart."

Kirk could see the utter astonishment in the blue eyes just as McCoy turned to look at Spock.

"I should like to explain to you, Doctor," Spock said huskily, "that the captain is endeavoring to protect me from exposure—"

"Spock!"

"I know the Vulcan's mind, Captain, as he knows mine. The odds are very high that he would concur with my judgment, although for manifestly different reasons."

"What Vulcan?" McCoy asked blankly. "There's no other Vulcan on the *Enterprise*."

"Dr. McCoy, I suggest that we adjourn this discussion temporarily and resume it in Sickbay." Spock pushed his tray away, his face ashen. "I have a rather lengthy story to tell you, much of which the captain also has not heard. But I would prefer to tell it in private."

Much later, in the middle of the ship's night, the captain and the chief medical officer sat alone in the captain's quarters, trying to get drunk. But although they had consumed almost half a bottle of brandy in the last hour, sobriety dogged them like a relentless nemesis.

"Pigmentation," McCoy said softly. "His pigmentation wasn't changed, any more than the pigmentation of Exar's children . . . child was changed. That's why the change in skin tone wasn't noticeable to anyone but me—a physician who's observed him over a period of time. Jim, his blood's AB positive."

Kirk took a long drink. "Is he anemic?"

"He's in perfect health. Blood pressure slightly above normal for his age and weight, but considering the strain he's under—God, this is incredible!" It was perhaps the tenth time the doctor had used that word that evening.

"Then there's a good chance the . . . rejoining will work?"

"In context, I'd say a very good chance. Oh, I can't quote you the odds . . ."

"I'll bet," Kirk said tightly, "that he can."

McCoy sighed. "Yeah." He was silent for a moment. "What hell he must be going through. And even for the two of us to know . . . Worse for him if the crew knew than even for you that time. Not sure either of them could take it." McCoy sighed again. "I would give one year's pay to see them together. Just once." And he drained his glass with scientific efficiency.

"So would I. *Permanently* 'together.' "

Their apologies had been exchanged hours before— one of many such exchanges in a long and eventful friendship. Now McCoy's gaze reflected only his concern. "Damnit," he said gently, "why is Spock always right?"

"About what—this time?" Kirk smiled tiredly into his glass.

"About you. You look like you're in worse shape than he is." McCoy rose. "Get some sleep now. You'll need it. I hope he gets some. Both of him. Good night, Jim."

"Good night, Bones. Sleep well."

But Kirk did not sleep well himself that night. He had to make Spock let him in on this. *Let me help.* And did he have the help to offer? Was it true that he was still so unsettled that he would be useless to his friend in this? No, he would not believe that. He had, by

God, accepted the "wolf" and taken it back in, whether he liked that darker side of himself much or not. And that would have to do.

But it was going to be even harder for the Vulcan. Both of him.

"Yes," said the captain, "Of course I'm beaming down with the landing party. I'm the only one on the ship who's been on this planet before."

On the last day before the *Enterprise* was to reach Starbase Ten, the ship's "milk run" status had changed abruptly. An urgent communiqué from Star Fleet Command had ordered Kirk to divert briefly to Iota Ceti VI. The mission: to rescue a stranded Federation survey team in danger of being captured by the natives—intelligent but bearlike creatures known to consider Human flesh a rare delicacy.

Kirk had chosen the rest of the landing party from among the non-Human members of the crew. When he announced that he too would beam down with the rescue team, he could not miss his first officer's reaction.

The expression that flitted across the Human Spock's face was most un-Spockian—disapproval, impatience, almost anger.

"Captain," he said, "let me remind you that these creatures do not attack non-Humans. Only Humans."

They were in the briefing room: the captain, the first officer, the chief engineer who would be in charge of the beam-up, and five non-Human crew members. Six pairs of eyes turned to Spock in astonishment; no one had ever heard him speak in that tone before—let alone to the captain. Kirk knew that the others heard a raw emotion that sounded like insolence. He himself heard fear—fear for the captain, who was also his friend. He was touched by Spock's concern for his safety, always before kept under firm control. But even more, he felt tension. If Spock weren't careful, he would reveal his secret to everyone in the room.

"Let me remind *you*, Mr. Spock," he countered lightly, "that I was in the first landing party ever to land on this planet. I've had experience with—"

"Experience," Spock snapped, "will not keep you alive."

"That's entirely beside the point. I know the planet."

"The landing party has been thoroughly briefed. They are all competent officers."

Calm, Kirk thought. Keep calm. "Mr. Spock," he said slowly, "let me put it to you once again. These officers are indeed qualified—"

"Then let me put it to you, Captain." Spock's words came only a shade more rapidly than usual, and his tone was only a shade more emotional. But that tiny difference was like the sound of distant thunder before a summer storm. "You would rather risk death yourself than risk feeling responsible for the death of even one of your subordinates."

"That's enough!" It was more than enough. Kirk was too furious to think about what he was saying. "If you can't control yourself, I suggest that you go and get your . . ." He stopped, horrified at what he had almost said.

The others had averted their eyes.

"A most . . . appropriate suggestion." It was scarcely more than a whisper, and Spock's lips barely moved. He rose, his eyes as bleak and empty as Kirk had ever seen them. But now he exhibited a desperate control that evoked a wrenching empathy from his captain, in spite of Kirk's anger. "As I am, I can be of no help to you. That is more than obvious. Request permission to . . . leave the briefing, sir."

A few moments later, the two Spocks faced each other in the first officer's quarters.

"I can't help him," the Human was saying. "Alone, I can't protect him from himself. If for no other reason than that, we must be rejoined."

"Affirmative." But the Vulcan was more interested in the present than in the future. He had risen from the desk, forgetting to turn off the tape reader. Now he moved purposefully toward the door. "I suggest filing a Five-six-seven."

"Dereliction of duty? But the ship is not in danger. Only Jim."

He watched the Vulcan control his rising anxiety;

they were both Spock, and logically, Spock's decisions must be arrived at jointly by the two of them. "The captain is not expendable personnel. According to Star Fleet regulations, Book—"

"I know. I know. But . . ." The Human stopped in mid-thought. "Filing a Five-six-seven would stop him from beaming down. By the time the matter was settled, the mission would be over."

"Precisely." The Vulcan was on his way to the door. Then, abruptly, he hesitated.

The contact between the two Spocks was tenuous— empathic rather than telepathic. Yet the Human did not need telepathy to know the words that were echoing in his alter's mind: *The ship is not in danger. Only Jim.*

"It would be illogical," the Vulcan began, "to permit an exemplary Star Fleet officer to risk his life—"

The Human interrupted with one short word—the Vulcan semantic analogue of a nonliteral obscenity that Jim Kirk had been known to use on occasion. "Jim will know," he went on quietly, "that we do this as his friend, just as he knew why I objected to his beaming down. Our . . . his first officer's logical explanations of emotional motivations have never fooled him. Not even in the beginning."

The Vulcan turned, about to argue. But the eyes that met his were his own. Here, between these two, there could be nothing hidden.

"It was you," the Vulcan said tightly, "who were emotionally motivated."

"No. It was Spock."

"I am a Vulcan."

"You are Spock, as I am. And it is Spock who has . . . doubted."

In the dim light, the Human saw his alter's face change. *So,* he thought abstractedly. *Even with full control, how clearly the emotions show. I must remember that.*

But now he was remembering other things, as he knew that his alter was remembering. For their memories were one.

Glimpses. Fragmentary insights that had troubled

the entire Spock since he had first lived among Humans. Fascinating creatures—appallingly enslaved by their passions. And yet, now and then, a brief insight that he could not forget.

And Spock would think, very briefly: Can this be completely wrong—this "feeling"?

Very briefly. Until he met Jim Kirk.

Here was a man whom Spock admired above all others—a man for whom he felt friendship, perhaps even what Humans call love. *Why?* he had asked himself a hundred times, in secret. Why? Here was a man who could feel emotion unashamed, and did. Yet Spock trusted him with his life, and with the lives of all the crew—had fought beside him many times, would choose to serve beside him before he would choose even a Vulcan commander. *Why?* he had asked. *Can it be that I trust him more because he feels?*

Both Spocks had shared these thoughts, thoughts leading nowhere except to an ominous unsteadiness in the very foundation of Spock's Vulcan creed of non-emotion. The Human Spock could not know with complete certainty what his Vulcan alter was thinking now. But he sensed that each seeing his own doubts reflected in the other had brought them to a new self-knowledge that, if it yielded no answers, at least yielded questions. And it was Spock's Vulcan father who had taught him that the path to any truth begins not with answers, but with questions.

"Time grows short," the Vulcan said quietly. "I must go to him now."

"Go, then," the Human answered in the same tone, "as long as you know *why,* Spock."

It was the first time either of them had called the other by name.

At that moment, the intercom whistled.

"Mr. Spock?" It was the captain.

"Spock here," the Human answered, remembering that he was on duty.

"I'm on my way to the Transporter room," Kirk announced unceremoniously. "You have the con."

"Captain . . ." the Vulcan began. But the intercom was dead.

The two Spocks stared at each other, this time knowing each other's thoughts without a doubt.

The Human Spock was on duty, and had been ordered to the bridge. If the Vulcan was to reach the captain before he beamed down, both of them would
have to be out of their quarters at the same time. And
if they were discovered . . .

Gossip.

Curious eyes, intruding, prying.

Pity.

For a Vulcan, torture.

"I will wait thirty seconds," the Vulcan said quietly.
"Go."

The Human nodded without hesitation, and left the
room.

When Kirk saw his first officer at the entrance to the
Transporter room, his guilt overcame his irritation. He
gestured to the attendant to wait, and approached
Spock, determined to apologize for his behavior in the
briefing room.

"Spock, I . . ." Then he stopped, scanning the other's
face intently. The Vulcan?

"Captain, I would like a word with you in private."

Kirk hesitated. But there was no reason why the
beam-down could not be delayed another five minutes.
"Very well. But just a few minutes."

"Understood, sir." They moved out of the Transporter room, into the deserted corridor.

"Now, what's this all about? I told your . . . the
other—"

"Sir, you are familiar with the content of Star Fleet
regulations, Book Five, Section Six, Paragraph Seven."

There was a moment of crackling silence. Then Kirk
said softly, "You're bluffing."

"A Vulcan does not bluff."

"You'd file a Five-six-seven on me—for *this?*"

"I am a Star Fleet officer," the Vulcan said, half-
quoting. "You are my immediate superior. The regulation in question is quite specific: if I have evidence of
dereliction of duty on more than one occasion . . ."

"What evidence," Kirk asked, deadly calm, "do you intend to submit?"

"The present situation is a case in point. On one other occasion, you beamed down to the fourth planet in the Tychos star system, risking your life—the life of the ship's captain—to plant an antimatter bomb for the purpose of killing a creature that fed on Human blood. At that time I pointed out to you that, as a Vulcan, I was immune—"

"I know the story," Kirk snapped. "You've got me cold, haven't you? Once you file your damned accusation, I have to stay on the ship. By the time I untangle the red tape, the mission will be over." Bitterly: "I have to hand it to you, Mr. Spock. You are very thorough. But just why did you bother to warn me about your little plan? *He* could have filed your Five-six-seven from the bridge, snarled me up in red tape before I knew it. You could have stayed in your quarters, kept me from beaming down without fear of detection. . . ."

Kirk's voice trailed off as he realized that the Vulcan's act could have been motivated only by friendship. Now, at last, the Vulcan looked away.

"I have done," he said softly, "what must be done."

"Was it his idea, or yours?"

"We were in complete agreement on the proper course of action."

"I see." Kirk sighed deeply. "They shouldn't have to go down there alone," he added apparently irrelevantly, and then grimaced as the Vulcan looked up again, now gazing at him steadily. "I know. Your Human 'half' is most intuitive, Mr. Spock. Why didn't you ever do anything like this—before?"

"A part of me was indecisive, and there was conflict. But on this particular issue, that conflict no longer exists."

"Obviously." Kirk winced a little. "I . . . consider myself warned."

Kirk relieved the Human Spock on the bridge with a "Thank you, Mr. Spock," which might have been formal, and which both knew was not.

The Human bowed his head gravely and left. Probably knew, Kirk thought, that he needed to sweat out the mission alone now—and come to some terms with this new turn of affairs before dealing with either Spock again.

The sweating was no easier than the coming to terms, but it was shorter. The mission came off, after some hairy moments when he clutched his hands at his helplessness, damning himself and both Vulcans for putting him out of touch with the actual events. It was not possible to command only from the bridge, and a first officer who challenged that . . .

But some small voice of inner logic told him that this was a time when his presence would have been a questionable risk, perhaps even increasing the danger to others.

He sorted out the details and got the ship back on the "milk run," and then he went to them.

Somehow he didn't care to use the intercom or the door signal. Outside their cabin, he put his hands to the wall. *May I? Both of you?*

They could always pretend that this signal did not exist. He was not entirely certain that it did.

Both of us, seemed to come from somewhere, and the door opened.

He held himself against the sight and the sense of both of them and thought that he found a small smile somewhere as the doors closed behind him.

"If it helps any," he said ruefully, "I see your point. I don't necessarily have to like it. And I may break both your heads if you try it again."

Twin eyebrows lifted and the Human traded glances with the Vulcan and spoke. "We . . . consider ourselves warned," he said with no more than the faint glint of humor that the Vulcan would have permitted himself.

"However, still not in conflict on that issue," the Vulcan added.

Kirk nodded. "I'll slug that out with you—later." He let his face go grave. "But you do see what it means? You did something today—together—which you could never have done separately."

The Vulcan nodded. "Nor even . . . together."

"Yes," Kirk said. "But you could now, because you have learned something from your division—as I did from mine, and even, from yours. I needed the strength of the wolf, even a dark and . . . hungry strength. And I had to find a way to . . . love even the wolf. Not the same for you, I know. Harder. But I think there is still . . . need. And I know that I need my friend—both of him—together."

The Vulcan came closer to him, but stopped at a little distance. "We also understand, in logic—even I." He permitted himself a glint of the same humor, over a deeper pain. "It is only that what came first to you will come . . . last to us." He took a deep breath. "Perhaps last of all to me, if it comes."

"We know the necessity," the Human said in a Vulcan tone. "Intellectually, in logic, inescapable. He has solved the mathematics, and we will build the equipment with the facilities of the Starbase. But that emotional acceptance which you found quickly, and whatever carried you the last step to be reunited—we are not certain that we have. We are both . . . Vulcan."

"And both Spock," Kirk said. "You'll make it. I'm not sure that I ever understood it intellectually, doubt that I do now. Maybe that's been the trouble. But . . . I think what carries that last step is . . . sheer cussedness." He allowed himself a grin. "And you've both got plenty of *that*."

He turned quickly to the door. Get out while you're ahead, before anybody gets too un-Vulcan. He turned back for an instant. "I'll go with you, you know."

We know. But neither had spoken.

He moved out then, fast.

On a night ten days later, Kirk wound his way through the Base hospital toward the renovated operating theater that now housed the gigantic instrument of Spock's rejoining. It was the last night before that event was to be attempted, and he knew that the two Spocks were still awake, still checking out their equipment. In fact, he suspected that neither of them had slept much in the week since planetfall.

Both of them were distracted and preoccupied, barely speaking to each other except when they were working on the rejoining apparatus. Kirk suspected that the
situation was much the same when they were alone
together, and was beginning to suspect the reason as
well. Their separation had now lasted ten days more—
ten endless days of asking "Can this be *me?*" Small
wonder if whatever emotional unity they had managed to attain was wearing thin with the strain of waiting.

He found them as he had known he would find them:
the Vulcan tinkering compulsively with the computers, the Human standing in the shadows of the huge
room, hands behind his back, staring at the machine
that he and his alter had constructed with the help of
three carefully chosen technicians. The technicians, of
course, had long since gone to bed.

Kirk walked slowly toward the machine, finding that
he was not immune to its fascination. It was still difficult to remember the trauma of seeing himself a thing
apart. And now, as his reflection seemed to walk toward him out of the machine's polished, gleaming surface, it was almost as though he again faced the darker
side of his own nature.

Can this be me? He moved past the Human Spock,
barely aware of him. The reflection advanced at the
same speed—blurred, distorted, somehow threatening.
Kirk paused, and he and his reflection appraised each
other in silence.

His gesture came without conscious intent, before
he was aware that his hand was moving—an abrupt
upward thrust of the middle finger, a simple symbol of
a simple concept, both born of Earth and both of ancient origin.

Simultaneously he realized that both he and his reflection were grinning, and that the Human Spock had
made a small sound midway between a groan and a
chuckle. Turning, Kirk saw that his friend's expression
was a rather extraordinary blend of amusement and
disapproval.

"Jim, that's not the answer." It was almost a sigh.

But Spock's Humanity was unable to maintain an objective sobriety.

"It'll do for openers." Spock shook his head wearily, and Kirk jerked his toward the oblivious Vulcan a few feet away. He went to the Human and laid his hand on his shoulder, steering him purposefully away from the machine and all its implications. "Come on, now. Enough's enough."

But as he approached the Vulcan, a curious reticence overcame him once more. *This is a Vulcan. Vulcans don't like to be touched.* His free hand, half-raised, fell to his side.

At that moment, the Vulcan looked around, directly at his captain. Kirk was sure that he had never seen Spock—whole or divided—so totally depressed. *He hasn't slept at all.* That certainty flashed through Kirk's mind, and with it the reason: the Human Spock might relax for a moment, might even chuckle with a friend on the eve of the trauma of his rejoining; but the Vulcan had no such outlet. His own private hell of apprehension leaped from his eyes in one unguarded moment, and Kirk responded in the only way he knew. He laid his hand gently on the rigidly tense shoulder and squeezed it briefly.

"Time to turn in, my friend. Tomorrow is a whole new day."

The muscles of the Vulcan's face did not move; Kirk knew that this Spock could never smile at anyone as the Human had smiled on the bridge. Yet he could feel the lean, blue-clad shoulder relax beneath his hand, and the bleak dark eyes seemed to shine quietly with renewed life.

Silently the Vulcan's gaze shifted to that of his alter —almost as though he were seeking a way of expressing himself there.

After a moment the Human asked softly, "Kipling's Thousandth Man?"

"Indeed." The Vulcan's response was almost immediate.

At a loss to understand what they were talking about, Kirk glanced from one to the other as their gaze held. Their emotional unity at that moment was almost palpable, and he wondered briefly if the fact that he was in physical contact with both of them made him some sort of telepathic conductor. Well, whatever the reason, the unity was there, and perhaps really for the first time. It might even get the two of them through until tomorrow.

"Come on," he said again. Then, only half-joking: "That's an order, Mr. Spock."

Two right eyebrows rose. "Yes, sir." The response was almost in unison. The Vulcan turned to reduce the computers to silent darkness. Then the two of them left the room, with Kirk walking between them, one of his hands still resting lightly on the shoulder of each.

And perhaps it was the same thing, whatever it was, or sheer cussedness, which carried them the final step the next day while he and Bones watched solemnly.

> **Captain's log, Stardate 5763.7. The crew having enjoyed the shore-leave facilities on Starbase Ten, for ten solar days, the Enterprise has been ordered to proceed to Sector Five for exploration and mapping operations. The crew seems rested and in good spirits. All present and accounted for.**

As he had done so many times before, Kirk clicked off the recorder. But this time he added silently: *Thank God.* "Prepare to leave orbit, Mr. Sulu."

"Yes, sir."

"Mr. Spock?" The chief medical officer's voice sounded behind Kirk. "My instruments have been recalibrated just for you, and this watch is almost over. Any time you're ready, sir."

"That, Doctor," Spock responded from his station, "is a very interesting figure of speech involving the Human proclivity for saying in five words what could be said in three." A slight pause for emphasis. " '*I* am ready.' "

"I," McCoy repeated amiably, "am ready."

"But *I* am not, Doctor."

There was a moment's silence, and then McCoy began ominously, "Spock . . ."

"I," Spock continued with what no one but McCoy

would have dared to call smugness to his face, "shall be on duty for another two-point-six-one minutes. If you will consult Star Fleet regulations, Book Three, Section—"

"SPOCK!"

"Bones . . ." Kirk turned in his chair, grinning up at McCoy. "Give up."

"Thank you, Captain," Spock said lightly, not looking around.

Then, slowly, he turned to look at Kirk. When he spoke again—in an entirely different tone—the bridge became for both of them a mirror image of a time long gone, a time when Kirk had been the one who had only recently become a unity once again.

" 'From both of us,' " Spock finished.

"Speak for yourself," McCoy began, and stopped, suddenly realizing that somehow Spock's last words had nothing to do with him or with their argument.

The captain and the first officer continued to lock gazes as Kirk's grin faded but did not entirely disappear. And in his mind he saw the words of Rudyard Kipling that he had located in the ship's library.

> One man in a thousand, Solomon says,
> Will stick more close than a brother . . .
>
> But the Thousandth Man will stand by your side
> To the gallow's foot—and after . . .

The only answer Kirk's grin got was a faint echo of the Human Spock's smile—just before the first officer of the *Enterprise* turned again to his duty.

Introduction to Intersection Point

by *James Doohan*

It was thought in the early days of *Star Trek* that there would be little use made of the Chief Engineer, because, after all, he was down in the "engine room." However, the writers kept slipping Scotty in there, and naturally, he was able to fix anything. Here in a suspense-filled short story by Juanita Coulson, Scotty, with the help of Mr. Spock and others, comes through again.

But how Scotty was able to bear the tearing, ripping, and puncturing of his beloved *Enterprise*, we will never really know; but we do know he was weaned on impulse engines and played with dilithium crystal blocks just a short time before he read the "Theory of Concupicity," which put him on a very rigid course of learning from which he never wavered.

Intersection Point

by *Juanita Coulson*

Jim Kirk nibbled on his thumbnail and glared at the viewscreen, feeling more irritable by the minute. In the center of the screen, dominating it, a milky veil swam, and the stars beyond were obscured, fuzzy. Three hours, and they'd almost circumnavigated the phenomenon, and what did they have to show for it? "Mr. Spock." The science officer turned toward him even as Jim swiveled his command chair.

"Nothing conclusive. Scanners continue to indicate the interference with the total spectrum is constant. It is apparently spherical, approximately three hundred thousand kilometers in diameter. But without a closer approach, it may be impossible to learn more."

"You suggested that earlier. But before we commit the *Enterprise* to a deeper probe I'll need—"

"Captain," Sulu broke in, "it's shifted direction."

Spock bent over his sensors. "Confirmed. Field expanding rapidly—in our direction. Loss of star field magnitude progressing geometrically."

"Reverse power, Mr. Sulu. Warp Two." The mist on the screen now crowded the corners of the viewer.

Levelly, Spock warned, "Field diameter now eight hundred thousand kilometers, and contact imminent. . . ."

Suddenly Sulu's hands were jolted from the helm, and the entire bridge seemed to slide out from under the crew. They spilled from chairs or clutched at the equipment and railings. Jim gratefully clung to the solidity of his command chair; from the corner of his eye he saw Sulu clawing at the controls, trying to execute that last, unfulfilled order.

Kirk's ears hurt, and he realized that a claxon was ringing—a claxon he could not recall having heard throughout his years on the *Enterprise*—the signal of a collision.

And what was wrong with the lights? They went out

completely for a split-second, and when Scotty man-handled the controls at the engineering station, they came back on, but with only half their earlier brightness.

Dislodged crew members were scrambling back to their posts, Uhura was monitoring departmental check-ins, Spock was once more intent on his sensors, and Sulu finally got his hands firmly on the helm, muttering, "Those deflectors should have . . . Captain, we have no control. No power."

"Everything acts frozen," Chekov complained, arguing with his own board.

Scotty was already on the com to Engineering. "Jerry, cut out all nonessential systems. Divert power to helm. Gi' us all you've got."

"Sir, we can't. . . ."

"If we get power," Kirk said, "perhaps we can ease away from whatever . . . What's the problem, Engineering?"

"Severe damage in Level Three. That's why we can't feed you any power. The impact was there."

Uhura said, "Damage Control on their way."

"I would recommend all speed."

Kirk glanced over his shoulder at Spock, not liking that tone.

"To be precise, Engineering Section 68-C is the impact point. Sensors indicate that both hulls have been penetrated."

For a moment Kirk was too stunned to speak, stricken, thinking of an open, possibly mortal wound in the *Enterprise.* "What . . . what did we hit, Spock?"

"We seem to have collided with nothing."

Instantly the captain was on his feet, at the railing lining the upper bridge, glaring up at the Vulcan. "Both hulls, and you say there's *nothing?*"

Spock blinked at the accusatory tone. "We have indeed suffered a collision, but at this point the physical nature of the other object is unknown. According to the sensors, there is nothing there. That is also, incidentally, why the deflectors failed to operate."

"Mr. Scott," from the intercom. The speaker's voice sounded strained. "Break confined to panels five and

six in lower J. Oddly enough, our life support seems
intact. No loss of heat or air, and pressure's normal.
Minor casualties."

Jim leaned over Spock's arm and punched the intercom at the science officer's station. "Can you see the
break from where you are? Can you see what hit us?"

"I . . . Yes, sir. But I think you'd better come and
have a look for yourself, Captain."

"Very well. Scotty, come with me. Spock, I want
some answers," Kirk insisted as he started for the turbo. "And no more 'nothing.' Some specifics."

The door closed on Spock's patiently aggrieved "Understood."

By the time Kirk and Scott reached the Engineering
Section, the corridor was a tangle of Damage Control's
equipment cables and wet with leakage from ruptured
ductwork. They had to wend their way through a crowd
of techs and staff, and the young red-haired lieutenant
in charge was obviously relieved by their arrival. "I've
set up monitoring on life support and this weird power
drain, sir."

"Very good. Dubois, isn't it?" Kirk said. He was remembering Scotty's increasingly laudatory record en-
tries during the six months Dubois had been assigned
to Engineering.

"Aye!" And Scotty beamed and slapped Dubois on
the shoulder. "We couldn't have wanted a better man
down here in a . . ." He paused and followed Kirk's
gaze. Dubois, too, turned and then nodded.

"As Mr. Spock would say, fascinating, isn't it, sir?"

"Horrifying," rather, was the word that came to Jim
Kirk's mind. A jagged tear gaped in the side of the
Enterprise, glistening metal poking out into Engineering, deck to overheads across two levels. It was as
though a huge invisible missile had torn its way through
both hulls. And through the rent the only thing they
could see was a swirling mist—dizzying, multicolored,
coruscating, and blending in constant movement. It left
a queasy feeling in Jim's stomach.

"What's this?" Scotty exclaimed over a piece of
equipment Dubois cradled in his hands. "Not the whole
circuit!"

"Afraid so. That's why we couldn't give you any power. Lissa, anything on the monitor?" A pretty dark-haired technician looked up from her equipment stationed before the tear in the hull. She shook her head, then blushed under Dubois's grin.

Spock's voice beckoned from the intercom, and Kirk hastily punched it up. "Preliminary survey: there is a constant severe energy drain in all sections of the ship, Captain."

Kirk squinted up at the feeble lights.

"Our power has been reduced by at least half."

With his other ear Jim heard Scotty telling Dubois to rig something called an RG unit, and Dubois's protests that such a thing could take hours. Then something in Spock's tone drew all of Kirk's attention.

"We have one reading of special significance. There is metallic debris in the immediate area drifting in space."

Kirk stared unseeingly at the intercom. "From the *Enterprise?*"

"No. However, it is from a Federation vessel, a scout of the Avenger class. Records show that a vessel of that type disappeared two parsecs distant from these coordinates, while on patrol, a solar month ago. Jim . . ." And Spock's voice lowered to a register that made Kirk's throat ache.

"I understand. Scotty, can you get us any maneuvering power at all?"

The chief engineer's eyes widened, and he shook his head emphatically. He and Dubois were still holding that piece of equipment tenderly, as if it were a wounded crew member. "We *can't.* It's even worse than I thought, sir. We can put temporary plating over the breach . . . but moving is out of the question."

Jim left the circuit open so that Spock could hear. "It's necessary to get us out of here *now,* to be on the safe side."

Lieutenant Dubois held out the broken equipment, and Kirk glared at it with annoyance. "When we hit, sir, we lost our main circuitry coupling. Feedback took out every alternate we've got. And now there's that power drain. The whole thing is useless . . . without that main coupling."

"Where is this coupling? What do you mean, you 'lost' it?"

Scotty held up a broken cable. "They found this leading in . . . in there, Cap'n." He pointed toward the opening, aswirl with mist.

The briefing room was a luxury that, in time, they might not be able to afford, but Jim thought perhaps they could all think more clearly away from that alien hole in the side of the *Enterprise*. But with Scotty, Dubois, and Technician Hart constantly on the intercoms checking progress down at the scene, he was beginning to think it hadn't been such a good idea after all, adjourning here. McCoy drummed his fingers on the table and looked sour; he pounced on the chance to snap at Spock when the science officer arrived. "Well?"

"The debris is definitely from the USS *Halcyon*."

"What destroyed her?" Kirk demanded, and the others gave the Vulcan complete attention.

"Logic, and what little data we have, suggest contact with this field or area with which we have collided."

Smothering his impatience, Kirk said, "And just what *is* this . . . field or area?"

Spock seated himself and made a steeple of his forefingers before he spoke. "I do not like to speculate, but the time factor and element of danger force me to do so. On our findings thus far, we may theorize that the field is most likely an interdimensional contact point . . . or, more properly, an intersection point."

"Interdimensional . . ." Kirk whispered.

"Y'mean like that world we stumbled into where everybody had a double?" Scotty exclaimed.

"No, I do not, Mr. Scott. This is something far different, and infinitely more dangerous. We can be certain of one fact: the field does not remain constant. It may enlarge quite rapidly, as when it moved toward and collided with us. Or, it may contract."

"How much?" Dubois asked, and Lissa Hart began to look scared.

"We have no way of knowing, Lieutenant. I suggest we do not experiment by remaining here to discover its vanishing point, as it were. Presently, this contact is maintaining the integrity of our life support; but that is insufficient reason to continue to risk the *Enterprise*."

"But we can't move!" Scotty said desperately.

"We'll have the RG unit ready in three hours," Dubois offered.

Kirk looked anxiously at Spock. "Current status of the field?"

"Difficult to assess accurately, but I would estimate 750,000 kilometers." Spock lowered his head slightly and spoke slowly. "The field is beginning to contract. And as it condenses, it presents a clear and present danger to the *Enterprise*. If it should contract and *close* while we are still touching it, we shall in all likelihood join the *Halcyon* as a collection of debris."

Kirk exhaled forcefully. "Then we have to get out of here."

"There is also the power drain to be considered. It hampers our efforts."

"Aye! Even if we get the RG unit in place in time, it may not function well enough," Scotty said mournfully. "The only thing that'll guarantee us bare minimum power is that coupling."

"And it's . . . over there. How about waldos, Scotty?" Kirk suggested. "Can't we reach into this . . . this other dimension and grapple the coupling and drag it back?"

The engineer looked hurt. "We thought o' *that* right away, Cap'n. But with the power loss, waldos operate at only half efficiency. It limits the grasp we can apply. And . . . well, even if we did close on something, we have no way of knowing it'll be the coupling. Electronic visual devices don't work over there, either."

"That is true," Spock said soberly. "We might blindly grasp something of immensely dangerous potential. And if that something were returned to the *Enterprise* . . ."

"We have to *know* it's the coupling," Scotty finished firmly.

Kirk pursed his lips, then turned to McCoy. "What's over there, Bones? Your bio labs got a report?"

Frowning, McCoy said, "Unlikely as it seems, Jim, there's an apparently solid floor surface of some sort and a nitrogen-oxygen atmosphere; a man could at least breathe the stuff."

"Then we can go in after it," Dubois said simply.

"Now, just a minute, young man," McCoy growled. "I said you could breathe the air. I didn't say you could live over there."

"There could be . . . factors as yet unknown to us," Spock added, and McCoy looked grateful.

"Temperature, Bones?"

"Forty degrees centigrade, plus or minus. Tolerable."

"The mist?"

McCoy spread his hands. "Nothing our labs can analyze. We've broken down I don't know how many specimen samples of the stuff. The bio comps just sit there and gibber."

"Understandable," Spock said. "Our physical laws would not apply. In fact, the odds against there being such an unusual similarity in atmospheric composition are . . ."

"Please don't," Kirk muttered. "McCoy, in your judgment, could a man survive over there long enough to retrieve this coupling?"

The doctor's eyes were haunted. "I can't say that, Jim. It's possible. But, as Spock says, there could also be things we can't even guess at."

"But if we don't try, and quickly, we could all be very, very dead."

"It's gambling with a man's life."

"Bones, we don't have any choice!"

"I know the equipment on sight, Captain," Lieutenant Dubois said eagerly. Lissa Hart laid a small hand on his arm, and he patted her fingers reassuringly.

"If anyone goes . . ." Scotty began.

"But I can't handle the reinstall, Mr. Scott. Only you could put it together in time."

"I think I'm the best judge o' that."

Kirk cut in on them both. "Gentlemen, we can't waste time debating. For all we know, the crew of the *Halcyon* hesitated too long. Miss Hart, contact Stores; get a safety line and rig and whatever else we're likely to need." McCoy leaned farther back in his chair, crossed his arms, and glowered. Spock lowered his head till it almost touched his steepled fingers. "Now, Scotty, how big is this coupling?"

Narrowly eyeing Dubois, the chief engineer said, "Three kilograms, maybe a bit more."

"Small enough to carry. Good. Now, if and when we get it back, how long will it take you to put it back where it belongs?"

"Once the inputs are set, a minute, maybe two."

"And to feed power to helm?"

Scotty made a face, seeing the drift. "Another two, maybe three minutes."

"Mr. Dubois, assuming Scotty were incapacitated, how long would it take *you* to do the work?"

Dubois and Scotty eyed each other levelly. Mingled with respect was an undercurrent of reverse rivalry—each trying to make the other less expendable. Finally Dubois said, "It'd take me at least five minutes, Captain."

"Ye could do it in . . ."

"I can't *guarantee* I could do it any faster. I haven't Mr. Scott's experience."

Kirk had let them have it out, appreciating Scotty's desire to take the risk on himself. But now he had to ask the question the chief engineer had obviously been dreading. "I need an honest answer . . . and if anything else goes wrong, I need you to get us out of here, Scotty. Can Lieutenant Dubois locate the coupling as well as you?" With great reluctance, Scotty nodded. "Then we'll . . ."

The intercom buzzed on, and Spock received a status report. They all listened to the information that the field was drifting, the *Enterprise* with it, and that it was beginning to contract.

But it wasn't until Jim saw Dubois squirming into the safety harness that he began to experience the gut worry he'd anticipated earlier. Scotty was all efficiency now, but plainly he, too, was worried, frustrated that it would be Jerry rather than himself going into the mist. Damage Control had sealed off part of the rent, but a doorway still gaped into those swirling colors. And in all their minds was the knowledge of the risk inherent in venturing into that unknown territory.

"All set, Captain," Jerry Dubois said confidently. Lissa Hart winked up at him, then stepped back beside her monitoring equipment. Scotty nodded encouragingly to his lieutenant and grinned.

"Good luck, lad."

Jim glanced around the now-crowded engineering section. McCoy, Nurse Chapel, and other medical staff waited by the doors, hoping they wouldn't be needed. And now Scotty was clearing himself an aisle directly to the coupling input, ready to install the missing unit as soon as Jerry brought it back. Damage Control stood ready to seal off the remaining gap in the hull. Uhura stood close by the mist-filled tear, a nonmechanical listening device connecting the bulkhead and her ears.

Taking a deep breath, Kirk gave the order. The safety crew began paying out the line, and Lieutenant Dubois stepped through the rent, walking unhesitantly.

"If we could only gi' him a com unit . . ."

Spock sounded tired. "Mr. Scott, you should certainly be aware that even as the alien field has a dampening effect on all sound, the power drain makes electronic equipment useless beyond the dimensional barrier. Our experimentation—"

"I know, I *know!*"

Uhura began relaying a running commentary from the unseen Dubois. "About five meters beyond the opening now . . . it's very difficult to see. He says the colors are everywhere, not thinning a bit. And there are . . . strange things. Things that are . . . He thinks he sees a break ahead. Moving ahead now. Very strange things all around. Odd sounds. Eight meters now. Ten . . ."

The room was as still as an operational engineering section could be, everyone intent on Uhura. Her expression was that detached one people adopt when they listen to something closely. "Twelve meters now. He thinks he sees . . . sees . . . It may be a . . . break . . . in the . . . the . . . fed . . . el . . . tu . . ."

"What?" Kirk said softly, stiffening with apprehension.

"Colors. Too many. Too many things. Jerry says . . ." And her beautiful face contorted as though she were struggling desperately to escape. Escape what? "Too many . . . No!" Her hands flew to her ears, and disbelief and horror took over her expression. "He couldn't . . . can't. CAN'T! No! I shouldn't be able to hear that frequency. I CAN'T HEAR THAT FREQUENCY! I CAN'T . . ." And her mouth opened in a soundless scream.

Kirk, Spock, and McCoy all moved toward her simultaneously, but McCoy and the Vulcan were closer. They lifted her bodily away from the edge of the opening. Spock gently disengaged the listening device from her trembling hands, then threw it aside with startling violence. McCoy gestured with a free hand, and Nurse Chapel was there immediately with a tranquilizing hypo as Uhura collapsed, weeping hysterically.

"The line!" Scotty shouted. "It's gone slack!"

"Pull him in!" Kirk ordered. The safety linemen hand-over-handed, tugging as though there were a behemoth on the end of the cable instead of a lone human. Kirk ran to the head of their line and helped pull, expecting to see Dubois's unconscious form slide out of the swirling colors.

But when the young lieutenant appeared, he was on his feet. His eyes were wide open, and his hands were clutched across his belly. Was he in pain, or trying to return to a fetal position?

His hands! Jim realized with sinking dismay that the young officer's hands were empty. The coupling was still somewhere . . . over there.

Lissa Hart pushed between the linemen and Jerry. Her hands framed his sweating face, but he gave no sign that he saw her. His eyes were not terror-ridden, as Uhura's had been; they were vacant. The girl shook him lightly, pleadingly at first, then with increasing panic. It was not until she screamed that Jim had the heart to pull her away from Dubois.

Except for Lissa's sobbing and Nurse Chapel's murmured words of comfort, the Sickbay was quiet. Kirk
wished he could drag his eyes away from the examining
table where McCoy labored over Dubois's open-eyed,
unmoving body. When the surgeon finally turned toward him, Jim tensed in dread of the verdict. "Well,
he's not exactly insane," McCoy said with bitter weariness. He held out a medical log, and Kirk looked at it
numbly; Spock finally took it from the doctor's hand.

"Bones . . ."

"He doesn't recognize us, or anything else. Whatever he saw or experienced over there in that . . . dimension, it's wrecked his mentality. Wiped it out. *Destroyed* it. I don't know what he encountered, but you
can write him off for the rest of his life."

"Which won't be long," Kirk said grimly, "for any
of us." He couldn't shut out the sound of Lissa's grief,
but he tried to force his mind to the greater problem.
"It was my responsibility, Bones. No option. If we
don't get out of here soon . . ."

"Aye, Captain." Scotty came in, took a long an-
guished look at Dubois, then squared his shoulders.
"The computer's given us a hard deadline. One hour,
maximum."

"This RG unit replacement?"

Scotty sighed and shook his head. "Another hour
and a half."

"You did the only thing you could, Jim," McCoy
said gently. "Dubois was trying for the only chance we
had, and he just might have made it. You couldn't
know."

"Doctor, these medical data on the lieutenant . . ."

"Must you, Spock?"

The Vulcan blinked at McCoy's irritation and went
on, "It appears that some of the hyperencephalograph
readings are unchanged."

"Not the *important* ones," McCoy snarled.

Jim eyed Spock curiously. "What's your point?"

"The tracks which have been so disastrously affected
in Lieutenant Dubois are largely those which are nota-
bly different in Vulcan hyperencephalographs."

Scotty stared blankly, but in the momentary silence

Kirk knew that he and McCoy were coming to the same appalling conclusion about what Spock was proposing. McCoy found his voice first. "We've ruined one man's mind, Spock. Do you insist we ruin a second?"

"Vulcan hyperencephalograph patterns *are* different on the critical factors, are they not, Doctor?"

And suddenly Lissa Hart was there, clawing at Spock. The Vulcan held her wrists and kept her nails from his face, but he stolidly bore the tattoo of her boots against his shins. Jim tried to drag her away from the science officer, wincing under her screams. *"You* could have gone instead of Jerry! He did it all for nothing! Nothing! It should have been you!"

McCoy's hypo hissed against her arm, and as he guided her to a chair he spoke with no-nonsense firmness. "Now, listen, young lady. Quit jumping to conclusions. Jerry knew what he was doing. It was a calculated risk. For all we knew then, it could have been *more* dangerous for Spock to attempt it. It *still* may be." He finished off with a warning glare at Spock.

"The fact remains, Doctor, that we have little choice. There are no alternatives."

"I'm afraid you're right," Kirk agreed unhappily.

McCoy's tone was acid. "All right, Spock. Let's assume a miracle—that you go over into that whatever-it-is, get the coupling and get back, and *still* end up like Dubois!"

Jim didn't say anything, but he saw the flicker of something haunted in Spock's face. He ached to speak, but held it back; after Dubois, and despite the time element, he couldn't. He looked angrily at McCoy and hoped Bones could read his thoughts: Did you have to remind him of that? We both know that life without mentality is a more horrifying possibility to him than death. At least let him try it with as few thoughts as possible along that line. McCoy pouted and looked a trifle embarrassed for his remark.

Clearing his throat, Spock said, "Have I your permission to attempt it, Captain?"

Kirk waved his hand helplessly, then nodded. As Scotty and Spock hurried out to prepare, he paused for one last mournful look at Jerry Dubois; Lissa Hart was staring down at the lieutenant, as if praying to wipe the last hour away.

Here we go again, Jim thought, watching Spock buckle himself into the safety harness. The room was not so quiet this time; there was a rustling edginess among those present. Techs dropped things, safety linemen swore at each other and stepped on each other's feet. And every so often a soft time-check report would come over the intercom. Jim turned to tell someone to shut the thing off, then saw Uhura monitoring it and thought better of the idea. She was dry-eyed now, but still looking shaky.

McCoy paused beside her, touched her arm solicitously. "You sure you're okay?"

"I'll be fine, Doctor."

"Let's hope the same for us all," Scotty muttered. Kirk managed a lopsided smile, and the engineer returned it, a bit weakly. "Aye, we'll take her right down the wire, sir."

"I believe I am ready, Captain."

Kirk was loath to waste time but wanted to delay that confrontation with whatever had ruined Dubois. "Do you think you can block it out with mental techniques or something?"

Spock's expression was unfathomable. He was thoroughly inside his Vulcan suit, and Jim knew he shouldn't try to drag him out of it, now, of all times. Finally he nodded, and Spock turned and walked slowly and deliberately toward the colored doorway remaining between emergency bulkheads. The linemen paid out the cable behind him carefully.

This time there was no running report from Uhura. They all stared at the opening, at the swirling colors, occasionally forced to look away. My stomach's turning at the sight of it, Kirk thought, and Spock's right in the middle of it. Why did I agree to let him try it? If we're going to go, the only decent way would be intact, not with Spock a mindless . . .

It seemed they'd been waiting for an hour already. How long had it really been?

As if in answer, Uhura relayed softly, "Time check thirteen minutes. Field diameter five hundred kilometers . . ."

"And closing . . ." Kirk finished.

Suddenly the safety line moved, jerked from the end, disappearing into that fog of colors. "That's the signal!" one of the techs exclaimed jubilantly. "He wants us to take up the slack!"

Even as they began to pull, another twitch snaked the line, more violently than the first; then another, and another. The head safety man was nearly pulled off his feet. Thinking of unknown monsters struggling with Spock, Kirk lunged to the line and added his strength. "Pull! Everybody! Pull him back! Now!"

There was resistance, but they leaned to it. The cable was definitely coming into their hands. Just about reeled in. . . .

"Damage Control—ready to seal off the moment Mr. Spock is clear. Don't wait! We've got to get back on our own life support."

And then Spock was back through the barrier. But unlike Dubois, his eyes were closed. His lips were drawn into a thin, grim line, and his body was stiffly rigid. Jim's memory raced back to Spock in a Vulcan trance, but it didn't look like that. It didn't look like any attitude he'd ever seen Spock assume.

"He's got it!" Scotty yelped, and Jim was brought back to the greater problem. Spock *was* holding a tubular metal device—clutching it tightly.

Jim dropped the line and took Spock's hands and tugged. The only response from Spock was even more rigidity and a tightening of the muscles in his forearms. Jim's shouts made no impression.

"Captain, don't!" Scotty warned. "Be careful! We've seen what he can do. If he clamps down on it, he can crush it."

Uhura's voice, shaking, cut in. "Time eight-point-thirty minutes to closing."

"Bones!"

McCoy was already there. He stood beside Spock, stared at him calculatingly a moment, then held his autohypo up to dial something.

"Hurry!" Jim pleaded.

"You want me to kill him?"

"You want to kill us all? We've got to have that coupling!"

McCoy selected something, and the hypo hissed against Spock's arm. The Vulcan's eyes opened, and Jim was momentarily delighted; that look wasn't vacant—it was stunned surprise. And then Spock collapsed like a spilled sack of grain. Scotty caught the coupling, and Jim and McCoy caught Spock.

In the background, Jim could hear Scotty's shouts to his techs. And McCoy was simultaneously yelling for a litter. Spock was ashen, his eyes once more closed, but this time relaxed, not fiercely squinted shut. Kirk felt like shaking him, or feeling for a heartbeat, if he could remember exactly where Spock's heart was. "What did you give him?"

"Something nasty. You wanted him to let go right now, didn't you? That didn't leave me too many options."

There was a great clatter from the Damage Control techs, and very little sound at all from the group around the input where Scotty sweated to install the retrieved coupling. McCoy waved to his aides as they scooted up with a rolling litter. Jim helped them lift Spock onto it; the Vulcan was a dead weight, seemingly lifeless. Kirk looked up and was struck by two particular faces in the crowd: Nurse Chapel, wearing a mask of professionalism that didn't quite succeed in covering her concern; and Uhura, over by the intercom, once more on the brink of tears, staring at Spock.

"It's in! Go!" Scotty shouted. Uhura didn't move. Kirk got there in several steps and gently moved her aside.

"Helm . . ."

"We're registering buildup of power," Sulu's voice crackled back. "It'll take a bit to . . ."

"Impulse will do, Mr. Sulu. As soon as you have any indication you can move, pull us away from here."

Over Sulu's acknowledgment, the chief of the Damage Control crew gave an exultant yelp. "Cap'n!" Kirk turned and looked to where the colors had been. Shiny new and somewhat unmatched plating now covered the area, and one of the techs was collecting sealing tools. There was an odd, ugly bulge where a smooth bulkhead had been, but the chief signaled that it would serve.

The thrum of power from the engines began to dominate Engineering. Jim glanced to his left as McCoy and a herd of medical staff wheeled Spock out the door, but he remained by the intercom. The deck vibrated beneath his feet now, and Scotty was busy running from station to station, checking progress. Then Sulu's voice rang over the intercom, triumphant: "We've got helm control! Reversing now!"

Jim could feel the ship move, a slow, throbbing slide away from the now hidden swirling colors, first very gently, then with gradual acceleration.

"Easy, Mr. Sulu, until we're well away."

"Thirty-five kilometers, forty . . . fifty . . ." Chekov recited.

And then another voice interrupted him—Mr. Leslie's, Jim tentatively identified it, imagining him filling in at Spock's station. Permanently? He threw the idea aside and listened. "Field diameter one-point-three kilometers and closing rapidly."

"Sulu, don't get us sucked in by some undertow."

The helmsman's voice was confident. "She's handling nicely, Captain. Seventy-five kilometers . . ."

Leslie: "Ten meters and . . . It's gone!" There was a pause, and then Jim heard muffled cheers from the rest of the bridge crew. "Sensors registered a kind of implosive force at the moment it disappeared—but there was nothing there to implode."

"Like the *Enterprise*," Jim said, sighing with relief. "Mr. Chekov, plot a course for the nearest starbase. We're going to need repairs. I'll be in Sickbay."

Lissa Hart stopped him as he entered the medical quarters. She'd been beside Jerry Dubois, who still lay motionless, staring vacantly at the ceiling. That sight softened Jim's impatience, though it did nothing to quell his anxiety.

"Captain"—and she was softly embarrassed—"I'm sorry for the way I acted earlier. I heard what happened."

"I understand," Kirk said gently, and started to go on. She touched his sleeve.

"I . . . I hope it hasn't happened to Mr. Spock, too."

Dreading even to consider that, Jim came in and found McCoy staring worriedly at the medical scanner over the examining table where Spock lay.

"Bones?"

"I don't know, Jim. I'm not really sure what I'm looking for, since his physiology is so damned unique."

"That drug . . . whatever you gave him?"

McCoy glanced at the scanner again, then down at Spock. "It's wearing off right now." Spock's eyes opened, no blinking. He didn't seem to see either of them. "Spock, can you hear me? This is McCoy."

Slowly, without inflection, Spock said, "I hear you."

Kirk was elated, but McCoy frowned and picked up a medical log to study. "It's intact, but is it functioning?"

"What?"

"I mean, it's possible his brain could respond to a direct question, but that . . . well, his ability to *initiate* thought is gone." McCoy bit off his words. "Not wiped clean. More like a lobotomy. Or a form of insanity. What did he see over there? What happened to him—to both of them—to destroy Dubois's mind, and Spock . . ."

The Vulcan was still staring unblinkingly at the ceiling. "Maybe," Jim hoped, "maybe it's only temporary. Is that possible, Bones? Like shock?"

"I don't . . ."

"A test! Something to focus his attention, to bring him out of it." Jim paced, softly hammering fist into palm, wondering if he were not speaking out of desperation. "Something scientific, or mathematical."

McCoy looked dubious. "One of us, think up a math problem for Spock?"

"Not a problem. A reminder of a tool he needs to use in his work—but something he'd have to *think* about. Something to bring him back to . . . to . . ." He suddenly bent over Spock. "Spock, this is . . . the captain. I need . . . data. Give me . . . give me the value of pi."

The doctor grimaced disapprovingly. "That's awfully . . ."

Tonelessly, Spock began to speak. "Three-point-one-four-one-five-nine-two-six . . ."

Kirk's initial grin faded. McCoy looked bleak. "Listen to him, Jim. There's no inflection there at all. Like an automaton."

Despairing, Jim caught Spock by the shoulders. The science officer was still reciting numbers, and that recitative ability that had irritated him so many times before now plunged him into black depression. Agonized, hardly realizing he spoke, Jim murmured, "Spock . . ."

Those deepset eyes blinked, and then Spock looked directly at him. Jim could have sworn there was a twinkle behind that solemn gaze. "To how many decimal places did you wish me to carry . . . ?"

"*Spock!*" McCoy roared, obviously torn between fury and joy.

"Must you, Doctor? I assure you my hearing is quite unimpaired."

Jim shook him half-playfully, weak with delight. "If you hadn't just saved the ship, I'd . . ."

The veiled amusement went out of Spock's eyes. He sat up, then said, "But I did not, as you put it, save the ship."

"But the coupling! You went in there, found it, and brought it back."

Spock shook his head. "Perhaps I did carry the device over the threshold—I have no memory of that —but I did not find it. I was incapable of doing so."

Interested, McCoy asked, "What was in there, Spock? What happened to you and Jerry?"

"I doubt that I shall ever be able to describe it accurately. There are no words, no terminology, for what I saw, heard, felt. I was able to block out some of it with mental disciplines. But not all. There were . . . beings there. I cannot . . . The mind was assaulted with incomprehensible images and sensations. Colors one could taste, sounds one could smell. Round objects with sharp angles."

Captain and doctor listened and watched with fascination. Spock plainly was still disturbed by the memory, though equally plainly he was once more himself.

"It finally became impossible to refuse the impressions. And when it did, I felt myself slipping into . . . insanity. That is not the proper term, Doctor. But my mind refused to accept what was being received by it, and . . ."

"Began to cease functioning. That's what must have happened to Jerry. Only he didn't have your grace period, when you were able to shut out the other dimension for a while."

Spock's voice was husky. "Losing control was a bit like losing consciousness—but only partially. The last thing I remember was *the coupling being pushed into my hands.* And then the safety line began to drag me back."

"But you . . ." Jim said confusedly, "you pulled on the line to signal us."

"No, Captain. *They* did."

"They?"

"I never really saw them, but I sensed their presence. And I sensed . . . an urgency. A sensation almost of desperation—as if our contact with their world was endangering them."

"As if," Jim said, speaking faster and faster, "they were working against a deadline, too! Maybe they *couldn't* pull free. They had to depend on us to detach from them."

"And they got one look at Spock," McCoy snorted, "shoved the coupling into his hands, and pushed him toward the door just as fast as they could. Very sensible people."

Spock's eyebrows were functioning perfectly, and he used them to express an acid opinion of McCoy's remarks.

Jim turned and snapped on the miniviewer, punched up a shot of the bridge viewscreen. The friendly stars, unveiled, filled it, appearing to move aside as the *Enterprise* bore toward a repair station. "Yes, very sensible people. And generous. I hope they got home all right."

Introduction to The Enchanted Pool

by *Nichelle Nichols*

Not only in the "bloopers" is Uhura occasionally tempted to say, "Mr. Spock, sugah." She has been known to tease him, even in song, and she is hardly the only one, present or future, who would be delighted to find some enchantment by which to disturb his Vulcan cool.

More seriously, Uhura is often seen today as a symbol of women and their role in the *Star Trek* universe, and as her alter ego I am often asked to speak on that role.

In fact, it is a question that has interested me and one that Uhura and I plan to deal with in a book now in progress with the editors of this anthology.

It was, of course, the intention of the creator of *Star Trek* to show not only the beauty of differences but also the delight in the diversities as well as the similarities of women; to show them as capable of responsibility, achievement, initiative, courage, compassion—fellow beings reaching for nobility, heroic in their quest.

For instance, the story of "Number One," the female second-in-command, played so beautifully in the first pilot of *Star Trek* by Majel Barrett, was always inspiring. "Nurse" Chapel was, in fact, a doctor and researcher in her own right.

Uhura, likewise, was highly respected as exceedingly qualified in her field, and a first-rate officer, even by the exacting standards of Mr. Spock. She was regarded as quite capable of saving the entire spaceship because of her expertise, and in a pinch, fully able to hold her own as a "gladiator." The *Enterprise* had security "men" who were women, and ran into doctors, lawyers, and Indian chiefs who were women—commanders, matriarchs, and the like.

If *Star Trek* ever lapsed from that standard—and it must be admitted that even Uhura was heard to com-

plain about saying, "Hailing frequencies open, sir," for
the umpteenth time—we should still remember that it
was only *Star Trek* that began to set that standard,
long before we heard much about it in our real world.

I can't help believing that *Star Trek* was a forerunner
in the real world for the inevitable movements for
liberation for anyone who ever felt misclassified by
form or face or color or creed.

We have come a long way since the last of the old
voyages, and I think we would not have come so far
without them.

We still have a long way to go. But I see people
working to get there. (It is significant that many of
them are women; for example, the writers and editors
of these stories.) So long as we are still working, writing, talking, thinking, loving, we are under way on
warp drive to the world and the future we want.

These are the new voyages. . . .

And they may be just a little different.

Logical, Mr. Spock, sugah.

P.S. Hailing frequencies still open, Cap'n Honey.

The Enchanted Pool

by *Marcia Ericson*

The three moons of Mevinna had risen two hours earlier, washing the glade in cool greenish light. Though he could see well enough to read his instruments, during all the past discouraging day they had revealed nothing useful, and Spock carefully closed the cases now and sank down at the edge of the pool roughly marking the center of the area that was, essentially, his prison.

Two time checks had come and gone without a sign from the *Enterprise*. Doubtless his last position report had not been received and they had no idea where he was. Nor would they even know, yet, that he was in trouble. Dutifully, because it was time for another check, but without real hope of an answer, he flipped open his communicator and tried to raise the *Enterprise*.

Silence—only the faint night forest sounds of small insects and the rustle of the long, graceful, gossamer pandella leaves swaying gently in the almost imperceptible stirring of the mossy-fragrant air. The glade might have seemed a haven of peace and beauty were he not a prisoner, were he not failing his assignment.

They had had the first hint of trouble when Uhura's voice came over the intercom. "Captain, you are receiving a Class A Security message from Admiral Benthoven at Starbase Six."

Twenty minutes later Kirk had his senior officers assembled in the briefing room. "Gentlemen," he asked, "have any of you heard of a new supersecret weapon developed by Star Fleet—code name Excalibur?"

The Excalibur was a top-secret weapon which was being transported by the USS *Yorktown* from a research lab on Earth Colony Seven to Starbase Six for final testing and evaluation. En route, the *Yorktown* had been decoyed by a false distress signal, engaged and damaged by a group of renegade Andorians. The

captain of the *Yorktown* had managed to dispatch a
shuttlecraft with the Excalibur aboard, and though
crippled, hold the Andorians from following for nearly twelve hours. The mission of the *Enterprise* was to
track the shuttlecraft and recover the Excalibur.

Five times in the days that followed, the *Enterprise*
had found and followed what appeared to be trails of
antimatter residue, only to have them play out into
nothing. As time passed, with the *Enterprise* making
wider and wider sweeps, her sensitive scanners closely
monitored around the clock, hopes dimmed.

It was Chekov who was on duty when the recorder
marker ejected by the shuttlecraft was picked up by
the scanners. The message read that the shuttlecraft
had been damaged by an asteroid bombardment and
was attempting to reach and land on the nearest Class
M Planet, Mevinna.

Spock hastily, but with his customary thoroughness,
gathered all available information on Mevinna for the
briefing session. Land area comprised one-sixth of the
planet's surface. Most of the land was covered with
forest. The planet was a geological oddity, containing
many rare though not valuable minerals, and was particularly rich in pyretimite. Spock's eyes met the captain's as he delivered that bit of information, and Kirk
swore softly. Pyretimite would play havoc with communications.

Humanoid life had not evolved on Mevinna; however, there were scattered small colonies of widely
divergent racial groups. With its natural beauty and
lack of civilization, it was a haven for back-to-nature
enthusiasts and for those to whom social and industrial
progress was inimical.

"I'm afraid our scanners won't help us in locating
either the crew of the shuttlecraft or the Andorians if
they were able to track the craft to Mevinna," Spock
said.

The *Enterprise* made two full orbits of the planet
without an answer to their radio calls. "All right," Kirk
said. "Beam-downs would be useless with this much
area to cover. I'm going to send out shuttlecrafts for
flyover. Spock, plot division of the land area into sec-

tors. You will command one shuttlecraft, with Bemis and Latrobe as crew."

They had been searching for nine hours and forty minutes when Latrobe reported to Spock, "I see a fresh cut in the underbrush, sir, as if a vehicle may have crash-landed, but I get no readings for the duranium we would expect if the craft itself were there."

"We'll go down and take a look," Spock said, and tried to raise the *Enterprise* to report their position. He got no answer except for a burst of static, and after repeating the attempt several times, gave it up. Only once during the search had he been able to get through the interference caused by the pyretimite and reach the ship.

"I think this must be it, sir," Bemis reported a quarter of an hour later.

"Yes," said Spock, busy with his tricorder. "There are still faint traces of antimatter exhaust discernible."

They fanned out, searching the area, and Bemis called out to Latrobe to show him something he had found. Latrobe approached him, and Spock had started toward them when he heard a strange humming sound. He called both of their names, though he did not know what he was warning them against, when suddenly, before his eyes, they—simply—disappeared.

Cautiously he approached the area where they had been standing, but before he quite reached the spot, he was jolted to a stop, and with a sick realization knew that a force field had been activated at the precise spot where his men had been standing and that they had been disintegrated in the field. Whether it was by accident or design that they had been caught, he did not know.

He spent the next hour defining the boundary of the force field. It was circular, covering about a square mile. He tried the shuttlecraft but could raise it only slightly higher than the tops of the trees. Though he was imprisoned, he still had a job to do, and he painstakingly began testing the area for any sign of the Excalibur, for any anomaly whatsoever.

He had found nothing, and so he sat now beside

the pool, fatigued and discouraged. He would do no more tonight. He would rest, even try to sleep, but within the confines of the shuttlecraft, not here on the seductively soft forest floor with starflies winking their gentle luminous sparks of light around him. Perhaps when he attacked the problem tomorrow his mind would be clearer and he would discover some clue that had so far eluded him.

He had tested the purity of the water earlier. Now, kneeling at the pool's edge, he scooped some up in his cupped hands and drank deeply. It was cold and fresh and tasted of moss and moonlight, though he instantly put that thought away from him as unscientific. The ripples he had created on the surface of the water cleared, and he could see the reflection of his face and of the three moons. Then, as he stared, bemused and weary, his mind played a trick on him, and in the depths of the pool he saw the delicate face of a nymph, pale and insubstantial as one of the moons. He felt a moment's alarm for his sanity, blinked, and leaned closer to the water, but the face did not disappear.

At a soft rustle beside him he started, whirled, and realized with chagrin that the face in the water had been only a reflection, but whether his mind was still playing tricks, he could not be sure, because the creature beside him did not have a look of reality. It was small and indisputably feminine, clothed in a strange garment of pandella leaves. Hair, silver and soft as thistledown, curved about the face. The skin seemed almost transparent.

After a long moment he forced himself to speak though his voice sounded strange to his ears. "Who are you?"

"Don't you know? I'm your true love." The musical voice was like ripples across the water.

He thought he had not heard correctly. "What did you say?"

"Your true love. Why else would anyone gaze into the enchanted pool on the night of the trine but to see the face of his true love?"

He decided to take one point at a time. "The trine. Can you explain the trine?"

"It is not to explain, but to observe." She pointed through a break in the trees. "When the three moons form a triangle that points to the heart of heaven."

He felt on somewhat firmer ground with an astronomical phenomenon, even though it was couched in fanciful language, but she went on. "On that night in the enchanted pool, you can see the face of your true love. As you have just done."

"I haven't done any such thing," he said sharply.

She gave him a disbelieving smile and began to dance around the water's edge. She moved so lightly that she almost seemed to float, and the swirling flutter of the pandella leaves and the stirring of the petals of her hair added to the illusion.

"Who *are* you?" he repeated.

She stopped dancing and turned shining green eyes on him. "I'm your—"

He interrupted quickly. "Do you have a name?"

She looked surprised. "Of course I have a name. It's Phyllida. Do you have a name?"

"I am called Spock."

She considered. "Cold Spock. There is a certain harshness to it."

"No, no," he said impatiently. "I am *called* . . . My *name* is Spock."

She brightened. "Oh, that is better. Spock and Phyllida. Spock and Phyllida. It goes trippingly on the tongue. Spock and Phyllida. There's assonance and rhythm there. We must tell it to the starflies, that they can rise up and write across the sky, 'Spock and Phyllida are one!' "

"We are *not* one," he said crossly.

She subsided at once with a look of hurt. "Your eyes are not so deep-seeing as they appear," she said. "They see me only as a wood nymph. They do not see that it is a transformation. I was a powerful princess till a wicked wizard cast a spell and turned me into a simple nymph and imprisoned me in the glade."

"If you were such a powerful princess, how could a wizard cast a spell on you?" he said with a touch of scorn, and was instantly abashed at having asked such an absurd question.

"Even princesses must sleep a little sleep," she said sadly. "And he is a *very* wicked wizard, with evil familiars." Then she brightened. "The spell can be broken, though." She came very close to him and turned her face up to his. "Don't you wish to know how?" When he did not answer, she said, "With a lover's kiss!"

Hastily he took a step backward.

She seemed bewildered. "You do not wish to break the spell? Perhaps you like me as a simple wood nymph." At his silence she said, "No? Then come with me to my cavern." She caught his hand, and with dancing steps tried to lead him.

"No!" He disengaged his hand abruptly.

She turned clear, stubborn eyes upon him. "You *must* come to the cavern. I am your destiny."

"You are *not* my destiny," he said firmly. "I am a Vulcan, and I do not accompany enchanted princesses to caverns or anywhere else."

"So that is what your people call themselves."

"You know of my people?"

"Of course. You are one of the fauns from a far part of the forest, come all this way to gaze in the enchanted pool and find your destiny. A daring enterprise."

He gave her a sudden sharp look.

"And you have found it. Come to my cavern," she begged, pulling at him, dancing before him, and as he set himself firmly against her wheedling, she calmed and grew imperious. "I command it."

"I do not take commands from you."

"Ah, perhaps you want to be the commander, Spock."

He blinked. Her face was innocent. "Are there others here?" he asked.

"Others like me?" She shook her head. "I am the only one. Why do you ask?"

"Earlier I felt as if I were being watched."

"The spirits watch," she told him. "The spirits have eyes and ears. They see every eyelash lying upon your cheek. They hear every sigh." Her gaze was intent upon his. Was it a warning?

"Can you help me find a path out of the glade?" he asked.

"There is no path. The wizard captured a whirlwind and stretched it into a circle and set it around the edge of the glade and pulled it into a canopy overhead."

A whirlwind like a dome, he thought. Perhaps in her fanciful way she was describing the force field. "Did he place the whirlwind to keep you here?"

"Oh, no, I am tied to this place till the spell is broken. But one morning I woke, and the whirlwind was here. I think he put it here because he feared someone would come and break my enchantment."

"Enough fairy tales, Phyllida," he said.

"You look so grim," she told him.

"Irrelevant," he said, but her words echoed oddly upon his ear.

"Perhaps you are afraid to break the spell," she said. "Perhaps you are afraid to have my power restored, lest it outstrip yours. Perhaps you recognize that I am a daughter of a third daughter and fear the power that the daughter of a third daughter wields."

"I thought that was the seventh son of a seventh son," he scoffed.

"How can I be a seventh son, or a ninth or tenth, when I am a daughter?" she said with scorn. "No, the magic is in being the daughter of a third daughter. My mother is one of nine daughters, but all her sisters are barren. It is from her that I inherited my power, and you do well to fear it—though I would not use it against my true love."

"I do not fear your power," he said dryly.

"I think you do not even believe in it," she said slowly. She drew herself up, and her eyes flashed. "You would do well not to anger me. Before the wizard cast his spell, I had such power . . . I tamed a lightning bolt and wore it above my heart like a jewel. I could make dark stars glow with fire. I kept a school of silver fish that swam the night sky and turned it ten times brighter than day. But now, because of the evil wizard, I must live in a cave, though it is a very nice cave. You would like it, Spock. It is hung with vines, and it has a glorious crystal waterfall, misty at the base, like the tail of a comet. And I keep twelve jadespiders to spin for me. The filaments they spin look fine and delicate, but they have great tensile strength. I weave them among the pandella leaves and press them into whatever form I like, and when they have dried in the sun, they make a permanent bond."

He was frowning. Her odd words disturbed him somehow.

She spun around now, spreading out her garment. "Do you like my dress? I think it is passing pretty, though green is not what I am accustomed to. I wore the color of flame, as befitted one of my station."

"How long have you been here, Phyllida?"

"Since the wizard enchanted me."

"Yes, yes," he said impatiently. "But how much time? How many days?"

"What does it matter? Time is relative. Perhaps a year. Perhaps fifty years. I grow no older under the spell."

"Have others been here? Anyone dressed like me?"

"Not that I have seen. None like you."

"Any others at all?" he persisted.

"Once, insects came."

He was disappointed.

"Insects the color of the sky"—she frowned, concentrating—"the sky on a day when the sun is a little dim. Insects that walked on two legs and spoke to me. Not like my insects that spin for me. Perhaps a higher order of insects."

Again he felt a startled flicker. Higher order of insects. Were the words only a random choice, or was she more sophisticated than she seemed? Did she know something of zoological classification? What was she describing? Pale blue insects that walked on two legs. Why insects? Antennae? He experienced a surge of excitement. Andorians?

"Tell me of these insects. What did they say?"

"They asked stupid questions. Has anyone come out of the sky. Have I seen a great box with wings. I do not remember more."

"Could you answer?"

"How could I? I had been sleeping for"—she narrowed her eyes—"oh, since before the suvis came to bud. Sometimes I grow bored with waiting, and then I sleep till the season changes. But I am not bored now that you are here." She smiled confidently at him.

"Did they threaten you?"

"How threaten? Why should they harass me? I explained that if I should die, the whole glade dies with me and vanishes like a puff of flower dust blown on the wind. It is part of the wizard's spell. I think they would not want to be blown like dust on the wind, do you?"

"It would seem a most undesirable experience."

"The hour is late," she said suddenly. "We have talked enough. Let us break the spell now."

"Yes, it is late. I am going to sleep."

"I'll make you a bed of the softest moss," she promised. "In my cavern."

"I will sleep in my shuttlecraft," he said firmly, and turning on his heel, walked toward it.

"Good night, Spock." Her silver voice was like a night bird's call echoing through the glade. "Dream on the words of your true love."

He did not look back.

The sun was bright when he opened the hatch next morning, and he could almost believe that Phyllida had been a dream, but when he dropped to the ground, she was waiting, sitting beneath a tree, her legs folded neatly beneath her. "Good morning, my love," she greeted him. "Your breakfast is waiting in my cavern."

"I have had my repast," he said. "I carry rations with me."

"It is quite possible that I shall cry," she told him.

"I trust not," he said politely. "It would avail you nothing."

He set to work with his tricorder. She disappeared for a time, and it was strangely quiet. Then suddenly her face appeared, peering over a shrub at him. "You leave no stone unturned seeking one blade among the million blades of grass. What are you searching for?"

The words "The Excalibur" almost slipped out, but he closed his lips on them and said instead, "For a way to leave this place."

"You don't need those absurd toys for that," she said. "It will take only a kiss. When I have my power back, I can whisk you wherever you want to go in the wink of an eye. You could ride on the back of Cygnus if you wished, or take your ease in Cassiopeia's chair."

"Indeed. I don't wish to be rude, but I prefer to rely on my absurd toys."

"But you *are* being rude. You haven't paid any attention to me all morning. Come dance with me." She caught his hands in hers and tried to spin him around.

Pulling away, he walked to the pool and set his tricorder once more.

"What a delicious idea. We'll go for a swim."

"We will not go for a swim," he said.

"Yes, we will. *I* will." He heard a rustle and looked up to see that she was divesting herself of her garments. Hastily he averted his eyes.

"Put your clothes on at once," he said sharply.

For answer she gave a laugh, and then he heard a splash. Her face broke the surface of the pool directly below where he was standing. The water had darkened her fair hair, and it lay tight to her head and across her brow in flat gold tendrils, as if it had been sculptured. She lifted her arms to him. "I can teach you to swim, Spock. I can show you many things."

He backed away.

"First I'll teach you to dive." She started to climb out of the pool, but by the time her milk-white shoulders had appeared, he had made a hasty retreat. Her taunting laughter rippled after him.

In midafternoon she appeared carrying a woven leaf basket of berries and two large fruits. "Which shall it be, Spock. break the spell or have lunch?"

"Lunch," he said, as the lesser of the evils, though he had not intended to accept food from her.

"I'll show you how to open the lormos," she said, handing him one of the fruits. "Force a stick into the stem end and pull the shell apart. Then pour the juice over the tanniberries and eat the fruit."

The lormos fruit was cool and delicious, the tanniberries warm and sweet and sticky. The food and the heat of the sun, the drowsy hum of insects, had a soporific effect, and his eyelids felt heavy.

"You're sleepy," she said. "You had only a few hours' rest last night. Why don't you sleep now?"

"Perhaps I will," he said, and leaned back against a tree.

He awoke to find her lying beside him, raised on one elbow, regarding him intently. The breeze lifted the pale silk of her hair gently. The gossamer leaves rose and rustled with her breath. Her skin was no less delicate than the shimmering webs of her garment. And her face . . . He might have been looking into the heart of some newly opened flower, fresh-sprung from the velvet interior of the forest. She looked, in truth, a faerie creature—but he did not believe in magic. She had lied and lied again, but he could sense no malice in her. Had she believed her own mad words? Had she intended to deceive?

"Who are you, really?" he asked hoarsely.

"You have only to break the spell to find out," she said.

Baffled, beleaguered, not knowing what else to do, he leaned toward her. He did not know whether he had actually moved all the way to kiss her, or whether at his slight gesture she had come partway to him. Their lips touched, and her arms went around him. Her sun-warmed skin was fragrant against his cheek. Her mouth had the sweet taste of tanniberries. Somehow, one of his hands was curved against the down-silk hair at the back of her head. A faint wave of dizziness swept over him, and he felt as if the time and space in which they were wrapped were dissolving.

Something inside him asked, "Is it the spell breaking?" And slicing them cleanly apart came the inescapable Vulcan thought: "I am as mad as she."

He looked at her, feeling triumph that logic was vindicated and that she was after all unchanged, and yet there was a stab of something very like disappointment in the victory. "So," he said, his voice harsh, perhaps to ensure its steadiness. "The spell is not broken, after all."

She was trembling, but with an effort that moved him oddly, she calmed and spoke evenly. "A kiss is only part of breaking the spell. It must be delivered while standing under the crystal waterfall in my cavern."

"Why did you not tell me that in the first place?"

"I have begged you over and over to come to the cavern, but you were afraid and refused each time."

"Then why did you want me to kiss you here and now if you knew it wouldn't break the spell?"

She looked at him and sighed. "I thought you might like it well enough to follow me to the cave. I thought it might be pleasant enough to make you less wary. Was it so unpleasant, Spock?"

"Not unpleasant, precisely," he said carefully. "But serving no useful purpose."

She flicked him a glance compounded of wistfulness and exasperation. "Then come with me and do it properly, under the waterfall."

"You know it is foolishness."

"Is that what you fear so greatly—seeming a fool? Come with me now, Spock. Aren't you curious to see what I am as my true self?"

He thought perhaps it was the discouraged note of weariness in her voice that did it, as if the effort of going through it one more time was almost beyond bearing.

"Very well," he said. "Come." If it was a trap, so be it. He picked up his tricorder and started for the mouth of the cave.

It was cool inside, and as she had said, vines hung from the ceiling. The tricorder showed no living beings larger than insects. At one side was a small waterfall. It was an indication of Phyllida's fertile imagination that she could call this modest spillway a glorious crystal waterfall. "Not a very prepossessing cascade," he commented.

"Shall we try to make its magic work?" Then, with a quick movement she laid two fingers across Spock's lips to keep him from speaking, and pulling him after her, she stepped not toward the waterfall but toward one of the walls covered with pandella vines. She pulled the vines aside, revealing a narrow cleft in the rock wall, and motioning him to follow, slipped through. There was a pathway leading sharply downward, and she hurried along it, pausing only now and then to make sure he was following.

Sometimes the path twisted, but it always swung back, so that they were progressing steadily in one direction and always descending. At last Spock heard a roar that grew louder and louder, till suddenly they passed through another slit and came to a large cavern, bright with green phosphorescent lichens. And there at the end of the cavern, tumbling over a sharp cliff of rock, was Phyllida's crystal waterfall. The droplets sparked with flashing colors, and at the bottom, where it formed a swiftly flowing river through a rock channel, it boiled up feather-white.

There was a niche in the rock, with yet another passage opening off it behind the fall, and it was to this ledge that Phyllida led him now. As they stepped through the shining curtain of water, he gasped slightly. The water was cold but deliciously invigorating.

She turned to him and started to speak, but suddenly, looking at her face glistening with beaded water like a flower in summer rain, her gaze earnest upon him, he wished only to get it over with, to have done with deception, to hear no more lies, and abruptly he drew her to him. Her body was small and fragile in his arms, but with a supple strength that surprised him. Her cold mouth grew warm and alive under the pressure of his.

When he released her, he was almost regretful to see her proved wrong. "I hope we are finally done with such illogical foolishness." The words came out as a harsh whisper. "I have done as you asked, and you are quite unchanged."

"You are mistaken, Mr. Spock. I am transformed." There was none of the wanton, playful child in her tone now. It had deepened to a note of authority. "Lieutenant Phyllida Gaines of the USS *Yorktown*. We have passed under the perimeter of the force field. If my calculations are correct, the edge of it lies just the other side of the waterfall. We can no longer be heard by the Andorian sensors."

For a moment he could only stare, stupefied. Then he said, "Explain."

"I was one of the crew of the shuttlecraft that escaped from the *Yorktown* with the Excalibur on board. We crash-landed in the glade, and knowing it was possible that the Andorians might track us, we secreted the weapon while trying to repair the craft. It was several days before they caught up with us. Meanwhile, we had explored the area and found the cave—the outer room of it. We were using the small waterfall as a shower. That's where I was when the Andorians arrived.

"When I started back to the shuttlecraft, I heard their voices. They were so intent on trying to learn the whereabouts of the Excalibur from the other crew members that they didn't see me."

She looked away, her eyes haunted by old ghosts. "Several of my crew mates had already died. The others soon followed. The Andorians are not a subtle people." Her voice was bitter. "I had no weapon with me. There was nothing I could do. I returned to the cave, and knowing it wouldn't be long before they found me, I burned my uniform and fashioned a garment out of leaves. When they discovered me, I told them the same tale as I told you."

"I don't understand why they let you live."

"Whether I was mad or masquerading, they could have learned nothing from me if I were dead. They had discovered how readily we die under their form of questioning. Then too, civilization is newer to the Andorians than to your race or mine. I think they felt some element of superstitious fear that I might be telling the truth, and that if I died, the glade might be destroyed with me.

"They began their search, but they couldn't find the Excalibur. They put the force field in operation to keep out wanderers. When your shuttlecraft was sighted, they decided to let you in, then reactivate it to keep you here. They realized that your equipment and methods were more sophisticated than theirs and hoped you would discover the Excalibur for them. They can monitor by sight and sound everything within the force field—at least, everything outside the cave. They can hear what's going on in the cave, but they can't see inside. I had meanwhile discovered the passage behind the vines and blocked it up with stones before they searched the cave."

"Could you not have told me this sooner?"

She put her hands on her hips and gave him a look of total exasperation. "Haven't I been trying to get you inside the cave from the beginning?"

"There was no reason I should have trusted you," he said.

"They could hear every word I said, but I told you as clearly as I could that I knew who you were, that I was from Earth, and that I served aboard a starship. If only you hadn't been so stubborn. . . . You are not an easy man to seduce, Mr. Spock."

Hastily he said, "Where is the Excalibur secreted?"

"At the bottom of the enchanted pool."

He threw her a disbelieving look. "That is impossible. I have scanned the pool."

"The water contains minute particles of verilium, does it not?"

"Yes. A very rare element. But what has that to do—?"

"And of obsitrate," she said. "You are unfamiliar with the effect of the combination?"

He frowned. "Verilium and obsitrate almost never appear together." He searched his memory, and a light broke. "But when they do . . ."

"Exactly," she said. "They polarize negatively, forming an impenetrable screen that shows no sign that a screen exists."

"I have been a fool," he exclaimed impulsively.

"Yes," she agreed dryly, "on several counts."

He flashed her a quizzical look from under arched brows.

"Our science officer discovered this, and we sank the Excalibur into the pool. *That* is why I had to keep you away from it with your tricorder, you know. I was afraid you would figure it out and give the show away."

"One thing I do not understand. If when we passed through the waterfall we were beyond their listening devices, why . . . ?" He paused.

"Why what, Mr. Spock?" she said innocently.

"Why did you still . . . ? You allowed me to believe . . . You did not tell me a kiss was unnecessary," he finished uncomfortably.

"You said it wasn't *precisely* unpleasant," she retorted. "But if you wish, you can put me on report later. Now, however, do you think it's wise to stand here talking of kissing?"

He gave a guilty start.

"This passage leads eventually to the surface—outside the force field. We can use your communicator . . ."

"No," he said. "The pyretimite on this planet interferes with communication. We'll have to leave in the shuttlecraft."

"But how can we?"

"I have been thinking—M rays would destroy the field."

"How are we going to produce M rays?" she asked scornfully.

"I had given the matter considerable thought," he said, "but it won't work from inside the field. However, now that you have found a way to the outside, I believe I can construct a device by pirating parts of the communication and gravity systems of the shuttlecraft. It would not work at long range, but close to the field it should operate effectively enough. You would have to stay behind, ready to lift the shuttlecraft off and retrieve the Excalibur with a tractor beam, and then, if possible, to pick me up. The craft will not be easy to manipulate, with half its gravity system missing."

"I can manage," she said, "but, Mr. Spock, you can't just go out and start bringing electronic equipment into the cave. They'd know something was afoot."

He stared at her reflectively. "I could disassemble the necessary components as if I were simply overhauling the system. Then . . . I'm afraid, Lieutenant, that you'll just have to lure me back into the cave."

She groaned. "Mr. Spock, frankly I've *had* it with luring you."

"The prospect is not pleasing to me either," he said shortly. "Unfortunately, our personal preferences have no relevance in this matter."

He was seated on the ground, with all the parts that he needed from the shuttlecraft spread out around him, when she approached.

"What are you doing, Spock?"

"Just what it looks like—endeavoring to repair my communications system."

"That's not what it looks like at all. It looks like you're playing knucklebones."

He didn't deign to answer.

"Would you *like* to play knucklebones? It would be more fun than what you're doing."

"I am unfamiliar with the game, but I do not wish to *play* anything at all."

"You're angry with me."

He thrust the parts into a case and stood up. "I am incapable of anger," he said, starting toward the shuttlecraft, "but I see no reason to converse with anyone who speaks only lies."

"I haven't lied to you!" she cried.

He turned, his eyebrows arched. "No? I did as you asked. You told me your miraculous transformation would take place within the hour. I waited the requisite time. No transformation occurred. Your words are all lies."

"Did you ever stop to think that it was not my words but your performance that was at fault?"

The eyebrows rose higher.

"Yes, your performance," she said. "I told you it would take a *lover's* kiss to break the spell—not the kiss of a skeptic who was only trying to prove me false. Your performance was not . . . *proficient* enough to break the spell. Tell me, Spock, have you ever kissed a woman before?"

"That is of no concern to you," he said stiffly.

"But it is," she said. "I'm your true love. If only you'd stop doubting. . . . One part of you wanted me. I sensed it. But that disbelieving side of you wouldn't let you kiss me except as an experiment. Of course it didn't work. But we could make it work, Spock. Come back with me. Give in to your feelings. Give love a chance."

She put her hand on his arm, and as if hypnotized, he followed her, carrying the case of components from the shuttlecraft.

The *Enterprise* was in orbit around Starbase Six, the Excalibur having been safely transferred to a security station there. Spock was in the Transporter room with Phyllida, where she was ready to disembark to await the repair of her ship.

She looked trim and neat in her red uniform, every inch the efficient officer. It was difficult to believe she had ever danced in the moonlight garbed only in gossamer leaves, laughing her silvery laugh. On her uniform was the insignia of the Engineering section, the spiral lightning bolt that she wore above her heart like a jewel.

"And so our mission is accomplished," Spock said gravely.

"I know no other officer in Star Fleet who could have produced M rays with such inadequate equipment," she said.

With a rare lapse into informality he said, "You know I could not have done . . . any of it without your help, Phyllida."

"Nor I without yours."

"It is fortunate that my . . . ineptitude does not extend to scientific matters," he said dryly.

She shot him an astonished glance but did not pretend to misunderstand. "I was speaking for the benefit of the Andorians. I have confidence in your proficiency in every field. If there *had* been a spell, you would surely have broken it."

The signal came from the planet that they were

ready for her to beam down. She stepped onto the Transporter platform.

"So it's good-bye, Spock—for a little while."

"A little while?" The eyebrows rose.

Her lips curved slightly. "Somewhere, someday, we will meet again, Spock. It is destiny. You *did* look in the enchanted pool."

And then she was smiling the half-wild, half-sweet smile of old, and until he heard the whine of the Transporter and she faded from view, he saw only the delicately mischievous face of the wood nymph.

Introduction to
Visit to Weird Planet Revisited

by *Majel Barrett Roddenberry*

Even in *Star Trek*'s most serious moments, we were always inclined to have a bit of fun: over Christine Chapel's Vulcan version of chicken soup—excuse me, *plomeek* soup; or tribbles in the chicken sandwiches; or whatever.

And on the set it might be a certain Vulcan's bicycle hidden in unlikely places or a put-on staged for—or by —a certain producer known as the "Great Bird of the Galaxy," and by various other names bearing little resemblance to Gene Roddenberry.

It is always fun for us to see that the fans understood not only the seriousness but also that element of fun and humor—as in this story, which captures some of the atmosphere of the set in those days.

It also captures something more subtle: the feeling we sometimes had that the universe in which the *Enterprise* flew was, somehow, real—that on any day you might step off the transporter set and into the corridors of the real *Enterprise*.

What would we have done if we *had*—short of fainting?

Well, I for one would probably have headed straight for sickbay and turned myself in to my colleague Dr. McCoy.

What do you do if you *are* Dr. McCoy, or the Captain, or the Vulcan?

Somehow I have the feeling that De and Bill and Leonard might have done exactly what they do in Ruth Berman's delightful story—and pulled it off, too.

Meanwhile, do you wonder what we would have done with the real McCoy and Captain and Vulcan on the set? Or they with us?

Mmm. . . . Fascinating thought.*

*That story has been written, too. It is "Visit to a Weird Planet," by Jean Lorrah and Willard F. Hunt, which Ruth Berman acknowledges in her title.

81

Visit to a
Weird Planet Revisited

by *Ruth Berman*

The director counted off seconds to himself while his actors stood transfixed on the Transporter platform in attitudes of heroic attentiveness. "Action," McEveety said.

William Shatner stepped forward briskly, and the camera panned around to follow him. His foot slipped, and he stepped down with a thud.

"Cut. Oh, God," said McEveety. It was becoming more a genuine prayer than a simple curse by now.

Shooting had not gone well that day, and on top of everything else, he had a small herd—or horde—he wasn't sure which word fit better—of visitors. Normally, he'd have thrown them out, but they were high-up something-or-others, and he always felt hesitant about telling the producer to take his guests and get out.

"Sorry about that," said Shatner.

"Well, it wasn't your fault." McEveety sighed.

"The blame's a foot," said Shatner solemnly, then chortled at his own joke.

McEveety winced. "Take five while I recover from that," he said, and went into a huddle with the cameraman. Slips aside, he still wasn't satisfied with the smoothness of the pan.

Leonard Nimoy went to his chair and plunked down. One visitor came up and asked for an autograph, saying how much she liked Mr. Spock.

"Thank you, thank you!" said Nimoy, as cordially as late-afternoon sleepiness allowed, and pumped her hand vigorously. When he had signed the autograph, however, he excused himself and opened his script to check his lines.

The fan watched reverently for a moment, then wandered off to request other autographs.

Shatner chatted with the visitors, finding it easier to

83

relax in conversation than in sitting still, and DeForest Kelley joined James Doohan (waiting patiently behind the Transporter controls) for a quiet gripe-and-grumble over the odds against their finishing at a reasonable hour.

After a few minutes, they were called back to the Transporter, and dutifully stiffened themselves into the "beaming" pose. The clapboard slammed, McEveety counted the seconds needed to cover the special effect, and said hopefully, "Action!"

But the hope that this take would go right was promptly spoiled. For a moment the actors wondered if they were fainting; there were spots before their eyes, and they felt dizzy, as if they had been kneeling and then had stood up too quickly. But their vision cleared, and they were still standing on the Transporter platform. Shatner, hoping to salvage the take, stepped forward and said authoritatively, "Scotty, get a report on that power source and meet me in the briefing room."

"Power source, Captain?" said the man behind the panel in a tone of utter bewilderment.

"There goes the take," muttered Nimoy disgustedly. "What's the matter with you, Jimmy?"

"The captain's all right, to all appearances, but, begging your pardon, Mr. Spock, are you?"

Nimoy suddenly noticed that they were in a room with four walls and a ceiling, and with no camera or lights around (except for normal room lighting, apparently coming out of concealed ceiling panels). Nimoy dropped characterization and broke into a wide grin as he looked around. "Beautiful!" he said. "Whose idea was this? Justman's? This mock-up must have cost a mint. How'd you get us here?"

"I . . . I think there's something wrong," said Kelley.

"Aye, Doctor, there is that, seemingly."

"How about dropping the accent?" said Nimoy.

"Mr. Spock!" Lieutenant-Commander Montgomery Scott blazed with righteous indignation.

Kelley spoke quickly. "Captain, will you give me a hand getting him to Sickbay?"

Shatner nodded, and they each took one of Nimoy's arms, prepared to hustle him out into the corridor. By this time, however, he too had counted up the costs of scene design and construction. James Doohan could have gone on improvising in the tones of outraged Scottishness all day without breaking, but Matt Jeffries just didn't have the budget to have built the room they were in.

The door swooshed open at their approach, and all three knew, even before they got past it, that they were on board the *Enterprise.* The pneumatic door-sound was supposed to be added by Glen Glenn Sound. They had never before heard it in real life. The door swooshed shut behind them, and they stood still for a moment, feeling totally lost.

"Nice going, De," said Shatner, trying to recover some poise. "Now, how the hell do we find the Sickbay?"

"Go to the elevator and say 'Sickbay'?" suggested Kelley.

"Yeah," said Nimoy, "that's right, they work on voice commands, don't they? Sorry I blew it."

"Well," said Shatner, "if it weren't impossible, it's exactly the sort of thing Justman would pull."

"Sort of thing you'd pull, as far as that goes, if you thought you could break me up," Nimoy grumbled.

The elevator obediently took them down a few levels. Fortunately, they found the Sickbay a few doors away, saving them the embarrassment of being caught reading the labels beside the doors. Kelley shivered at the sight of the familiar room. He picked up a diagnostic instrument. It looked just like its counterpart, but it was heavier than the salt shaker. He cocked it experimentally at Nimoy. It promptly emitted a wavering whistle, and he dropped it.

Shatner and Nimoy burst out laughing.

The tension eased a little.

"Well, it's, you know, spooky," Kelley complained, restoring the instrument to its place in what he had always thought of as a glorified medicine cabinet.

"You mean 'Spocky,' " said Shatner.

"Wait'll we get on the bridge, and see how you feel," said Kelley, ignoring the pun. "Say, Leonard, tell me what goes on in that viewer of yours, okay?"

"We're not going to pretend we really are those guys, are we?" said Nimoy.

"Why not?" asked Shatner wickedly. "No, you're right," he said, thinking better of it. "Scotty would be the senior officer, wouldn't he? Let's go back and—"

Something buzzed.

It took Shatner a moment to identify it as the sound effect—no, the sound—of the intercom. He stepped to the table and flicked the intercom switch with the nonchalance of long practice. "Kirk here," he said to the face that appeared on the screen.

"Captain, we're under attack," said Sulu.

"On my way," said Shatner, and switched off the intercom. He stood, wondering what he was waiting for, and realized it was a director to say "Cut." He looked helplessly at the others and shrugged. They headed for the door together.

The elevator took them to the bridge on their command. Shatner was startled by the size of the bridge. It took him several steps to get to his chair, not the few he was used to. It seemed strange to sit down and stare at a main viewscreen with a picture already on it. It showed a typical view of stars-and-planet. The planet showed flat black—they were over the night side. There were no larger lights that might be moons or other planets. Shatner found the loneliness of the dull-black-on-deep-black sight depressing.

Kelley crossed to a point behind the chair and stood there wondering, not for the first time, if the doctor really had any business being there. Nimoy went to Spock's station and looked into the viewer. To his disappointment, it was dark. He suspected that the dial on the side turned it on, but realized it would look odd if he tried it and it was wrong. He sat down in Spock's chair, feeling useless, and glanced at the others, wondering if they felt as ill-at-ease in the masquerade as he did. They at least were real humans, if not real Star Fleet officers, whereas he might be spotted as a fake alien.

"Report, Mr. Sulu," said Shatner crisply.

"Smart-ass," muttered Nimoy, unable to keep himself from resenting Shatner's (seeming) confidence in his ability to keep up appearances. He spoke a little louder than he meant to, and drew a look of shocked disbelief from Uhura. He raised an eyebrow in a typically Spock look of surprise at her, and she turned back to her board, wondering if she was hallucinating. Nimoy, suddenly feeling better, turned a Spockishly cool look of expectancy on Sulu.

"Nothing the deflectors can't handle, Captain," said Sulu. "The Klingons are trying to warn us away."

"That doesn't seem like the Klingon thing to do," Shatner commented.

"There's the treaty," Kelley said doubtfully, and was relieved to see both Sulu and Chekov nod in agreement.

"Still no claim made to the planet by the Klingons, sir," Uhura said.

Chekov shifted uneasily in his seat, obviously on fire with some kind of curiosity. Shatner was afraid that he'd have no hope of answering anything the young man might want to ask of Kirk. He reflected, however, that a question might contain in its phrasing the answers to some of the questions he could not ask. "Yes, Mr. Chekov?" he said.

"Was there anything on the planet's surface to explain Klingon interest, Captain?"

Shatner hesitated. He didn't know what Kirk and his landing party might have found. But he couldn't very well say yes, so . . . "No."

"Illogical, Captain," said Nimoy.

Shatner turned around in his chair and stared.

Nimoy continued. "If the landing party found nothing, it does not necessarily follow that there was nothing there to find."

Shatner went on staring, and clamped his teeth shut over the giggle. He sat quite still, except for the jerking in the muscles at the back of his jaw.

Nimoy stared back, and felt his own control going. "Further research is indicated, Captain," he said quickly. He knew that hastiness was wrong for Spock, but he had no choice. He headed for the elevator without waiting for permission. Once inside, he leaned against the far wall, let his head droop against his chest, and laughed himself out of breath.

Caught on the bridge, Shatner held himself rigid and tried to distract himself with thoughts of the Klingon menace. The ploy took sudden effect as it occurred to him that he could actually get killed by Klingon phaser-banks or photon torpedoes, or other equally improbable gadgets. "Uhura," he said, "try hailing the Klingon captain."

"Aye, sir," she said, and played a little medley of electronic bleeps on her board. "Ready on visual," she said after a moment.

Shatner turned his head back to face the screen and marveled as the picture blurred out, came back into focus, and showed him the familiar gray, armorial uniforms. To his surprise, he found the face above also familiar. "Commander Kor!" he said.

"Not exactly," Kor said. "My rank is now equivalent to commodore. Perhaps the Federation does not appreciate your true worth, Captain."

"Perhaps," said Shatner, smiling affably. Even if he had felt a truly personal interest in the insult, he would have been distracted by the sight of Kor's aide. Kor had the common dark skin and bifurcated eyebrows, but the officer behind him had light skin and un-branched eyebrows. The two were clearly from different races of the same species. "Fred Phillips should be here," Shatner said to Kelley.

Kelley nodded, remembering Phillips's anguish at discovering he'd done inconsistent makeups on Klingons the second time they used them.

"Indeed?" said Kor. "And who is Mr. Phillips?"

"Well," said Shatner, "let's say he's a student of the Klingon face."

"A spy," said Kor thoughtfully. "Inactive, I assume, or you would not reveal his name."

"Yes," said Kelley, "by now he'd be dead." His feet were beginning to hurt from standing so long after a hard day's work, so he went to Spock's chair and sat down heavily. Kor mistook the weariness for emotion.

"Mr. Phillips was a friend of yours, gentlemen?" he said with mock sympathy.

Shatner grinned. "Yes. But tell me, Commodore, do you generally use peaceful vessels for target practice? You fired at us, I believe?"

"Scarcely that, Captain," Kor said. "Call it a salute. We have both, after all, been exploring this planet—I have reported it to the Empire under the name of Kahless. If you have not thought to give it a name of your own, perhaps you would do well to adopt this one."

"But that could be a trans*parent* trick?" said Shatner. There was a pause, while the translation devices footnoted the pun for the Klingons and Kirk's crew puzzled over the captain's unusual turn of humor.

"Hostility can be a spur to endeavor," Kor said at last. "My scientists have found nothing of value on Kahless, I admit, yet your interest in it has caused me to report to our governments that I claim it for the Klingon Empire. If you wish to dispute the claim, of course, we must arrange for arbitration. Unless you care to return my fire?"

"I'll take it under consideration," said Shatner. He detected a real enthusiasm for battle in the Klingon's offers. "Kirk out."

The screen blurred back to its picture-postcard view.

"They must have found something!" exclaimed Chekov.

"Not necessarily, Ensign," said Shatner. He tried to think of a way to get more information. "De . . ." he said softly, finding himself at a loss.

"Who got—" Kelley started out. He paused to re-phrase it, to suggest that he knew the answer. "After all," he said firmly, "who got here first?" Surely some-one on the bridge had the temperament to answer rhetorical questions.

"Wery true, Doctor," said Chekov.

Kelley spread one hand out toward Shatner in a you-can't-win gesture. He halted it midway as Chekov went on, "But, then, why did they wait to exercise right to claim, when they had clear priority?"

"An excellent question, Mr. Chekov," said Shatner. "I think it merits discussion." He stood up and nodded at Kelley. "Bones . . ." He turned to Uhura. "Lieutenant, have Spock and Scotty meet us . . ." He hesitated, wondering if he could figure out a way to find the briefing room. ". . . in Dr. McCoy's office."

Nimoy was already there when they reached Sickbay. He would have preferred the privacy of Spock's quarters, once he'd gotten over his spasm of laughter, but he couldn't remember what level it was supposed to be on, and so had gone back to a place he was sure of finding.

Nurse Chapel had come in once, looking for Dr. McCoy. Nimoy, covering for his fellow impostor, had said that the doctor was helping investigate the current Klingon problem. Then it occurred to him that he had better cover for himself too, so he'd said he was also researching the problem and asked to be left alone. By then he was curious enough to want to try looking into it himself.

Shatner and Kelley found him seated at McCoy's table, staring intently into the viewer.

"What're you doing?" asked Kelley.

"Looking at the landing party's report," said Nimoy.

"What?" said Kelley.

"How?" said Shatner.

Both men crowded around to look over Nimoy's shoulder. The viewer showed a shifting scene, taken during daylight hours. Apparently whoever held the tricorder was turning in a circle. The view went around from sparse meadowland reaching out to khaki-colored mountains, to dry sand blowing in a heavy wind and ocean beyond, and across a high-water mark to wet sand and a wide bay of bright blue. A seagullish, sandy-yellow bird swooped into view, grabbing some kind of mussel from among the sea creatures caught out on the wet sand. A crab scuttled away from the bird's attack, and made it to the safety of the water. Meanwhile, the view kept turning, sweeping rapidly across the bay, and coming back up past wet sand and dry sand to the meadow.

"All it needs is a boardwalk," said Nimoy dreamily.

At the meadow, the view had stopped, becoming a still picture. Nimoy touched a switch, and the screen cut to a computer print-out of information on the life forms present.

"You've really got that thing under control," said Shatner admiringly.

The door opened.

Nimoy said, "Well, I called the computer on the intercom and asked how to run this thing, that's all."

"Amnesia, Doctor?" Scott asked Kelley, staring at Nimoy with deep pity.

"Sit down," said Shatner. "You're in for a shock. We're not who you think we are."

Scott, without moving, examined them minutely. "Aye," he said. "It's a brilliant job, but I can see where the ears went on. May I ask why you're telling me this?"

"We need your help," said Shatner.

"Do you, now?" said Scott. He had slowly been moving his hands down. One hand suddenly came whipping up with a phaser in it. "You're three to one, but I'm armed," he said softly. He would not have been carrying a phaser aboard ship normally, but they had been on yellow alert since discovering the Klingon ship, and Kirk had had phasers issued generally before beaming down with the landing party.

The three actors couldn't help grinning at first. It was difficult for them to believe that the little object he was pointing at them was a weapon, not a prop.

Scott was surprised at their reaction, but did not let it stop him from backing toward the intercom.

"Wait a moment," said Kelley. "What do you think we are?"

"Klingon spies."

The accusation provoked open laughter, and Scott halted in surprise.

"Scotty, this is going to be hard for you to believe," said Shatner.

Scott nodded grimly. "I agree," he said.

"We're actors," said Shatner. "We come from the past—the past of another universe entirely, I suppose. Damnit, it's a TV series," he said, throwing his hands out at the room around them. "This room's a set; the ship's a model; we're actors in a science-fiction show."

"It's like that script where we went into a parallel universe where the *Enterprise* was run by cruel people, sort of like pirates," said Kelley helpfully.

"The ISS *Enterprise* of the Terran Empire," said Scott. "I was there."

"That's the one," said Nimoy. "Where Spock had a beard."

Scott jerked his head over to stare at Nimoy. "That detail wasna in the captain's report." He sighed, shook his head, and put the phaser back on his belt. "Well, gentlemen, and if you're not them, then where are they?"

The actors looked at each other. "Back at the studio?" asked Kelley.

"Probably," said Shatner. He turned to Scott. "They're in Los Angeles, California, in the twentieth century. We think."

"A multi-parallel, space-time inversion," said Scott. "It's a pretty problem. I'll do what I can to find a way to reverse the situation, but you gentlemen had best stay away from the bridge meanwhile. There's no call to alarm the whole ship, especially at a time like this." He started out, muttering, "If the paraspatial anomalies . . ."

"Er . . . Scotty," said Shatner hesitantly, "could you at least tell us what's going on? What *is* all this about the planet?"

Scott stopped. "So you truly dinna know? Well . . . no more you would." He looked grave. "It's like this: these Klingons have found a star system. It isn't much of a system for anything we can see—no strategic importance, one star, one planet, no satellites, no minerals to speak of—but there they are, and no signs of budgin', although they wouldna claim it until it looked as if we might. You took—that is, the captain took a landing party down to investigate the planet."

"Have you looked at the reports they sent up while they were on the surface?" asked Nimoy.

"No, I had to deal with the Klingons while the reports were coming in. And after that . . ." Scott shrugged. "I wasna aware that I was in command. If you'll excuse me, there's work to be done." He turned to go.

"What if Kor wants to talk to the captain again?" asked Shatner.

"Aye," said Scott thoughtfully. "And, at that, I could keep a closer watch on what you're up to if you're on the bridge."

"We've done a pretty good job of playing our parts so far," said Kelley tartly, resenting the implications of a close watch.

Scott looked at him closely, then nodded. "Thank you, gentlemen," he said, and left.

"Back to the salt mines," murmured Shatner.

The three started out the door. As they passed the table, Nimoy leaned over to turn off the viewer.

Shatner watched him thoughtfully. "Why did you ask if he'd seen the reports?"

"Oh, I dunno, Bill. Somehow I got the feeling he hadn't, but . . ."

Kelley winced as the door swooshed open for them and closed behind them. The noise was getting on his nerves.

Chekov looked up hopefully as they came back on the bridge.

"No conclusions, Mr. Chekov," Shatner told him. On impulse, he added, "Do you have any theories?"

Chekov looked pleased to be asked, but shook his head. "No, Captain. What would anyone want with that moonless, peopleless . . ."

"Moonless?" said Nimoy.

"Yes, Mr. Spock," said Chekov. "Observations of system—"

"But it has tides." Nimoy had grown up in a coastal town, and liked to sail with his family. He knew what a lunar tide looked like. "Check the coastlines, and you'll see."

"They could be solar tides," said Uhura. She looked over at Nimoy for an opinion on the suggestion.

Nimoy, lacking Spock's scientific training, was quite unqualified to give any such opinion. He sat still, trying to think of a way to avoid answering.

Shatner recognized the danger and used Kirk's authority to get around it. "That's a possibility," he said. "Chekov, let's see you test it."

Chekov left his post and came over to Spock's station. Nimoy made room for him, and the young man bent over Spock's equipment. Nimoy gazed over his shoulder, trying to look critical.

"Solar influence not great enough to account for tides," Chekov reported a minute later. "Lunar influence seems necessary."

"Very good, Mr. Chekov," said Nimoy judiciously.

Chekov, however, looked unhappy. He worked a few moments more, then said, "Perhaps you should check me, sir. Sensors show nothing in position indicated for moon by tidal action."

"Unnecessary," said Shatner quickly.

Chekov smiled sheepishly, pleased and a little surprised at winning unqualified approval from his demanding superiors.

"Perhaps . . . an invisible moon," mused Shatner. "Sounds like Romulan work."

Uhura said, "But these are Klingons—" She broke off, reconsidered, and ended her sentence "—and they have an alliance with the Romulans."

Sulu jumped in excitedly, "And we know the Romulans have been working to improve their cloaking devices. But the power involved in blanketing a whole moon . . . !"

"Well," said Shatner, "just goes to show what researchers will come up with, left to their own devices."

"Very funny," said Kelley. "Now what do we do, go steal the new, improved cloaking device?"

There was a silence, during which the three actors realized that the junior officers thought it quite possible that they ought to try just that.

"It's an engineering advance," said Shatner when he had his voice under control. "Uhura, locate Scotty and tell him what we've uncovered. I want his opinion."

A moment later Uhura had Scott's image on one of the smaller viewscreens. A Transporter console, with some of its panels open, was visible beside him. His irritation at being interrupted faded out as Uhura briefed him.

"No wonder they had to claim the planet," he said when she was finished. "If they'd gone on squatting there with no pretense of interest, it would ha' dawned on us in the end that they had to be interested in something else." He grinned suddenly. "Well done . . . Captain."

Shatner grinned back. "Any suggestions on how the Federation gets hold of the new cloaking device?"

"How the Federation . . . Oh, I take your meaning," said Scott, realizing that Shatner wanted to know what Kirk would do and if he ought to do it. Scott shook his head. "We'd maybe do best to let them think we're fooled. Given the hint, our scientists can find the way to do what they've done. We'll have the advantage of knowing what they know—and beyond that, the advantage of their not knowing that we know." He hesitated, and then said slyly, "For the matter of that, sir, I think I could show you a bonny trick of disappearing, if you'll meet me down here."

"Very well, Scotty," said Shatner casually. "Kirk out." He nodded to Nimoy and Kelley. "Gentlemen . . ."

Scott hadn't been able to tell them exactly where "down here" was, but they assumed it was the same Transporter they'd appeared in. After a little confusion in finding the right level, they located it easily enough.

"But, Captain," Scott was saying as they entered, "we've got to pull you back in the next five minutes, before the anomaly shifts." He glanced sideways at them. "And I've got three gentlemen here very anxious to go home."

"Right, Scotty. Set it up, and we'll get onto the platform. Kirk out."

Nimoy and Kelley shot quick looks at Shatner to be sure he really hadn't spoken. Shatner himself felt a little unsure. He found it upsetting to hear his own voice coming out of someone else's mouth.

"Ah . . . gentlemen . . ." Scott nodded at the Transporter.

They hurriedly placed themselves back on the little circles.

Kelley asked curiously, "Do you really think they shouldn't try to steal the cloaking device?"

Scott shrugged. "That's my opinion. The final decision'll be up to the captain." The fact seemed to please him.

The room faded out, and when it came back, the fourth wall was gone. Hot lights blazed down at them through a nonexistent ceiling. All three sighed with relief.

Shatner stepped forward and said eagerly, "Gene, you will never *believe* where we've just been!"

"Cut!"

Another take ruined. The director gave up and called a halt for the day.

Introduction to
The Face on the Barroom Floor

by *George Takei*

I am particularly delighted to be asked to introduce a story that captures two things that were very important to me in *Star Trek*—a touch of humor and a genuine joy in diversity.

Sulu could unabashedly have dreams of D'Artagnan and nightmares of a samurai, and it is only fitting that the dignified Captain Kirk can have eyes for a samurai suit, and the courage to let go of a bit of that dignity for a time.

In a way, that's a symbol of all that was best in *Star Trek*. We could trade jokes, even trade dreams and nightmares and traditions.

Sulu has been described as "Oriental but not inscrutable." His tastes were wide-ranging—from the swashbuckling swordplay of a musketeer's dream to the exotic biology of excitable plants. He could swap a joke with Chekhov or be left in command of the *Enterprise* in the toughest moment of the outbreak of war with the Klingons.

Star Trek said, not only in words, that people can be proud of their cultural roots, but not bound by them, not limited, not divided. People can choose from the best of any culture—love and respect for each other as individuals.

I am proud to have been part of that statement, and proud of all the diverse people of our time who have responded to it. It has been a joy to me to meet them, to see what they are doing in writing, in art, in life.

It is my greatest hope that they will work ever more to realize the ideals they see in *Star Trek* in this life, this world, this time.

Much of my energy for many years has been devoted to that aim, and the same is true for many of the others of the cast and crew, who have the same feeling on this spaceship Earth as aboard the good ship *Enterprise*.

It is my hope that those who see the dream will not settle for the dream, but will make it reality.

And let us, by all means, still find time to smile in the doing, and not always stand upon our dignity. Sulu would get a good chuckle from the events of this story, and so would Kirk. In fact, my guess is that they would fall on each other's shoulders in a belly laugh, and laugh until there were tears in their eyes.

When we can all do that, without doubt or division, that will be my dream.

The Face on the Barroom Floor

by *Eleanor Arnason and Ruth Berman*

Spock turned away from his panel of sensors to observe the captain cautiously. Kirk was quickly and efficiently handling a number of tasks: scanning the leave schedules and power-consumption reports brought in by yeomen for his signature; exchanging formal greetings with the captain of the *Deneb Queen,* a freighter also in orbit around Krasni, and discussing the possibility of asking Engineer Scott to give the *Queen* a hand with some trouble they'd had in their drive alignment; checking with Scott that he didn't mind; recording his log report. . . .

If Spock had not been a Vulcan, he would have fidgeted.

McCoy, not being a Vulcan, was under no such constraint. "Hurry up, will you?" he said.

"I'll be just a moment, Bones," said Kirk.

McCoy frowned. "Shall I make it doctor's orders? Even captains need to go on leave."

Kirk paid no attention.

McCoy sighed. The whole crew was still on edge after a rough passage through ion storms, and Kirk was obviously feeling still too jittery to enjoy the thought of visiting Krasni, the most populous of a number of inhabited planets within the star group. The outer members of the cluster were highly active, making it difficult to reach the inner stars. The *Enterprise* had just completed a difficult escort journey, guiding a shipload of would-be colonists through the least active of the outer segments to one of the cluster's habitable planets. After leaving the colonists, the *Enterprise* proceeded to pay a courtesy call at Krasni to exchange news, make repairs, and take shore leave.

Spock stood up and poised his body to walk toward Kirk's chair. Unconsciously, Kirk got up too. "Mr.

Spock, you have the con," he said, as Spock slipped into his chair.

A yeoman came up with another report. Spock took it from her so smoothly that it did not look as if he had grabbed it.

Kirk looked at Spock quizzically as the yeoman retreated.

"My responsibility, sir," said Spock.

Kirk looked first startled and then amused. Spock seized his advantage. "I am in command of the ship ... Captain," he said.

Kirk laughed and joined McCoy, waiting not very patiently by the elevator, and Helmsman Sulu, who was also ready to go on leave.

The doors closed after the three of them, and Spock leaned back in the captain's chair, alone on the bridge, except for Chekov, at the navigational console, and Uhura, at her communications board. Spock, like humans, needed a rest now and then, much as he hated to admit it. With most of the crew down on Krasni, he had the ship almost to himself, and he looked forward to a restful day of silence.

On Krasni's surface, Kirk left the port-of-entry Transporter chamber with McCoy and Sulu. As the planet had rather primitive institutions, they had to stop at a bank to get currency, and then had to begin spending it by getting moneybags to hold it in. They were the last of the crew to come down, and so found themselves going out as a group together in search of amusement, rather to Sulu's surprise. The helmsman was a convivial soul who enjoyed being with people, but he was a little in awe of Kirk. He could not help watching the captain as they walked along girl-watching and window-shopping, to see if he was really human. McCoy, for more professional reasons, was doing the same.

A neo-samurai outfit in the window of a clothing store caught Sulu's eye, and all three stopped to look at it. It was gaudy, with metallic interweaving, and completely different from the austerity of their plain uniforms. "Nonsense," said Kirk. "When would you wear it?"

"Off-duty," said Sulu. "But it doesn't look like my type, anyway."

They wandered on to the end of the block, where they paused again to consider a large bar, the Krasni-Xanadu, suspended in midair above an artificial lake. A fountain in the center spurted up a jet of water that ended just beneath the floor, so that the building appeared to be held up by the water.

Sulu whistled. "That's quite an anti-grav unit they've got there."

"Shall we?" said McCoy.

Kirk hesitated. "It looks a little ostentatious."

"Suits your rank," said McCoy. "Besides, I have expensive tastes."

They started up the ramp. Kirk stopped halfway up.

"What's the matter?" said McCoy, halting a few paces farther up.

"Nothing. You go ahead, and I'll be there in a moment. Thought of something I should tell Spock."

McCoy gave him a sour look, but went in with Sulu.

Kirk took out his communicator. *"Enterprise,* Kirk here."

"Spock here, Captain," said Spock's voice.

"It just occurred to me that there's no reason for Scotty to report back when he's through on the *Deneb Queen.* He ought to go on leave from there directly."

"Very well, Captain," Spock said patiently.

Kirk got the impression that Spock had already had the same bright idea and acted on it. He shrugged. "Kirk out." He closed the communicator and stood absently for a few moments, enjoying the play of light on the water.

When he went inside, he discovered that the floor was transparent from inside, giving a view of the fountain. He also discovered that McCoy and Sulu had acquired a table and three women.

". . . Yes, but uniforms are *drab,"* one was saying. She stopped as McCoy looked up and waved.

"Renee, this is Jim," McCoy announced to the one

who had spoken. "Take his mind off his work." He looked at Kirk half-mischievously, half-anxiously.

"Hello, Renee," said Kirk pleasantly.

"Welcome to the Folly," she said, matching his tone.

"The Folly?" said Kirk.

"Krasni's Folly. The planet," she explained. "But they don't like jokes in Records."

"They've got us down on the charts as just Krasni," said one of the other women.

"What was so foolish about Mr. Krasni?" asked Sulu, making conversation.

"Well, to begin with . . ." said Renee. "Oh, good!" she interrupted herself as the table opened and their drinks arrived.

"Bones!" Kirk protested.

The doctor had ordered a round of mint juleps.

McCoy shrugged. "Order something you like better." He pulled the remaining chair out from the table for Kirk.

Kirk pulled a face and said jokingly, "Watched pots never relax."

McCoy correctly refused to take it as a joke. "Well, there's a cure for that," he said.

"There is?" said Kirk.

McCoy nodded. "Go away." He took a mouthful of his mint julep and meditated for a moment on the coolness of it. "And don't go back to the ship."

Kirk looked at the door and tapped his hand on the back of the chair.

"And don't worry about whether I'll be back on time for my shift. That's Spock's problem."

Kirk grinned. "All right, Bones. Sorry, Renee."

McCoy looked glum as Kirk swung away and disappeared out the door.

"Relax," Sulu suggested.

"I tell other people that," snapped McCoy. "All the same . . ." He picked up his glass again.

Outside, Kirk meandered down the street and halted in the middle of the block, staring again at the glittering, warlike suit that had caught Sulu's eye.

He looked at himself in the semi-mirror of the store

window, one half of him yellow, one half black. A bit of braid, a small badge. It wasn't drab, exactly. It was efficient, comfortable, tailored to move to his actions.

After buying the suit, Kirk walked out of the store feeling foolish, but free. He looked at himself again in the window, enjoying the shifting of the light against his new clothes. His uniform was a neat brown-paper package bulking under one arm. Looking at it, he realized that it was a nuisance to carry. He hurried back to the port and dropped a quarter-credit into a voice locker, stashing the uniform inside. "James T. Kirk," he told the locker, and sauntered out, name and uniform behind him.

A short stroll in the direction away from the Krasni-Xanadu brought him to a rougher section of town, and he stopped at the first bar he came to. It was full of men, and the buzzings of conversations. Kirk went in. The neo-samurai clothes stopped conversation for a moment within a radius of three meters or so, and the number of raised eyebrows around made Kirk think of Spock. He felt suddenly lonely for the *Enterprise*. Then the conversation resumed. ("It's not the blue eyes I mind, it's the pink tentacles," was all Kirk heard before the general buzz covered individuals.) He began threading his way between tables to the bar.

Kirk gave the barmaid his very best prince-charming smile, but she reacted professionally, looking him over carefully and suspiciously.

"I'd like a beer," Kirk said.

"Right," she said, taking down a glass. "You new around here?"

"Yes. My name's Harry Leroy. I'm a relief helmsman on the *Deneb Queen*." It came out quite smoothly.

The woman looked displeased. "The *Deneb Queen*," she muttered. "Here's your beer. One credit."

Kirk gathered that *Deneb Queen* men were well known and not particularly welcome. "Why is the planet called Krasni's Folly?" he asked as he paid for his drink.

The woman softened a bit. "Now, that's a story . . ."

The objector-to-pink-tentacles came up just then, a giant ox of a man, wanting refills for his table.

". . . but it'll have to wait."

On board the *Enterprise*, Chekov was studying Andorian history. He had started at the back of the tape, with the exciting part (meeting of Terrans and Andorians), and was now regretting it as he worked his way diligently through their Age of Exploration. He glanced behind him. Uhura was frankly dozing over her board, and Spock was probably meditating, but it looked much the same to Chekov. He considered imitating them and decided that his conscience would let him nap if he kept going another ten minutes.

Just then something began buzzing at Uhura's board. She woke up with a start, and Chekov put his viewer aside. Perhaps something more interesting was coming in.

Kirk fired a dart. It hit the board, on the outer edge.

"Not bad," said his opponent encouragingly.

The second dart hit the wall.

"The thing of it is, you've got to be able to think like a navigator—the vector of the force you put on the dart, combined with the vector of gravitational—"

"Thanks," said Kirk. He threw the third dart, and it hit the wall. He gathered the darts up and handed them to his opponent.

The first dart hit the center ring.

"By the way," said Kirk, "why is the planet called Krasni's Folly?"

"Ah, that's a yarn and a half. Wait till after the game's over."

The second dart hit the edge of the center ring.

"Starship *Enterprise* acknowledging," said Uhura. "Starship *Enterprise* acknowledging. Your signal is weak."

"Yes, I know," said a tiny voice. "We can't help it."

Uhura put the volume on high and set the computer to compensate for static.

"Can you hear me?" the voice blasted out of the speaker.

Uhura winced. "Affirmative," she said. "You don't need to shout."

Spock came and leaned over the communications board. "Commander Spock, *Enterprise* here. Please identify yourself."

"Antonio Pérez, on board the passenger ship *Starfarer*. Where's Jim?"

"The captain is not on board at present."

"What?" said Pérez. "But Kirk and his ship come in a set. Like a hermit crab and its shell. How'd you get him out?"

"The captain is on shore leave," said Spock. "Can I help you?"

Pérez snorted. "If you can't, tell Jim to think of me from time to time. . . . He'll know when. The *Starfarer*'s had some kind of blowout. I can't be precise, because it hit the bridge, and the auxiliary controls are affected. *And* the bulkheads slammed down to keep the air in. There're about three hundred of us alive. We think. We haven't finished counting. If we all keep on breathing—and no one's volunteered to stop—we should be out of air in five days. Where are you?"

"In orbit around the planet Krasni, of Krasni's Star."

"Krasni . . . Oh, that Krasni!" They could hear a hurried consultation in the background as Pérez and a *Starfarer* officer discussed position and power. "We can get our full speed, but that puts us eight days away from you."

"That is satisfactory. We will rendezvous with the *Starfarer*," said Spock. "What is your present position?"

Pérez gave him the coordinates.

"Mr. Chekov, compute route and time to rendezvous; Lieutenant Uhura, notify Krasni port that we will break orbit in ten hours."

"That's not very efficient," said Pérez reproachfully.

"We have to recall the crew, Commander. A skeleton crew can operate the ship, but should another emergency arise . . ."

"Don't quote the relevant regulations," said Pérez.

Spock closed his mouth, reconsidered, and said, "What caused the *Starfarer's* malfunction?"

The officer whose voice they had heard in the background before took the communicator from Pérez. "Second Navigator Lo Chah here," she said. "Sir, we don't know. We began to lose air, and the inside locks failed to close immediately. The fore section lost all its air." Her voice was beginning to sound strained. "Your pardon, sir," she said.

In the distance they heard Pérez's voice. "Go lie down, lackbrain." He took over the communicator again. "Sorry, Mr. Spock, but an injured second navigator is the best we can do for technicalese, and we're saving that to keep the ship running. Who knows what happened? It's a new ship. My father always told me: Don't try anything new. Wait and see if anyone dies from it. And here I am, wondering how such a smart man got such a half-wit for a son." He sighed. "Pérez out."

Spock returned to the command chair and looked thoughtfully from Uhura to Chekov. Uhura had notified the Krasni post, put out a general alert for *Enterprise* men, and begun specific calls to her fellows in Communications and to Transporter men—both groups had hard work ahead in finding and retrieving two-thirds of a crew.

In the second round, Kirk took aim, sighting along the dart, and moved his arm back and forth experimentally without releasing the dart. Then he threw it, and it landed precisely in the middle of the glass of the man who objected to pink tentacles.

"Watch it, willya?" said the objector. "Trying to kill someone?"

Kirk reached for the dart with one hand, and with the other tried to mop up some of the spattered green liquid. He was never quite sure which of his elbows knocked over the rest of the drink.

With a roar, the objector rose out of his chair and took a swing at Kirk, who ducked.

"Lay off," suggested one of the objector's drinking mates. "Leave the little guy alone."

In astonishment, Kirk stared at the men still seated at the table. One was a small, thin-faced man, who could have no business calling Kirk a "little guy." The other . . .

"Yeah? Wanta stop me?" said the objector.

"Why not?" said the other, rising endlessly out of his chair. The objector had a good four inches on Kirk, but the other was big and burly enough for a Rigellian warrior.

Kirk mentally dropped his objection to the other's description of him and set about trying to restore tranquillity to the atmosphere. "Now, look," he began.

"Let's see you try," said the objector to his companion, and the two behemoths fell on each other, the two nearest tables, and half the occupants thereof. The occupants, with shouts of protest, piled into the brawl.

Kirk looked at the dart he still held in his hand, with a futile sense of great-oaks-from-little-acorns.

"You *Deneb Queen* guys," said a disgusted female voice at his shoulder. "You can just stand there looking pretty and get a fight started. No sense of responsibility." The barmaid clicked her tongue.

Kirk winced, scowled, and examined the brawl carefully. For just a moment he could see the two behemoths flailing in the center of it, their thrashings bringing even more tables, chairs, and people into the hog-pile. Kirk sprang, at that second, and he heard with a sense of pleasure a gasp of wonder from the onlookers as he not only reached, but separated the behemoths, chopped one to the floor, and turned to deal with the other.

Then the rest of the brawl closed in on him. It had gone too far to be stopped by removing the two who had begun it. Kirk had one last picture, vivid as delirium, of the little man from the behemoth's table crawling on the floor among the floundering bodies with an alert expression of deep interest on his face. After that, the press of bodies and furniture was too close to let Kirk see anything, and his one thought was to keep breathing and get out. As if from far away, he heard the barmaid's voice. "Port security? I got a riot going on. . . . Yeah. . . . Thanks."

Uhura finished tracking down all the Communications and Transporter personnel. It had not been an easy task. Lieutenant Palmer, now seated beside her at the board with her blonde hair hanging damply down the middle of her back, had been under a hair dryer. Lieutenant Kyle had been with a woman, and he expressed his unhappiness in a set of curses that fascinated both Spock and Uhura and shocked those on the bridge for whom English was a native language. Kyle returned promptly, however, and Uhura went on with the individual calls, leaving it to Palmer to acknowledge the responses coming in to the general alert.

"Captain Kirk, please acknowledge," she said, touching the frequency to signal his communicator. "Captain Kirk, please acknowledge."

Down in the bar, the small, thin-faced man squirmed himself out of a tangle of arms and legs and seated himself in a dark corner to count his collection of moneybags. One of them began bleeping, and he made a worried noise, sucking his lips against his teeth as he realized that he had picked up someone's communicator. He held it firmly shut and moused his way through shadows to a disposal chute. He slipped the communicator in, and then began taking money out of bags and dropping bags and nonnegotiable contents down the chute after the communicator. He estimated that he had time to do that—and avoid the risk of being picked up with identifiable property in his possession—and still get clear before the riot squad arrived.

However, he estimated wrong.

Someone at the door gave the ancient cry of "Cheezit!" and the brawl went thundering out the door and vanished into the streets. The man at the disposal chute was farthest from the door. He was therefore the last one out the door, and he caromed into a large red chest.

" 'Scuse me," he said, trying to sidle past. A large red arm blocked his way. He looked up. "Oh. Hi, Bud. How're you?"

"Fine, thanks," said Bud. "How're you, Morrie?" Bud twitched Morrie's moneybag out of his hands.

"Now, look, I wasn't fighting anyone. She'll tell you that," Morrie complained, turning around to point at the barmaid. He stopped with his arm out in the air and whistled in amazement at the change in the bar. The floor was peaceful and serene, with only the fragments of splintered furniture and one man in a gaudy neo-samurai outfit, out cold on the floor, to bear witness to the brawl.

"Morrie, you got too much money on you," said Bud sadly, and handed him over to another security man. Bud came further into the bar.

"You took long enough," said the woman.

"All gone?"

"All but Sleeping Beauty, here."

Uhura, feeling puzzled, reported to Mr. Spock her failure to reach the captain, and went on with individual calls to Dr. McCoy and Mr. Scott.

Kirk spluttered and gagged as a liter of cold water hit him in the face. "Wha . . . what is it?" he said, trying to sit up.

Bud pulled him to his feet. "Come on, mister."

"Wait a minute," said the barmaid. "At least this one can pay for his own drinks."

"Oh . . . sure . . ." said Kirk, trying to take the words in. "How much?"

"Two-ten."

He fumbled for his moneybag. "I've been robbed."

Bud sighed. "That figures. Well"—he looked at the barmaid—"Morrie's haul looks as if it's enough to pay your costs and damages, and"—he looked at Kirk—"there'll probably be some of your share left over to help pay your fine. We've got laws against public brawling on this planet, mister. What's your name?"

"James T. Kirk, of the—"

"That's not what you said before, Leroy," said the barmaid. "His name's Harry Leroy," she added to Bud.

"He *was* involved in the brawl?"

"Oh, yeah."

"You're under arrest, Mr. Leroy. Come along."

McCoy made a face as his communicator sounded. "You know," he said to Sulu, "I think a fellow could get to like this *sake* of yours—if he ever got a chance to try it properly. McCoy here. Take two aspirin—"

"Sorry, Doctor," said Uhura. "All leaves canceled."

At the jail, Bud booked Kirk in for the night. "Sleep it off, and call your captain in the morning," the officer at the desk told Kirk in a fatherly way.

"I *am* my captain . . . I mean, I am Captain James T. Kirk of the starship *Enterprise*."

"And I am Marie of Romania," murmured Bud.

"Look, let me call the Xanadu. A couple of my shipmates are there."

"The Xanadu? Well, well!" The officer and Bud exchanged a look of surprise. The officer shrugged and put through the call for Kirk, but no Dr. McCoy answered the page. Neither did a Mr. Sulu.

"It's not the end of the world, son. This your first time in quod?"

Kirk nodded.

"Well, look at it this way: it saves you the price of a hotel room, and your captain will bail you out in the morning. Just once won't hurt your record much, and you'll know better another time." He turned to Bud. "Lock him up."

"But . . ." Kirk gave up and submitted to the inevitable.

"And you do not know where the captain went?" Spock asked.

"No," said McCoy shortly. "Spock, what all is going on here?"

"We received a distress call," Spock began.

"Here it is again, sir," Uhura said.

Spock punched the voice on. "Yes, Commander?" he said.

"We have the figures on our population and life expectancy ready now," said Pérez. "You got Jim?"

"We have not located him yet, Commander," said Spock.

"You've lost Jim? You took him out of his shell, and now something's eaten him."

McCoy grinned despite himself.

"You spoke of more precise data." Spock changed the subject.

"Oh, that. We have 311 survivors and enough air for four days ten hours, plus or minus three. If you leave as scheduled, that gives us a margin of two to eight hours."

"Thank you," said Spock.

"You're very welcome, Mr. Spock. May I suggest that the margin could be fattened up a little if you left sooner?"

"We will attempt to do so," said Spock. He cut the connection and asked Uhura, "Estimated time for recall?"

"We have enough of the crew to leave now, sir. It looks as if we'll have almost everyone back soon." She waited, but Spock made no comment on the fact that Communications and Transport were doing a good job.

Lieutenant Palmer leaned over and whispered, " 'Once more, dear friends, into the breach.' " Uhura chuckled, and the two went on with their manhunt.

McCoy said in a low voice, "Spock, you softy!"

"Doctor?"

"You don't want to leave Jim behind, because our schedule's so tight we won't get back for three months, and he'll miss that visit he's got lined up with his nephews while we're at the Starbase."

"You overlook the fact, Doctor, that the purpose of our visit to the base is to give the ship its periodic repair and updating. The captain knows the ship better than any other single officer, and the work cannot be done adequately in his absence; the *Enterprise* is overdue for its checkup, and further delay would be unsafe."

"You're a softy," repeated McCoy, and beat a retreat to the lift before Spock could tell him he was being illogical.

Kirk paced back and forth in the little cell that he shared with the little man he had last seen on the floor in the brawl. Bud had introduced him as Morrie Singh.

Morrie lay on the right-hand bunk, watching him, and kept count up to fifty turns, at which point he decided that his cellmate had had his fair share of nuisance-making. "Hey, Leroy, will you cut that out?" he said. "I can't sleep with you padding around like an imitation tiger."

"Wh . . . ? Oh, sorry," said Kirk, sitting down on the left-hand bunk and holding his head in his hands. "I'm worried about my ship."

"Why, you the captain or something?"

"Something," said Kirk grimly.

"Well, calm down, you'll get tried tomorrow afternoon, maybe day after tomorrow. . . ."

"But my ship was scheduled to leave tomorrow afternoon."

"The *Deneb Queen?* No, it isn't."

Kirk's shoulders slumped. How far had his innocent lie circulated? "Not the *Queen.* The *Enterprise.*"

Morrie eyed Kirk's battered face and the gaudy clothes, ripped at the shoulder. "If you say so. Make enough of a fuss tomorrow morning, and they'll maybe get you tried early. So they'll fine you maybe a hundred for drunk-and-disorderly, and you'll call your ship and get the captain to pay the fine and dock it off your salary. What's to worry?"

"I don't think the captain will be in when they call."

"Oh, first mate got it in for you?" said Morrie, nodding wisely.

"No, he . . . Forget it," said Kirk.

"Yeah, that's what I told you. Now, me, I got a real problem."

"Oh?" said Kirk, without enthusiasm.

"That rat, Bud."

"Who's he?" said Kirk, beginning to feel faintly interested.

"The nosy who arrested me tonight. He could have waited till tomorrow night. I mean, I might've spent the money by then, but I'd probably have had most of it left. But the thing of it is, I wanted to be free tomorrow. And he knew it. I told him so way last week when I got Charlie's invite. Charlie's getting married tomorrow. And he's my only brother."

"That's too bad."

"Yeah. Charlie always throws a good wedding." Morrie sighed noisily, got up, and began to pace. "My turn," he said apologetically, and went from wall to wall, back and forth, like a Ping-Pong ball in a volley.

"If it was anyone else," he said at one wall, "I wouldn't mind so much," he said at the other. "But Charlie's a great guy. . . ."

"Why don't we break out?" said Kirk sardonically.

Morrie halted with his nose up against a wall and tapped his fingers against it meditatively, then turned around and took his seat on the bunk. "That's a good idea," he said. "You got a pick on you? Bud always confiscates mine."

"A pick?" said Kirk. "For an electronic lock?"

"Sure. It gets the classical music stations, too."

Kirk eyed him doubtfully, but he seemed to be serious. "Well," Kirk said, "one of us could pretend to be sick and call for the guard, and then we could jump him when he came."

Morrie winced and addressed the wall plaintively. "All the cells in the world, and I get one with a cornball in it. There's no justice!"

"It can't hurt to try," said Kirk. "Just fake a little delirium, can't you? Babble of green fields or something." He got up and tested the bars. They were solid. "I wish we had Spock here," he said aloud to himself.

"Oh? He's good at getaways?" Morrie had overheard him.

"Well, he . . . Yes, he is." Kirk grinned as it occurred to him that he and Spock actually were an accomplished pair of jailbreakers, what with one hostile society and another. Even without Spock, he thought, he should be able to manage something. "Do you want to play sick, or shall I?"

"No." Morrie rolled his knuckles along the blanket, looked at Kirk, then hopped to his feet. "You want to do it cornball, we do it cornball. But we don't do it so one of us has to be lying down when the guard shows up. We fight."

"Fight?" said Kirk, not immediately comprehending.

"Leroy, you purple bloodworm, say that again!" shouted Morrie, putting up his fists.

Kirk looked bewildered as Morrie advanced upon him, waving a fist in the general direction of his nose.

"Call me a dirty ground-crawler, will you?" said Morrie.

"No," said Kirk in a smug tone of voice, catching on, "I call you an arrant malmsy-nosed knave, and I'm going to wipe the floor with your head." He fastened his hands loosely around Morrie's throat.

"Help! He'll kill me!" Morrie thrashed about a bit. "Get your hands off me, Baby Face!" Kirk's hands tightened involuntarily at that particular insult, and Morrie's next "Help!" sounded convincingly choky.

"Say that again, you crack-brained garbage-head, and I'll—"

A guard came to the door and aimed a phaser in through the bars. "Cut it out, boys," he said soothingly.

"All right," said Kirk, dropping Morrie and grabbing at the guard's arm. Morrie simultaneously went low to grab at the legs, and the guard's stun beam went high, hitting on the ceiling in a burst of pretty red fireworks.

Kirk snatched the phaser away and stunned the guard. Morrie caught the body so that it fell where they could reach out and get the keys.

As they opened the door, an alarm sounded.

They sprinted down the hall. Morrie flung the door open and announced, "I *told* Bud I wanted out," then ducked as the officer at the desk fired at him. Kirk leaned in and fired back. The officer slumped in his chair, and the two of them went on through the main door, pulling it shut after them just in time to block the phaser beams of two more guards, roused too late by the alarm from their graveyard-shift napping to catch the fugitives.

It was a good thing, Kirk thought, that phasers were routinely left on stun. A full-strength shot would have killed him and/or Morrie right through the door, not to mention doing considerable damage to the door.

Outside, Kirk followed Morrie as he skittered down the block to an alley, cut into the alley, and ran one mile, with scarcely three yards of it in a straight line, and slid into a dark doorway to wait for some brightly lit traffic passing in the street ahead of them to go past their current alley. "Do you need a hideout?" he said hospitably.

"No, thanks," said Kirk. "Just tell me how to get to the portmaster's office."

"Take the third door from the end on the right, and sneak down to the basement. Go through the door marked 'Keep Out.'" Morrie scowled, his eyes squeezed shut as he visualized. "No, no," he said, opening his eyes, "not that one, the one that says 'Keep This Door Locked'—go through the tunnel, into the warehouse, out the back door, and turn . . ." He stopped again, his body twisting in the imagined turns. "No, there'll be a Nosy directing traffic at the corner. Well . . . go out the window with the loose catch on the east side and cut across the lot to Third and go . . ." He stopped again and squinted up at Kirk. "Are you getting all this?"

"Yes," said Kirk uncertainly.

"Okay. Well, you go left two blocks, and there's another Detention Station, so go through the all-night shoe store to the alley, and . . . Or, no. It'll be blocked. This was Mrs. Krasni's day to move her pianos. So you go through the . . . No, that doesn't work. So you take . . . Leroy, you know something?"

Kirk shook his head.

"You can't get there from here. You come to the wedding. Charlie'll find you a guide."

"But . . . How about the nearest public-communications outlet? I could call the portmaster."

"Should be one on the corner. You got any change on you?"

Kirk sighed and shook his head.

"Well, come on, then. And keep your head down." Morrie slid out into the alley, and they headed into the night, hugging the darkest shadows.

Uhura rubbed her eyes and stretched in her chair, then swung it around. "That's the last of the bars, sir. He isn't in any of them."

"He isn't in any of the restaurants, nightclubs, or bordellos," added Lieutenant Palmer.

"The portmaster scanned the Security and Hospital Services reports for us," Uhura said, by way of appendix, "and nobody has a record on James T. Kirk. Nobody."

McCoy sat down in Spock's chair, leaned back in it, and stared down his nose at Spock's head, rising over the top of the command chair. "You know, Uhura," he said wearily, "I wonder if James T. Kirk could be a mass hallucination dreamed up jointly by the crew of the *Enterprise*."

Uhura wrinkled up her face as if tasting a lemon. "You have a morbid imagination, Doctor."

"Oh, I don't know," said McCoy. "Spock, can you prove you're not the real captain?"

"Affirmative, Doctor," said Spock, without looking around at him, and raised one blue-sleeved arm in the air. The double line of braid denoting commander's rank caught the light.

McCoy blinked, trying to decide if Spock was taking him literally or making fun of him, and fell silent.

The two fugitives darted through the last of the shadows into an obscure doorway, its surface made of the same violet plastic as the wall and set flush with it so that the entrance was almost invisible. Kirk glanced nervously up at the sky and around the street. The sky was getting light overhead, and he could make out figures even at a little distance—the windows across the street, a few early risers visible behind them, the fashionably crenellated line of the rooftop.

Morrie told the door, "Let me in."

It creaked and stuck.

"Let me in!" Morrie bellowed.

The door groaned open, and a blast of noise hit them. Kirk involuntarily covered his ears, thinking that it was a wonder the door could respond to voice cues at all in that racket.

Morrie beamed.

The tail end of a conga line came tramping past the doorway, and it reeled inward to make room for the newcomers to enter.

"They've started the party already," Morrie explained unnecessarily.

The door slammed behind them.

The last man in line dropped off and embraced Morrie, exclaiming, "Morrie!"

"Charlie! Congratulations!"

"Drinks that way, food that way, bathrooms that way," said Charlie, waving expansively. "The ceremony'll be that end of the room at noon. Got it?"

"Got it."

Charlie hugged his brother again, pumped Kirk's hand, saying, "Any friend of Morrie's . . ." and ran to rejoin the conga line.

Morrie trotted over to the food and began stuffing an improbable set of ingredients in between two slices of orange bread.

Bud slammed the corridor window down so hard that its crystal structure chimed once like a striking clock.

His assistant squatted down and retrieved his phaser, turning a look of reproach up at Bud all the while.

Bud sat down on the windowsill, cutting off the silvery note. "What the hell were you doing?" he asked in a tone of courteous interest.

"I was *trying* to stun them before they could get inside and get away. Sir."

"Nonsense," said Bud. "Nobody goes to Charlie's wedding and just gets away like"—he snapped his fingers—"that."

"How do you know?"

"Off-worlders!" Bud shook his head at such ignorance. "Same way I knew Morrie'd come here. If he went to all the trouble to break jail, we can at least let him stay for the wedding." He looked out the window meditatively, then turned and started back down the hallway to the lift.

"What are we doing?" his assistant said, hitching his phaser on his belt and running to catch up.

"Going to crash the party. We can't keep an eye on them from out here . . . and Charlie always throws a good wedding."

As trusty native guides go, Kirk decided, Morrie was a frail reed. He gave up trying to get the little man's attention, turned his back on the dance, and went to the wall. He began prowling along it, looking for a communications outlet.

Bud's assistant cleared his throat as softly as he could and still expect to attract his partner's attention.

"Right. You keep an eye on Morrie." Bud slipped into the crowd, heading to the other side of the room, where the fugitive was exploring the wall.

"Jim!" said a high, clear voice. "Jim?"

Kirk came to with a start, as he realized that someone was actually calling him by his own name. He turned. "Hello, Renee," he said quietly, feeling suddenly too tired after a sleepless night to show surprise.

"I didn't know you knew Charlie."

"I don't. I came with Morrie."

"Oh, you did!" she said, looking half-surprised and half-amused. "Looking for a hidden safe?" she asked as he continued his inspection of the wall.

"No, a communicator."

"Well, you won't find one there. It's in the next room." She led the way.

The next room turned out to be a small office, thickly carpeted and hung with heavy Rigellian tapestry work. The sudden quiet beat on Kirk's ears. He flung himself into the desk chair and said to the communications outlet, "Portmaster's office. James Kirk speaking. Relay to the *Enterprise*." His sense of relief was marred only by the fear that, somehow, something could still go wrong.

And something did.

The door slid open, and Bud appeared in the entrance, just as Kirk said, "Beam me a—"

"Why, Bud Krasni! What's going on?" Renee said.

"Get out of the way, Renee," said Bud, and side-stepped around her before she could obey, even if she had intended to. The door closed behind him, and he fired.

The whistle of the phaser beam and the hum of the Transporter beam sounded together. Kirk fell, sprawled over the top of the desk, turned gold, and vanished.

Bud pulled out his communicator. "Calling *Deneb Queen*."

"*Deneb Queen?*" said Renee. She looked from Bud to the desk and back again. "I think I need a cup of coffee," she said. She pursed her lips. "I think you need a cup of coffee, too," she added. She marched out the door and headed for the refreshments.

Lieutenant Kyle signaled the bridge. "The captain's aboard, sir." Then he refocused his eyes and said, "I think."

"Confirmation requested, Mr. Kyle," said Spock's pedantic voice.

"Yes, sir. It's the captain. He seems to be unconscious, though," said Kyle, not daring to try a description of what the captain looked like.

Spock ordered McCoy to go examine the captain, and told Sulu to take the ship out of orbit.

The *Enterprise* practically purred as it picked up speed. They were already beyond Krasni's Star and approaching the outer members of the cluster as McCoy told Kyle, "Looks as if the captain's been phaser-stunned." McCoy proceeded to slap Kirk's face lightly, several times.

Kirk grabbed his assailant by the throat, rolled him down, and raised one hand to strike, but happily woke up before his instincts could complete the reaction. "Bones!" he said, looking down at the startled and annoyed face of his chief surgeon.

"Yes, and I'd like to keep mine in working order, thank you," wheezed McCoy, removing the other hand from his throat.

"Oh. Sorry," said Kirk. He sat back on his heels and let McCoy up. Then he put his hand to his forehead.

"Headache?"

"Yes."

McCoy sat up, straightened his tunic, and picked up the kit bag he had dropped. He took out a hypo and gave Kirk an injection of Masiform-D. The stimulant took effect quickly, and Kirk stood up, reaching to straighten his own tunic as he did so. He cringed as his hands met the fabric of the neo-samurai outfit.

"I see you got it." McCoy nodded at Kirk's clothes, grinning.

"Yes," said Kirk forbiddingly, and changed the subject. "How long till we leave orbit? I ought to call the portmaster and arrange . . . to have some things straightened out."

McCoy shrugged. "You can call the portmaster, but we're already out of orbit."

"What?"

"We received a distress call several hours ago from *Starfarer*, sir," Kyle said.

"From Antonio Pérez," McCoy added.

"Tonio?" Kirk set off for the bridge, with McCoy close behind.

In the elevator, the double-take McCoy was waiting for hit Kirk. "Received several hours ago?" he asked.

"Yes," said McCoy. "There was some safety margin, so . . . Spock waited."

"I see." They reached the bridge and found Spock explaining to the *Starfarer* that the *Enterprise* was now on its way to their rendezvous.

"I take it you found Jim," said Pérez.

"Yes," said Kirk, leaning down to speak into the communicator at Uhura's station.

All eyes turned to the captain and stayed there.

Kirk looked down at his clothes and cringed again. Then he carefully ignored his crew and went on in a cheerful voice, "Having a little trouble, Tonio?"

"A little trouble? The second navigator is holding the ship together with baling wire and worry beads, if that's your idea of a little trouble. Where were you, anyway?"

Kirk sighed and decided to brazen it out. "In jail."

"James T. Kirk has a record?" said Pérez.

"No. Besides, I was innocent."

"That's what you said the night the goat turned up in my Uncle García's bed."

"Give him my regards the next time you see him."

"Uncle García or the goat?"

"Both. Kirk out." He inspected the bridge with a look that dared anyone to say anything. After a suitable interval he announced, "Mr. Spock, you have the con." He turned, and turned back again. "Oh, and, Spock . . . thank you."

"Captain?" said Spock with a puzzled air.

"For waiting."

Spock opened his mouth.

"Don't bother," Kirk said. "I'm sure you had a good reason. Thanks anyway. I . . . appreciate it." He yawned more widely than he needed to, smiled sweetly at them all, and left the bridge.

"Mr. Spock," said McCoy, gazing at the closed door of the lift, "next time . . . you take shore leave, all right?" He turned to face Spock.

Spock steepled his fingers and looked into the hollow of his hands for a moment, then looked back up at McCoy. "Your suggestion, Doctor, is . . . highly logical."

Introduction to The Hunting

by *Sondra Marshak and*
Myrna Culbreath

Our own hunting has been good—both for stories in the wilds of *Star Trek* fiction and for the introductions that the stars and makers of *Star Trek* graciously took time to give by way of returning thanks to the fans.

Yet certain quarry eluded us. Without an anthology of a hundred-odd stories, it would be impossible to include a word from each of the many guest stars or semi-regular members of the *Enterprise* crew who have developed followings of their own in *Star Trek* fandom.

Yet they are an important part of the *Star Trek* phenomenon, and should be represented. At any convention, fans can be seen tracking down pictures and memorabilia of their particular favorite. That guest star may have appeared once, years ago, on *Star Trek*, yet is still instantly recognized at a *Star Trek* convention or when seen on another television show. He or she very probably remembers that *Star Trek* role with fondness—perhaps even as a high point in a career.

Almost every guest star has received such attention: a Klingon villain, a Romulan commander, an android, even a monster. Most have had stories written about them in *Star Trek* fan fiction. Certain ones have become "legend"—by being invited as guests to conventions and received with great enthusiasm, or by having dozens of stories written about them.

In particular, what we might call the Vulcan contingent has captured the imagination of fans, as has the whole idea of the Vulcan culture behind Spock.

Only three out of seventy-nine episodes gave us a glimpse of other Vulcans, yet they have been engraved in our memories: T'Pring, Spock's intended wife (Arlene Martel); T'Pau of Vulcan, the indomitable ruler (Celia Lovsky); Ambassador Sarek, Spock's Vulcan father (Mark Lenard); Amanda, Spock's

Human mother (Jane Wyatt); Surak, the ancient Vulcan philosopher of peace (Barry Atwater); even Stonn (Lawrence Montaigne), who got T'Pring, and may have regretted it.

Arlene Martel frequently appears at conventions to answer questions both as herself and as T'Pring, and is phenomenal as both. Mark Lenard, as the grave and powerful Sarek, is another perennial favorite (and one of the few to have played two guest roles on *Star Trek*, appearing also as the Romulan starship commander in "Balance of Terror").

The interest which these and other stars still take in *Star Trek* and the seriousness with which they took their roles then and now, is a credit to them and to *Star Trek*, and we feel sure that they, too, would like to express thanks to the fans for returning that interest. Let us, then, express thanks for them—and to them.

Perhaps it is fitting that we do so as an introduction to a story about a custom of the Vulcan culture. In a sense, Vulcan culture itself is a kind of star in the universe of *Star Trek*. The fans' fascination with it is unique; whole sagas have been written about it: trilogies, epics, odes, sonnets.

Yet that is not so remarkable. It is a "fascinating" culture, and in some sense it stands for all of the alien cultures we glimpsed in *Star Trek*—for our interest in them and our "infinite delight in infinite diversity"— a Vulcan philosophy which some of us Humans share.

Here, then, the story of one Human's not altogether delighted sharing in one such diversity. Good hunting!

The Hunting

by *Doris Beetem*

Rhinegelt. It was a frontier planet—a few hundred kilometers of settlement surrounded by barely surveyed terra incognita. Shore leave would be limited either to hiking, hunting, and camping in the primitive areas, or to drinking and carousing in port towns reminiscent of the American West of three hundred years ago.

"You're getting old, McCoy," the *Enterprise*'s chief medical officer told himself. Roughing it, either in the forests or the port towns, didn't appeal to him. Perhaps he wouldn't bother leaving the ship this stop.

The Sickbay door swished open. "What shore party shall I assign you to, Bones?" Captain James Kirk asked. To the captain, nothing was more relaxing than a stable orbit around a safe planet, and a lessening of responsibility for the 430 crewmen he commanded: so the captain could always approach shore leave with considerable energy.

"I don't need leave," McCoy said. "Give it to somebody who can use it."

"A little rest'll do you good, Doctor," Kirk replied. "That's what you always tell the crew, anyway. Even Spock's taking leave."

"He is?" McCoy was startled by this unusual occurrence.

The captain was obviously greatly pleased. "Spock's been under too much stress lately—even for a Vulcan. He's been stretched both physically and mentally, although he'd never admit it. We've both seen it."

"And you know how stubborn Spock is about taking shore leave. He says it's illogical."

"By his own request, I put him down for shore party three. And Lieutenant Uhura tells me that he's already contacted Rhinegelt Port Control and arranged to take out a Primitive Area hunting permit."

Dr. McCoy reviewed four years of poking, prodding, and psychologically dissecting the *Enterprise*'s Vulcan

125

science officer. "Something's wrong there, Jim. Spock wouldn't kill a fly. A hunting permit, you said?"

"Why not ask him about it?" answered Kirk, apparently untroubled. "Sure you don't want shore leave?"

"Ye-es," McCoy answered slowly. "Guess I will, at that. Put me down for party three."

Kirk foresaw another McCoy/Spock bout, but complied with the request.

"Fool Vulcan! He can't be gone already!" McCoy, waiting impatiently outside Spock's door, signaled for admittance again.

"Yes, Doctor?" Imperturbably the Vulcan surveyed McCoy's collection of camping equipment, which was piled lumpily in the hall. McCoy was determined to be well prepared, and had packed everything from medikit to insect repellent to a small tent.

"Spock, I'm going with you," McCoy asserted, too proud to soften his statement to a request. "I'm all packed and ready to go."

Spock, staring quizzically at the heap of equipment compiled by the tenderfoot woodsman, replied, "I can see no logical reason—"

"Blast it, I've got a hunch," McCoy interrupted. "A Human, irrational hunch that you'll need my help. Now, am I going with you or not?"

Spock, after considering the matter carefully, answered, "You have the right. And I should have a companion. A Vulcan preferably, but you will do." While McCoy was deciding whether or not to be insulted, Mr. Spock, after picking up a small green sack of his own, slung a good part of McCoy's camping equipment over his shoulder. "Come, Doctor," he ordered, starting down the hall.

"But what about your supplies?" McCoy spluttered. "Don't you need to get ready?"

Spock shook his head and continued on his way. McCoy picked up the remainder of his equipment and followed Spock to the Transporter chamber. Once again he checked to make sure that his medikit was still securely packed.

Three days later, McCoy was still puzzled, although he was learning more about Spock's character than ever. He'd discovered that, given half a chance, the Vulcan would keep his mouth shut forever. However, no new information had been offered about the hunting expedition.

"Dr. McCoy, you have turned up your sonic screen to the point that it is audible to me." Both the doctor and Spock had edged quite close to their campfire—McCoy for protection against the native animals, and Spock because he found nights on the Rhinegelt savannah chilly.

McCoy grudgingly turned down the protective device. "By the time it's low enough for you, the wild animals it's supposed to ward off won't notice it," he complained.

"I am somewhat dubious about the value of a supersonic transmitter as protection. Were I a wild beast, I suspect that I would more likely be irritated into attacking than retreating," Spock said politely, but with a trace of resentment against the machine. Since the beginning of the hunt, he'd used no tools at all, and was eating various tubers he'd collected, without even bothering to roast them in the fire.

"Hasn't eaten anything but native plants since we came here," McCoy thought. "Some hunter!"

Above them, the giant planet Fafnir glowed green in the sky. It provided as much light as Earth's full moon, but in coloring, the landscape distorted vision. McCoy peered gloomily out into the savannah. "What game animals are found on Rhinegelt, Spock?" he asked suddenly.

"Scissorbuck, white mammoth, and owltiger. We are hunting an owltiger," Spock replied, answering the question that had been bothering McCoy more and more with time.

Scissorbuck were the brown antelope types with prongy white horns, McCoy knew, and the mammoth would be farther north. But . . . "How big are owltigers, Spock?"

"Approximately the same size as the Terran Bengal tiger."

"Then why," McCoy exploded, "are you hunting

one with no weapon? What are you going to do—give it the kiss of death?"

"I can stun it with a nerve pinch long enough to accomplish my purpose."

"What purpose, Spock?" McCoy asked. "You've got to let me know, or I'm likely to be a hindrance when the time comes." He was determined, this time, not to let the Vulcan lapse back into silence again.

Spock settled back, nodding reluctantly at McCoy's request. "I am engaging in a ritual hunt—one of the more important rituals of my people. Since I am a male of full physical strength and dexterity, I seek out the most dangerous beast of all. It is the *mok farr*— the time of remembrance."

"Another Vulcan ritual—and me with only a medi-kit," thought McCoy, appalled.

"The hunt does not end in a killing. Instead, I shall meld minds with the animal, as you have seen me do before. The purpose of the tradition is to see and understand, in the ferocity of the beast, the savagery of the Vulcan nature, which we have hidden and controlled so carefully."

"And then what?" McCoy asked skeptically, thinking privately that Spock, unlike young men on Vulcan, had doubtless already encountered more savage ferocity than he would ever require.

"Then I shall officially be an adult."

"You mean you're not?" McCoy asked, amazed.

Spock shook his head, shamefaced. "My human heritage impeded my telepathic ability, and I was quite young when I left Vulcan. I could not have successfully completed the ritual. Since then, I have had mind contact with many aliens—Humans, the Horta, a Medusan. Now I am prepared. I do not wish to further postpone the rite."

"Wouldn't it be safer to put it off until you could get to Vulcan?" McCoy ventured tentatively.

"Doctor. The *mok farr* is the Vulcan rite of passage into adulthood. If our positions were reversed, would you put it off?"

"I guess you've got a point."

Spock curled up like a cat on a pile of leaves—he

was carrying primitivism a bit too far, McCoy thought resentfully—and prepared for sleep. "The correct phrase would be 'Good night, Doctor,'" Spock said sleepily. McCoy crawled into his sleeping bag, and for a long time listened to the voice of the warm wind.

As usual, Spock was up at dawn, irritatingly alert, and as usual, McCoy slept half an hour longer, savoring each precious moment of sleep with an intensity he had not previously possessed. Once McCoy was finally wakened, Spock had them ready for the trail in practically no time at all.

In three days the Vulcan had taught McCoy something of the rudiments of stalking—enough to tiptoe quietly down the trail. Spock, who by this time had appropriated the carrying of nearly all of McCoy's pack, was more silent still.

"How long until we find your owltiger?" McCoy panted.

"We have been following a scissorbuck herd for two days now," Spock replied. "Eventually, one will make an appearance."

"Mmmph. Maybe."

"Dr. McCoy, do you know nothing of hunting?" Spock was watching the lithe brown forms of the scissorbucks move slowly in the distance.

"I've fished a little."

"I have never been able to comprehend the Terran attitude that fishing is a sport. Considering the mass ratio between man and fish, it can hardly be called an equal contest. At any rate, you may trust me. I know what I am doing."

At that moment Spock's keen eyes caught the leaders of the herd sniffing the air nervously. "Wait here," he commanded, slipping off the bulky pack and moving quietly toward the herd. After a few minutes, McCoy crept after him, clutching the medikit firmly in hand.

From a slight rise he watched Spock approach the now skittish herd. The Vulcan's Star Fleet uniform was relatively easy to spot—McCoy recollected the incredulous eyebrow-raising he'd encountered when he had suggested wearing different clothes for the occasion. Apparently Spock considered his uniform an auxiliary skin.

McCoy strained his eyes looking for an owltiger, then finally flipped open his medikit to check its life-form-sensor. He hadn't wanted to take one of the *Enterprise*'s tricorders on a private excursion, but the medikit would perform the same function.

Yes. Spock was cautiously approaching the location of a large animal only a few hundred yards from the herd. Then McCoy saw the owltiger.

It was huge, a mottled dun color, with a small white ruff. The owlish ears were what gave the beast the name owltiger, McCoy knew, that and the two wicked fangs placed close together, which gave the impression of a beak.

Had it seen Spock? The scissorbucks were beginning to scatter. Then McCoy saw Spock fling himself toward the giant carnivore at a dead run. The great cat roared, and responded by leaping toward him.

As the two closed, McCoy cursed the government regulation that made phasers in Primitive Areas forbidden. He watched helplessly as the beast attacked. Spock was almost under its paws, and then suddenly standing over the brute, which was twitching convulsively. "He's safe!" McCoy shouted thankfully, then added, "Knock on wood."

The owltiger's short red thoughts flooded into Spock's mind. Spock struggled with the problem of handling its bestial emotions without suppressing them, and attempted to calm the beast by mentally asserting, "We are one mind. Our thoughts are moving together." *Hurt, pain, attack, slash.* "No! We are unity—no need for that!" *Run, leap, bite, hurt.* "The twitching in the legs will stop. . . ." *Flesh rending food, the hunting* . . . Fascinating—all thoughts the same. Monomania . . . monom . . . mon . . . *Teeth, claws, kill,* kill, *kill* kill*kill*kill . . .

The owltiger shook itself and bounded off. McCoy watched it go with a feeling of great relief. "Well, that's that," he told himself, satisfied. He was startled, then, to hear an unearthly roar.

Or was it a scream? It's Spock! McCoy realized. "I'm coming," he yelled, and recklessly scrambled down the slope toward his comrade.

Spock was crouching on all fours, flexing and un-flexing his hands, looking at the strange blunt claws. He felt clumsy and off-balance. The whole landscape was full of confusingly different colors, sounds, and odors. Out of the corner of his eye he saw the scissor-buck herd, alerted and on the run, and he growled in irritation.

Some creature was crashing down the hill at him. Suspiciously, he prepared to spring. But foggily, from the back of his mind, he remembered that the creature had something to do with sickness and whirring things that hurt, and his own blood. Rattled, he got up on two feet and fled.

"Wait, Spock, wait!" McCoy puffed. He'd known that catching Spock was impossible from the moment that Spock had started to run, but had continued until the last glimpse of the blue shirt was gone in the distance.

"Damn!" McCoy remembered bitterly Spock's ten-dency to get so tied up in the mind of the being he was contacting that he had to be pried loose. "I'll have to bring him back to himself, or he'll be yowling at the moon for the rest of his shore leave." McCoy grumbled. Nagging at him was the recollection of Simon van Gelder. Spock had snapped back to normal im-mediately after being pulled away from him. Never before had Spock maintained mental identity with a being so far away from him. Worriedly, McCoy reached for his communicator to summon help.

It wasn't there. He'd let Spock carry it, along with most of his gear. The doctor scrambled over the dusty grasses to where Spock had dropped his pack, opened it, and rifled through. No—Spock had carried both their communicators securely on his belt. And they were both lost with him.

Glumly McCoy considered the situation. The near-est Wilderness Station was about twenty miles back along the river. By the time he could get there and call the *Enterprise,* Spock could wander off so far that the search operation might take months. And heaven only knew what would be happening to Spock, mentally and physically, in the meantime.

Grinding his teeth quietly, McCoy decided to follow the herd. Maybe Spock would return. He had to!

Midday. The sun's warmth comforted Spock, even as it disturbed him by revealing colors he'd forgotten how to name. Night was best, when the violent stars lit a gray landscape and he could prowl, scenting sharp living odors on the wind. It was too cold to hunt then, though.

He tried to doze, well hidden in the tall grass, lying with his head on his hands. Both legs were drawn up awkwardly to his body, showing great rents at the knees of his trousers where the dura-fiber had been worn away by too much clumsy scrambling on all fours. His knees were scratched and gashed, and his hands.

Spock's eyes gleamed ferally as his ears flattened at a small, suspicious sound. He had been hunted. Something was following his trail. Some . . . what? He couldn't remember what, but he didn't want it to find him.

He sighed. No way to hunt and run away at once, and now he was so tired. He kept wary guard regardless, but trusted his ears more than his eyes, which constantly drooped and closed. Suddenly his eyes snapped open. There was a rustle in the grass, and a small, foolish rodent ran in front of him. It was small . . . but he was *hungry!* Spock carefully lifted one paw.

McCoy watched the sun flee over the mountained horizon. His back straightened painfully as he unfastened the heavy pack. The light would soon be gone; he'd try again tomorrow.

"Why didn't I go back and call out the search parties?" he asked himself for the thousandth time. "Nine days—we'll be absent without leave in two more. Anything could be happening to him out there."

He rubbed a grubby sleeve against grainy eyes, and

strove to see one flicker of blue somewhere on the savannah in the fading light. Hopeless. Spock's Vulcan stamina could probably keep him ahead of McCoy indefinitely. Scrabbling through his pack, McCoy searched for a nutri-bar. He sat on a rock in the rapidly fading twilight and bit at the food concentrate. It would be another bad, cold night. His sleeping bag was at least fifty miles back, and he didn't dare light a fire for fear Spock would see it and run. Using the sonic screen was definitely out, too—Spock's sensitive ears might pick it up.

"Wait a minute . . ." McCoy smiled ephemerally. Then he searched out the screen projector in his kit. It had been too small and light to be worth leaving behind. Scrutinizing its control dial carefully, he saw that it allowed a considerably stronger broadcast than the labeled "protection" range.

"Wouldn't this just be audible to those Vulcan ears, though!" McCoy chuckled grimly. "And that feline fiend inside him will be madder than a wet hen when it hears this. Maybe even mad enough," he speculated, "to come and try to stop it!"

His plan was risky, McCoy knew. The supersonics might frighten Spock into running off. "But what choice do I have? I could be following him till doomsday." Decided, McCoy flicked the sonic device on and up to maximum.

The vibration made McCoy's teeth grate rustily in his mouth. He couldn't hear the sound, but it was palpable, and pushed on every nerve relentlessly. From far off toward the mountains he heard a bloodcurdling screech, and another, and another echoing it, from much closer locations.

McCoy considered morbidly the chance that his trick might prove fatal. Some maddened owltiger leaping on him with bloodlust . . . Or even Spock. McCoy formed the grotesque picture of himself as King Pentheus in reverse—ripped apart by a man who thought he was a lion.

Then McCoy remembered Spock, standing stiffly, and saying in a thin, precise voice, "Nothing can excuse

the crime of which I am guilty. I intend to offer no
defense. I must . . . surrender myself to the authorities."

"And he would," McCoy thought savagely. He
grabbed his ever-present medikit, pushed the med-rec-
ord button, and spoke. "To whom it may concern—
Jim, I guess. About the events occurring to Mr. Spock
and me on Rhinegelt." He paused and then added
peripherally, almost idly, "Damnit, Spock, don't try to
deny that I brought this on myself!"

Outlined on a ridge, a scissordoe trembled and
twitched her ears nervously. Then she ran toward the
mountains, as if scenting the acridness of a grass fire,
and nearly bowled Spock over in her uncautious
flight.

The rasping shriek caused even more pain to
Spock's sensitive ears than the doe's. He stood his
ground, wondering. No! It was not like a fire, or a
flood . . . something natural, to hide from. It was—
Spock searched through his muddled thoughts—*him!*
The following one. Spock remembered other times of
pain, when he had been strapped down so he couldn't
run, and the face of the following one. A face that
smiled too much.

"I will stop him!" And Spock, gathering up all his
will, waded painfully through the tall grasses in the
direction of the hurting.

McCoy thumbed his medikit and peered toward
the hills, deathly afraid. Hypnospray . . . sedative . . .
knockout drugs. He considered them all, then muttered, "Nothing organic's wrong with him . . . nothing
but the sanity of that alien Vulcan mind. What am I
going to do for him? And my God, what will I do if
I guess wrong?"

Over the absolute silence of the hypersound, McCoy
heard a sound—a branch snapping. And then hoarse,
heavy breathing, as if every intake of breath was half
a sob. Before McCoy could take a reading on his kit,
Spock appeared, gliding swiftly toward him, looking
ragged, muddy . . . and homicidal.

McCoy had been expecting savagery, belligerence—

all the emotions written nakedly on Spock's face—but not, somehow, the Vulcan's incredible, pantherlike speed. Before the doctor had time to more than yell, "Spock!", Spock had sprung. The lunge carried them both to the ground, where Spock dug his fingers cruelly into McCoy's neck with slowly increasing force.

"S-s-pock . . . s-s-stop . . ." McCoy hissed breathlessly. Then, as the Vulcan's lethal grip did not slacken, McCoy kneed him in the stomach. Spock panted, and released him. McCoy scrabbled off, feeling a little more confident, until he looked into the Vulcan's face to see a vicious smile. And recollected, with a dreadful certainty, how the cat toys with its prey.

The screen projector was sitting on a rock. Twisting desperately, McCoy reached it before Spock became aware of his intent, and grabbed it as his only protection. The projector vibrated fiercely in McCoy's hand as he jabbed it toward Spock. The diabolically feral look faded, and Spock covered his ears with shaking hands, pacing backward fearfully.

The doctor had tasted his moment of triumph for only an instant, when he realized that Spock was about to bolt again. Swallowing hard, he flicked the screen projector off, gambling on Spock's mental controls for his life.

It was still Spock—nothing could change that. The Vulcan seemed confused, as if memories were being awakened, or perhaps because he was being pushed into an entirely different pattern than the days of chase on the savannah; Spock would have to choose now, to think. McCoy waited.

He found himself looking into eyes that were neither bestial nor logical, neither a Star Fleet officer's nor an owltiger's. Spock simply stood immobile, projecting a mute doubt and horror. It seemed to McCoy in that moment that all the gambles had been lost.

Then Spock stepped forward and pleaded in an awkward voice, *"Alab hwallir k'len?"* McCoy could practically have hugged him for every incomprehensible, tongue-twisting Vulcan syllable. Spock was acting Human again!

The doctor had pried the communicator off Spock's

belt, and they were coalescing out of golden sparkles
onto the comfortingly safe Transporter platforms, before he remembered to amend that description.

It was nice to have the authority to certify yourself
medically fit for duty, McCoy thought. The captain,
after grasping the situation's seriousness, if not its nature, had wanted to argue that with him. The doctor
recollected how Kirk's grin at his friend's bewhiskered
appearance had faded when Spock had toppled unceremoniously to the floor. He was worried about them
both.

McCoy thankfully tugged on a clean shirt and hurried out of his office into Sickbay. Whether he'd be
able to certify Spock medically fit was another matter.
His med-scan had revealed Spock to be in acceptable,
if not perfect, physical condition, and Dr. M'benga had
agreed that he was suffering from no more than shock.
But whether Spock would snap out of it quickly was
another matter.

As Dr. McCoy entered the ward, M'benga approached him and whispered, "Mr. Spock has an unusually resilient mind, for either a Vulcan or a Human.
He should recover quickly now." He paused, then
asked, "It's not a medical question, Doctor, but this
wasn't anything you did to him?" Scowling, McCoy
returned to his patient.

McCoy sighed with relief as he saw Spock eye with
loathing the sponge bath M'benga was taking away.
The Vulcan was already back in thermal underwear
and was finishing dressing rapidly. "Look at it this
way," McCoy said soothingly. "It's better than a belly
full of fur balls."

Spock looked up at him sharply, and McCoy was
immediately aware that Spock was in no mood for the
usual feuding back and forth; he just wanted to talk.
"I believe I understand now the purpose of the ritual,
Doctor."

"To understand how to control emotion?" McCoy
ventured.

"No, to demonstrate that the alternative is attractive. I have wondered from time to time why there are
such extensive game preserves on Vulcan. It seemed to

me that the 'track and stalk' that is favored there had no logical value, since the prey was not killed. Now I know that there must be many who wish to re-create the experience of the *mok farr.*"

McCoy, as usual, was not quite sure that he knew what the Vulcan was getting at. "Wait a minute! You can't tell me that you liked running around in the bush regressed back to an animal."

"As you should know, not all of that was intended to be in the ritual." The Vulcan's face was unusually somber. "It is what you have always advocated—a life ruled by the nerve endings. More pleasurable, in some ways, than my own. But I shall not choose it."

"Why?" McCoy asked.

"Doctor. Choose the life of a wild animal?"

"No," McCoy explained, "not that. But you might live a little more according to your nerve endings, Spock."

"The end result would be essentially the same."

The Sickbay door whistled, and the captain of the *Enterprise* walked in, anxious about the condition of his friends. Catching the polite battle stance of his science officer and chief medical officer, Kirk extrapolated, "You must be all right, Spock. Bones never argues with seriously ill patients."

"Have him tell you someday, Jim, about the time he tried to walk out and go back to duty in the middle of an operation," McCoy cracked.

"All right, what's been going on, and why didn't either of you take my advice to rest during shore leave?" Captain Kirk demanded.

Dr. McCoy opened his mouth and prepared to give a long, aggrieved account of Vulcan rituals, uncomfortable nights of reversion to Boy Scouting, and a companion who alternated ignoring him and pouncing on him. The frozen look on Spock's face stopped him, and he closed his mouth carefully. "He wants to tell Jim slowly. In his own time. Or maybe not at all." Out loud he answered, "There was a Vulcan custom Spock wanted to go through. What was its name again, Spock?"

"The *mok farr,*" Mr. Spock replied thankfully.

"Oh," Kirk said, mystified. "Well, I hope it worked out all right."

"There was . . . some difficulty." Spock said seriously. "But Dr. McCoy solved the problem."

"How?"

McCoy grinned. "I took a thorn out of his paw!"

Introduction to The Winged Dreamers

by *DeForest Kelley*

It is a tremendous pleasure for me to be able to introduce this story for *The New Voyages*.

When I want to pat myself on the back a little, I remember that I was saying years ago, maybe before almost anyone else, that *Star Trek* would come back.

When I saw the enormous response to it in syndicated re-runs, the great outpouring of affection from the fans, I knew that nothing could keep it down forever.

Now, with new fiction and nonfiction, with plans for a motion picture, I'm beginning to feel as if the real McCoy can not only "cure a rainy day" but also give a pretty good prognosis for a new day dawning.

The patient is alive and well, and just may live forever.

It is a source of pride for all of us who were involved with *Star Trek* to remember the effort we put into it, and the love, and to see the effort appreciated far more than we ever expected, and the love returned a thousandfold, a millionfold.

Isn't that the dream of an actor's life—of anyone's life—to do something that moves people profoundly, something that makes a difference?

Star Trek made a difference.

And it will again.

The kind of difference *Star Trek* made was in people's thinking and feeling. There was a time when things looked pretty bleak, when kids—and adults—needed some hope for the future. Some of them, many of them, found that hope in *Star Trek*.

There are still times when the newspaper headlines look bleak.

If *Star Trek* can bring that hope again, it will once again give us the greatest pleasure.

When I realize that there are people out there who are thinking about *Star Trek*, writing about it, taking pleasure from it, seeing it as a living world after all these years, I am startled, but not surprised.

And when I think that this story, for example, comes from England, from a woman I have never met, but might, through the fantastic world of *Star Trek* fandom, and that even if I never do, she clearly knows Kirk, Spock, and a certain McCoy as well as I do—I am left a little breathless.

But I'll cheerfully prescribe a little Tri-ox, any day, and read on. This is just what the doctor ordered. Consider it a prescription for a rainy day—or a sunny day to come. I keep telling people I'm a doctor, not a . . . whatever. But a reader I am. And a reader of this new *Star Trek* fiction, I certainly am. I hope you enjoy it as much as I do.

The Winged Dreamers

by Jennifer Guttridge

Spock bent his head over his tricorder, a faint frown forming on his face. "Fascinating," he said, not for the first time that day. "A world of this composition and climatic condition is ideally suited, and yet intelligent life has not evolved here."

"McCoy was saying much the same thing only this morning," Kirk told him. "He can't understand it either. The plants and animals—they're in such abundance here. The planet is stable, secure, warm, comfortable. I don't understand why the cradle is still empty."

"A most poetic concept, Captain," Spock remarked with a raised eyebrow.

Side-by-side the two men followed the grassy bank. The water of the lake was dark and crystal clear; a light breeze stroked its surface, making it ripple and gleam in the sunlight. There were reeds at the water's edge, with silver-tufted tops, and graceful lemon-colored trees that dipped the tips of their slender fronds into their reflections. Beyond was a land of rolling hills and lightly wooded valleys. In the distance, purple forests swept majestically from foothills to mountains, where sun-gilded snow peaked through the thin, high clouds.

The sun was hot, the breeze fragrant and refreshing, the scent of the flowers pleasant and sleep-inducing. A cluster of cornflower-blue flowers nodded their heads drowsily in the soft breeze. Kirk and Spock stopped to watch two furry-bodied creatures sweep down out of the faultless blue sky. They hovered a few moments, riding the breeze with their iridescent green-and-gold wings stretched to transparency; then they settled on the flower heads so lightly that the nodding went on undisturbed. Furry antennae unfurled as they scented the air, and long, finely scaled proboscises uncoiled downward into the hearts of the flowers as they began to sip at the nectar.

141

"Beautiful, aren't they?" Kirk asked, moving on. He didn't expect an answer, and he didn't get one. Spock's appreciation of beauty was a very personal matter, and he rarely deigned to discuss it with anyone—not even with Jim Kirk, who was as close a friend to him as anyone had ever been. "This world will be ideal for colonization when the tide of advancement reaches this far," Kirk continued. "Crops can be grown here, livestock raised. There are no diseases we cannot vaccinate against, no creatures that attack unless attacked first. . . ."

"You are about to name this place a paradise, Captain," Spock informed him stiffly.

"And you don't approve?"

"I do not believe in perfections or idealisms. There is invariably a . . . 'fly in the ointment,' I believe you would say."

Kirk grinned. "Mr. Spock, you're a cynic."

"Agreed, Captain. I find that it avoids disappointments."

"Now, that is a Human trait that you have often denied allegiance to," Kirk accused, laughing.

Spock stopped walking and shot him a look from beneath shaded brows. Then he turned to survey the landscape, and changed the subject. "It will be a shame to destroy all this with the plow and the saw."

Kirk stared at him in amazement. "And now sentimentality, Mr. Spock?" he asked.

Spock gazed steadily at the distant mountains. "Philosophy, Captain," he corrected.

"Very well, 'philosophy.' " Kirk started walking once more, picking his way through deep grass toward a copse of blue-green trees, kicking up clouds of pollen high around his head as he walked. He didn't look back, but after a moment the Vulcan followed of his own accord, as Kirk had known that he would.

The trees stretched seventy feet straight up into the sky. The trunks were perfectly straight and unbranched to the very top, smooth and silver. The crown of each tree was a spreading flat table of branches, thickly clothed with round blue leaves. It was a large copse with several hundred trees. Beneath them, small five-petaled yellow flowers littered the ground, and a peculiar kind of grass grew there, short and even, yellowy-green, each tip stained with red, as if it had been dipped in human blood. All it needed to look exactly like the glen of fairy tales, thought Kirk, was a pixie and a toadstool. Then, watching Spock examine a flower, he corrected that simply to a toadstool.

He felt pleasantly wicked and sat down with his back against a tree trunk. "Come and join me, Mr. Spock," he invited.

The Vulcan looked toward him and then wandered over, but he remained standing stiffly, his hands clasped behind his back.

Kirk looked up at him. "The crew like it here," he said.

"Indeed."

"What about you? Do you like it here?"

Spock eyed him warily, sensing a trap. "It is a pleasant place," he said with care.

Kirk laughed softly. "You're a strange man, Mr. Spock."

"Captain?"

"You're always content with what you have, and yet you give me the impression that you're constantly striving for something more."

Spock's eyes took on a look very much like tenderness. "It is the lot of man to strive, no matter how much he wishes for contentment."

"Vulcan philosophy, or Human?"

Spock raised an eyebrow at him. "Like myself, Captain," he admitted, "a little of each."

Donna Michelli wove the stems of the red, silver-lipped bell flowers into her hair. She called them "tinkerbells," after an ancient children's legend her parents had carried with them from Old Earth. A sailor carried through the air toward her, its membrane spread wide and flat on the wind. Its body was furry brown and curled almost double beneath its canopy of brown-splotched white. It hit a tree branch with a soft thump, clung there, and began neatly to fold its sail membrane.

Donna gazed up at it, shielding her eyes against the

sun. They were a creature unique to this world. Someone aboard the ship had attached a long, complicated
name to them, but to everyone else they were "sailors,"
riding the wind on their single glistening wing. She
yawned. It was a warm day, and she felt sleepy. She
sat down on the grass and began to make a necklace
of the tinkerbell flowers as she thought of the planet
Earth, the home of her parents, the world of living
legend that she had never seen.

She looked at her busy fingers and sighed, and then
stared. The tinkerbells she'd been weaving were no
longer red; they were smaller, and of the brightest yellow she'd ever seen. She got to her feet and looked
around in alarm. She was no longer in the shade-
dappled glade, but rather on a green-clothed swelling
hillside. The sky was a beautiful clear blue, tufted with
feathery clouds. The sun was round and bright and
yellow. She heard a whistling sound and saw high in
the sky real birds wheeling in the sunlight. The yellow
flowers dropped from her hands. In the distance were
purple hills shrouded in white mist. An endless green
meadow stretched away before her, and there was a
silver-stranded wire fence that ran as far as she could
see in both directions. There were two remote spots
against the green carpet that grew rapidly nearer: a
man and a woman riding horseback. They reined in
on the other side of the wire and waved at her. She
recognized them: her father, dead six years past; and
her mother, whom she'd left gray-haired and ailing half
a galaxy away. But now they were both young, with
happy smiles on their faces. Donna scooped up her
buttercup chain and ran down the hill toward them,
waving her arms, shouting wildly. They smiled at her
and waved again. The scene wavered, and they and
the purple hills and the wheeling birds faded from
view. She was all alone, running through the shaded
dell, a string of crushed tinkerbells in her hand.

Langely stared around in amazement. Moments before, he had been walking through a cool glade, making his way back to the lake and the stationary
beam-down point, as he watched a formation of sailors

gliding high over his head. Virgin planets, no matter how beautiful, bored him. Langely was a man of sophisticated tastes, and his mind had been wandering. Now he found himself in one of the ornate pleasure palaces of Diad II. There were gold drapes and pale-blue-and-gold-design cushions embroidered with golden thread. Three identical female dancers swayed with movements so exactly matched that they might all have been images of the same woman.

Langely had a woman on his left and right, with swelling bosoms and creamy white skin. One of the women pulled gently at his earlobe. Langely smiled, and holding a glass of sweet wine in his hand, he began to enjoy himself. He wrapped an arm around the woman and lay back with her into the luxury of the cushions.

Kirk looked up at Spock over the top of the report pad he'd been reading, startled. "What?" he asked. "Say that again."

Spock shook his head, equally puzzled. "Forty-three men failed to return from shore-leave activities on the last watch," he repeated.

"Well . . . where are they? What happened to them?"

"They are still on the planet surface, Captain. They appear to be doing . . . nothing."

"Have you tried to call them back?"

"Affirmative. Those that have communicators do not respond."

Kirk looked at him a bit longer and then just shook his head, utterly astounded.

The turbo-lift doors opened, and Sulu quite literally bounced down the steps to relieve the man at the helm. Kirk and Spock exchanged glances and walked over to him.

"You seem very pleased with yourself this morning, Mr. Sulu," Kirk observed. "I take it you had an enjoyable time ashore yesterday?"

Sulu beamed at him. "Oh, yes, sir. I've never been to such a wonderful place. It was as if there was a whole city down there, and all the towers were made of gold. There was a marketplace, and they were selling

silks and spices. And there were the most beautiful
women you've ever seen."

Spock and Kirk looked at each other over his head.
Spock blinked.

"I had an experience very like that, sir," Uhura said
from the communication console. "It was as if I were
home with the palm trees and the moonlight and the
sea. And all my friends were there. It was very real."

"That's very odd," Kirk said. "Explanation, Mr.
Spock?"

Spock raised an eyebrow and shook his head. "None,
Captain."

"Mr. Sulu"—Kirk turned to the helmsman—"have
other members of the crew had these . . . experiences?
The impression that they were somewhere else than on
the planet?"

"Nearly everyone's had them, sir. You can be whoever you want to be. Do whatever you want to do. All
you have to do is think about it."

Kirk looked at Spock. "I think we'd better talk to
McCoy about this."

Carlos Durban looked around the lab in satisfaction. He was a biologist and had always taken a great
pride in his work. Mainly because of his own efforts,
the records of the fauna of the planet were complete,
and the environment cases comfortably filled with the
more unusual forms of small-animal life. Durban was
determined that one day he would lead expeditions to
the farthest unexplored regions of the galaxy and discover the strangest life forms known to man. Bizarre
manifestations of life held a fascination for Durban; in
fact, he was almost fanatical about them.

The lab lighting dimmed. Durban stared around,
wondering what sudden emergency could have caused
the power failure. The lab no longer existed around
him. Instead, he was in a deep dark pit with remote
stars high above his head. There was a reddish glow in
the bottom of the pit, and in the deepest shadowy
recesses something was stirring, pulsing. Durban felt
fear, the terror of the unknown, of being trapped; but
also, the curiosity of the scientist was aroused.

He stood his ground as the thing extended a long questing tentacle along the ground toward him. It touched his foot, his leg, then reached up and gently touched his face. In the gloom, the bulk of the thing quivered. Durban heard a message transmitted somehow by the tip of the tentacle. "Come, come closer." The being was intelligent. Excitement raced through Durban. He went forward, straining to see more of the creature. More but shorter and thicker tentacles reached toward him. Durban felt no fear now, only excitement and a growing wonder. The tentacles reached up. One of them wrapped firmly, tightly about his neck. Durban saw the jaws of the creature open. . . .

McCoy covered the dead man's face and went to wash his hands. Kirk—and after a moment, Spock— trailed after him. "Well, Bones?" Kirk asked.

"I don't know why he died, Jim," McCoy answered. "He just stopped living, and I can't find the reason for it."

"There must be a reason for it, Doctor!"

"I know that!" McCoy snapped back. "I'm simply saying that I can't find it!" The two men glared at each other, and after a moment McCoy looked away. "I'm sorry."

Kirk looked at Spock. "Do you have any means of . . . explaining the man's death?"

"Negative, Captain, though I have spoken to those who actually saw him die. It seems that he was clutching at his throat as if he were struggling with something that was choking him. But, of course, there was nothing."

"You can count out any form of strangulation, Jim," McCoy said. "There's no bruising or marks of any kind on his neck. If a man's choked to death, it shows."

"What about gas?"

"No sign of any, either in him or in the lab."

"A man can't just die like that!" Kirk insisted. "Could it have been a heart attack?"

"Except for the fact that it's not beating, his heart's as healthy as yours."

Kirk shook his head and sat down, locking his fingers together on the tabletop and studying them. "I . . . can't . . ." He let the sentence trail off with another shake of his head. "Could this be connected somehow with the other business?"

"The case of the disappearing crewmen?" McCoy asked.

"They are still alive, Captain," Spock replied. "They simply refuse to report back to the ship."

Kirk drummed his fingers on the tabletop and then looked up at the Vulcan. "Then we must do something about it. All remaining shore leave is canceled effective now. We'll take some security guards down and collect those men and beam them back up here, whether they want to or not!"

"Yes, sir." Spock left the room quickly and silently.

Kirk looked at McCoy. "Bones, when they get back here, I'll want a complete physical and psychological report on every man. And I want a thorough biopsy report on Durban."

"Yes, Captain," McCoy said.

Kirk met Spock and his security team of four in the Transporter room.

"I don't expect any trouble," he said, taking his place on the beam plate, "but if they resist, use phasers on stun. I want these men back here, and I don't care how they come."

"Acknowledged, Captain," Spock said.

Kirk looked toward Scott. "Energize," he ordered.

The engineer's hand moved across the console and slid the red levers upward. The beam generators pulsed and glowed redly as the six figures beneath them dissolved into a shimmer of gold and vanished.

The whine of the beams died away into silence as the six figures reappeared on the planet surface. The area seemed silent, at peace. The water of the lake ruffled gently, and the trees dipped their branches. There were no immediate signs of the *Enterprise* crew.

"Phasers on stun," Spock said, repeating Kirk's earlier order. He turned a slow half-circle, studying the landscape, and consulting his tricorder. "That direction," he said, pointing to the copse where he and Kirk had been the day before. "There seem to be several of them gathered there."

"What are they doing?" asked Kirk.

"Nothing." Spock shook his head. "They're just sitting."

"Take two of the men and round them up. Beam them up to McCoy. We'll go the other way, and we'll meet back here later."

Spock nodded, and the two teams set off, each in an opposite direction. Spock led the way around the edge of the lake, the men following in single file. A pair of sailors danced across the sky, twisting and wheeling about each other in an elaborate courting ritual. Spock glanced at them once and then ignored them. He had dissected one of each gender, and the species held no further mysteries for him.

One of the security guards let out a wild shriek. Spock turned, startled, and almost ended up in the water as the man pushed roughly past him on the narrow path and went charging headlong into the long grass, shouting at the top of his voice and waving his phaser above his head as if it were a scimitar.

Spock picked himself up and looked after him, holding the other man back with an upheld hand. The runaway was soon lost to sight, and his shouting became increasingly fainter, until it could no longer be heard. The lieutenant looked at his officer doubtfully.

"What could have caused that, sir?" he asked. "Porter has always been a well-balanced individual. I'd never have thought that . . ."

"There is something we don't understand on this planet, Lieutenant," Spock told him. "We must be increasingly vigilant." He moved on toward the blue-topped trees.

He could see figures lounging beneath them—the red-and-gold-and-blue uniform shirts of the missing starship crew. The men were just sitting idly on the ground or lying on their backs looking up at the sky. Some of them appeared to be sleeping.

As Spock and the guard drew nearer, the men got to their feet and gathered into a group, waiting for their approach. Spock stopped three yards away. His chill gaze swept over them. "You are to return to the ship immediately," he said flatly.

Langely, apparently the appointed spokesman for the group, shook his head. "We won't be doing that, sir." There was no insult in his voice; he was merely stating fact.

"The orders of Captain Kirk are that you return at once for medical examination," Spock repeated, his eyes narrowing. "If you fail to comply, I, also, have my instructions."

Langely shrugged affably. "No, sir. We're not going back to the ship. Not ever. We've no reason to. Everything we want is here." He gestured around at the trees and the rolling landscape.

Spock looked around carefully. As before, he found the place pleasant, unspoiled . . . but also unsophisticated and lacking in amenities. He failed to understand what Langely meant. He gazed back at the crewmen. "Your words are insubordinate, and your intentions are mutinous," he said quietly. "I advise you to return to the ship at once and surrender yourselves to the security force."

"We're not going back to the ship, Mr. Spock," Langely repeated more forcefully. "And you can't make us."

Spock gazed at him, and Langely returned his stare. It was a battle of wills. Even the wind seemed to drop into silence at the intensity of it. For one of the first times in his life, Spock found himself on the losing side of such a battle. The man stared him out. As a further threat to Spock and the guard, the errant crew members began to move about, encircling them on either flank, and more of the missing personnel were appearing through the trees. The numerical odds were increasing, and not in Spock's favor. He had the sudden feeling that perhaps he ought to retreat, but surveying the situation, he found that such a maneuver was impracticable. He raised his chin and looked at Langely out of wary eyes.

"What do you intend, crewman?"

Langely exchanged glances with the man standing next to him. "We . . . don't wish you any harm, sir.

We wouldn't have insisted that you come down from the ship. But now that you're here, we think you'd better stay."

Spock's phaser appeared at once in his hand, aimed at Langely's chest. The security guard beside him made no move at all. Spock looked at him sharply.

"Lieutenant!"

"Don't you see it, sir?" the guard asked. "It's so big, and so . . . beautiful."

Spock looked into the sky and saw nothing. However, it appeared that others did. Several of the men were gazing into empty air with the same intent fascination.

"Don't you see it, Mr. Spock?" Langely asked.

"See what?"

"Whatever you want to see." Langely shrugged. "There are no rules here. No regulations. You can have whatever you want, when you want it. All you have to do is dream about it."

"Dream?"

"Maybe it's different for you," Langely said. "But I'm sure it will come to you after you've been here for a while. It took time for some of us to get adjusted, to realize what was happening to us."

Spock's grip tightened on his phaser. "If you attempt to hold an officer against his will, you'll be committing a very serious offense," he warned carefully. "Return to the ship, and Dr. McCoy will proceed immediately with medical examinations to discover the cause of these . . . hallucinations you've been experiencing."

"We're not interested in discovering the cause, sir, and we're not going back to the ship. Neither are you."

Spock's finger reached for the white firing button. A strong hand locked onto his. The security guard looked into his face and shook his head.

"You mustn't fire that here, sir. You might damage it!"

He looked upward at whatever it was he saw in the cloudless sky. Spock tipped his head back and followed his gaze, frowning. He felt hands clasp his arms from behind, pulling them back. He struggled, his

Vulcan strength surging to his defense. He shook himself fiercely, and the hands fell away. He heard bodies thump to the ground, and turned, prepared to do battle. Something hit him hard across the back of the neck just below the skull. He felt himself falling and saw the flashing of stars before his eyes. And then there was blackness and oblivion.

Kirk returned to the shoreline of the lake later than he had anticipated. He and his two-man team had covered the area down to the river. Their tricorder had located two missing members of the crew, both women, who had offered very little resistance and who now walked meekly with the men. They moved as if in a daze, their faces blank and starry-eyed.

Kirk looked around. It was evening, and the sun was very near to setting. The tasseled tops of the reeds jostled each other in the light evening breeze, and the surface of the water rippled darkly. There was no sign of Spock or his men anywhere.

"He may have found more than he could handle," Kirk said. "Take the women back up to the ship and turn them over to McCoy. I'll see if I can help Spock." He set off around the lake and downhill toward the blue-topped trees.

The air beneath the forest was very dark and filled with the night scent of flowers. There was no sign of anyone, although in places the grass was freshly crushed, as if several people had rested there only recently. Kirk concluded, logically, that the Vulcan had collected the men and beamed up with them. He flipped open his communicator.

"Kirk to *Enterprise*. Transporter room. Lock on and beam one."

Once aboard, he made straight for the Sickbay. McCoy was there, halfway through a cup of coffee and waiting while his nurses undressed the women for examination.

"Coffee, Jim?" he invited over the edge of his cup.

"Later, Bones, thank you. What about the men Spock brought in?"

"What men?" McCoy scowled. "I haven't seen any men. I haven't seen Spock either, come to think of it. I thought he went with you?"

"We split up," Kirk said, frowning. "He can't still be down there, surely. It's almost dark." He leaned over McCoy's desk and flipped the intercom switch. "Kirk to Communications. Lieutenant Uhura, make contact with Mr. Spock on the planet surface."

"Yes, sir."

Kirk waited, his face impatient.

"Captain, he doesn't respond."

Kirk looked at McCoy. "Try the security team," he ordered into the intercom.

"I have, sir. No response."

"Thank you, Lieutenant." Kirk straightened. "Something's happened to nearly every man I send down there. Something's taking them away."

"It must be something pretty powerful to overcome Spock," McCoy remarked.

"Could it be some disease that . . ."

"You can forget about that. The planet's clean. I double-checked the tests myself."

"Then . . . what?"

"I don't know. Any more than I know what killed Durban. But I've an edgy feeling that they're connected."

Kirk looked at him sharply. "They could be in danger."

"They could."

"Bones, get your medical kit. I'm going to see Scotty."

Kirk found, to his alarm, that the ship was emptying. The attitude of the crew reminded him of lemmings, or, less complimentary, rats, abandoning a sinking ship. The *Enterprise*, however, gave no indication of "sinking." She swung on in her endless stately orbit. Kirk found that the officers of his crew, those who owed loyalty to him personally, showed no inclination of deserting their posts. Sulu and Uhura were on the bridge, maintaining the watch. Scott joined Kirk promptly in the Transporter room, and of course,

McCoy, with his medikit and tricorder, shortly joined them, to complete the threesome. All of which made Spock's absence odder.

"Scotty," Kirk said. "There's only one Vulcan life form on that planet. I want you to put us down close to him, but out of sight. We'll leave our communicator frequencies open. If you don't hear from us in an hour, beam us up, no matter what."

"Aye, sir. Ready to energize."

Kirk and McCoy mounted the steps to the Transporter platform and stood side-by-side on the base plates.

"Energize," Kirk directed.

Scott's hand moved across the controls and touched the levers. The Transporter mechanism screamed shrilly, the generators glowed an unnatural white, and the base plates beneath their feet spat fat white sparks. Kirk and McCoy fled the platform, leaving Scotty to battle manfully with the console.

As the smoke began to clear, Scott inspected the damage.

"What the devil caused that?" McCoy demanded, ruffled.

"A power surge, Doctor. It took the insides out."

Kirk frowned. "How long to fix it, Scotty?"

"If we work all night, we might have it goin' by midmornin' tomorrow."

"Can't you do any better than that?"

"No, sir," Scott said stiffly. "And I wouldn't attempt to use the other Transporter units either, if I were you. They all go through the same governor, and if they sent you anywhere, you might just arrive in little bloody pieces."

Kirk swallowed hard. "Thank you, Mr. Scott. Point noted. Nevertheless, we do have to get help to those people down there. And I can't afford to ferry a lot of men down to the surface. I'd lose them as fast as they arrived."

"Then what are you going to do, sir?" Scott asked.

"The doctor and I will take a shuttle down and see if we can locate Mr. Spock. I'm leaving you in command. Get those Transporters back on the line as fast as you can."

With grace and eerie silence, the angular shuttle dropped from her bay at the back of the starship's belly and began a slow, controlled fall through the atmospheric layers to the planet below. There was momentary discomfort for the two men inside as the blunt nose glowed cherry red; then Kirk turned the craft and landed it gently between the lake and the trees.

Kirk opened the door, and the two men looked out into the silver starlight.

This world was moonless, but because it was on the galactic plane, all the array of the hub stars spread it-self across the sky. Their radiance fell like a white cloak, casting shadows and streaming down through the treetops in shafted rays, to form pools of silver on the grass. The evening breeze had dropped consider-ably, and the surface of the water was mirrorlike, reflecting the star-encrusted sky.

The whistle of McCoy's tricorder broke the silence. He turned, studying it, and then settled on a direction. "That way. About a kilometer," he said, indicating the trees.

"Vulcan or Human?"

"Spock."

Kirk nodded and set out to lead the way, striding determinedly. McCoy settled the tricorder on his hip and followed on behind.

It was the sort of still, silent, altogether alien night that foretold nothing and forbade nothing. The trees stood as dark and stately forms lost in shadow. In places, the silver trunks stood out starkly, splashed with starlight. The grass crushed beneath their feet and sprang up once more when they had passed. The white trumpets of the lilylike flowers, which opened only be-tween sunset and the first light, watched them pass by with saucer-sized eyes. The most distressing part of this unworldliness was the peopled silence—peopled now with more than half the crew of the *Enterprise*.

Kirk knew that they had to have beamed down to this vicinity, because the Transporter settings had not been altered; yet, there was no sign of anyone. Wherever they were, they were being very still, very quiet. The thought made Kirk's back prickle.

It seemed to him that the darker shadows shifted in the dimness between the trees. He strained his eyes, but as he stared, the illusory shadows became still. He chided himself for a fool and pressed on, McCoy having to take an occasional running step to keep up with him.

Ridiculous, Kirk told himself angrily; the only large animals in the area were one-horned deer that grazed on the riverbanks. There was nothing and no one among the trees, and the trees themselves could not move.

The ground tipped slightly downhill. Kirk stopped. The whole of the wooded glade spread before him, silver-daubed. He frowned. Was it a trick of perspective, or were the straight trunks of the trees leaning together slightly at the tops? And was it imagination that made him hear the leaves shiver as if whispering together, conspiring?

McCoy walked into his back in the darkness, and they both stumbled. Kirk motioned the doctor's query to silence with a curt gesture. He fully thought that McCoy would see what he saw: the abnormality of the landscape they were about to traverse.

McCoy saw nothing unusual. To him, everything was as it should be—the same straight, tufted-topped trees, the same starlight, the very faint path running down the hill and vanishing into the trees on the far side of the glade. He looked at Kirk, puzzled.

For Kirk, things were very different. Visibly, the trees were moving, swaying together, dark and threatening. He heard their angry murmurs, sensed their enragement at his intrusion. The trees began to walk. They tore their massive roots up out of the earth and shuffled on them ponderously, closing on the path down which he must walk. Kirk had a sudden terrifying vision. Spock was somewhere just beyond those trees, and Kirk saw him crushed beneath their blind trampling, unable to defend himself or flee. Kirk knew it was going to happen, and he knew that he had to stop it.

He let out one frenzied shout, "Spock!" and then he was running down the path between the menacing trees.

They bowed down toward him, bending their slim silver trunks in two, so that their branches swept the path. He felt the clutch of their twigs tearing at his clothes and flesh. He felt the acid burn of leaves whipping against his face. He put up his arms to protect himself and rushed on, unseeing except for the vision of the Vulcan dying in a bloody pulp.

"Jim!" McCoy's voice shouted from a long way behind him. "Jim, what is it?"

McCoy was running too now, following Kirk's insane rush through the peaceful night-shaded glade. For him, there was no terror, only concern.

The branches of the trees were like steel bands trying to wind themselves around him and crush the breath from his lungs, splinter his ribs, squeeze his heart to lifelessness. Kirk fought them, forcing his way through. He had to get to Spock before it was too late. He had to get there! A twig tripped him. He went down onto his knees. He tried to lunge up once more onto his feet, but leaves slashed at his eyes, blinding him. A great bough fell across his back. His spine cracked.

Hands seized him from behind.

"Jim! Jim!" The voice shouting his name into his face was McCoy's.

"Jim! What is it? What's the matter?"

Kirk opened his eyes and looked. McCoy's face was very close to his. The ice-blue eyes blazed, boring into his own. The doctor's hands were gripping his arms painfully.

Kirk drew a deep breath and found that his lungs were no longer constricted. He could breathe again. He looked beyond McCoy, to the trees. They were still, silent, unmoving. They were now where they had stood for a hundred years. The earth around them was untorn. His ragged breath steadied. He got his feet under him and rose onto unsteady legs. Still holding on to him tightly, McCoy stood up with him.

"Jim, what was it?"

Kirk looked at him and shook his head. "I don't know, some kind of waking nightmare. The trees . . . they were moving . . . trying to kill me."

"The trees?" McCoy stared around incredulously. His eyes fell on something beyond the fringe of the wood—a dark huddle on the ground.

"Jim!" He pointed, and set off toward it. Kirk followed more slowly.

It was Spock. McCoy knelt down beside him and gently touched the side of his neck. The skin was warm, and at the touch of his fingers, the Vulcan stirred and lifted his head.

"Lie still," McCoy ordered, fishing in his medikit.

Spock was only too glad to obey. The pain in the back of his head was phenomenal, and moving made him feel sick. Kirk arrived beside McCoy.

"Is he all right?"

"Hm," McCoy grunted, loading a hypo. "He'll have a headache for a while. Something's hit him, and hard."

"Did you see it?" Kirk asked Spock. "What sort of creature was it?"

"Human, Captain," Spock said with an attempt at dryness. "Our own crew."

Kirk and McCoy exchanged glances. McCoy shot the contents of the hypo into Spock's shoulder.

"You can sit up now," he said.

Spock did so, too fast, and it made his head spin. He sat on the ground and nursed it.

"Are you sure about that?" Kirk asked. "Our own crew attacked you, their senior officer?"

Spock looked at him out of eyes drawn tight with pain.

"I'm sure, Captain. They . . . wanted me to stay here with them. They wouldn't go back to the ship. They seem to regard this place as a sort of El Dorado. Nothing would induce them to leave."

"And then they belted you," McCoy remarked, probing the discolored lump.

Spock winced. "As you say, Doctor. Oddly, they did

not seem to be violent until I refused to remain with them."

"Any more violence, and they'd have cracked your skull," McCoy said. "Jim, I want to get him back to Sickbay and check him over. He may have a concussion."

Kirk nodded and stood up. He looked back at the trees through which he had so recently run the gauntlet for his life. "I could go back and bring the shuttle around," he offered doubtfully. If the truth were told, he had no liking at all for the prospect of going back through those trees alone.

Spock saved him the worry. "I can walk, Captain." And to prove it, he clambered onto his legs and stood swaying.

McCoy looked at him unhappily and decided not to argue. He put an arm around the Vulcan to steady him, and when he didn't object, McCoy took his arm and placed it around his own shoulders. Spock glared at the doctor, but knowing in himself that he needed the support, he made no verbal objection. Still, McCoy could feel his muscles stiffen with distaste at the personal contact.

Kirk led the way as they slowly made their way back up the hill to the trees. Kirk eyed the woods warily before he stepped inside. All was as still as before.

"I came looking for you this afternoon when you weren't here," he said. "I didn't see anyone."

"Hardly surprising, Captain. It would seem that there is something on this planet which enables men to see exactly what they wish to see."

Kirk shook his head. "There's a fault in your logic, Mr. Spock."

"Captain!"

"Don't worry about it," McCoy advised. "That crack on the head has upset your thinking."

"You don't see what you want to see," Kirk elaborated. "It's more as if your thoughts come to life. Something's picking our brains and making us live what we think, as if they're real experiences, pleasant or not." He thought uncomfortably of the walking trees and rapidly dismissed the notion. He didn't want to go through that again.

Spock said no more and concentrated on lessening his dependence on McCoy for support. He went slowly, and they were just slightly more than halfway back to the lake when McCoy decided that Spock should rest. Kirk was reluctant, but gave in to the doctor's wishes. Spock sat down with his back against a very stationary tree and rested his head on his knees. McCoy passed his scanner over the motionless Vulcan and scowled at Kirk over the top of the bowed black head.

"He's in shock, Jim. Driving himself. The sooner we get him back to the shuttle . . ." He looked beyond Kirk, and his face brightened. "There it is! Come on, Spock!" He put a hand under the Vulcan's arm.

Kirk looked behind him. He could see nothing but the shadows beneath the trees. "It's not there, Bones," he said quietly. "You can see it because you want to see it."

"If I walk over there and touch it, it'll be solid. I know it will," protested McCoy.

"Yes. It will," Kirk agreed, "because you expect it to be real and solid."

McCoy blinked hard and deliberately looked away from the shuttle he thought he saw. "How do we know what's real?" he asked savagely. "If we can be deluded into seeing and hearing and feeling things that aren't real; if we can't trust the evidence of our own senses, how in God's name are we going to find our way back?"

Kirk looked at him uneasily. "I'm not sure," he replied honestly.

"We could wander around here the rest of our lives," McCoy continued. "We'd never know what we were really doing. We could imagine that we ate and drank . . . and in reality, we'd starve to death. No wonder the men that came down here didn't want to go back. Why should they! They can have everything the universe can provide, right here."

"But it doesn't always work," Kirk observed. "Sulu and Uhura, and the others, some of them . . . they came back. They gave up 'paradise' . . . to return to the ship and their duty."

"That doesn't solve our problem. I still see that shuttle, and if I went and got in, I know it would fly me back to the *Enterprise*."

Kirk looked where McCoy was staring. For a moment he saw it too—a ghostly flicker of a rectangular silver shape against the trees. Furiously he dismissed the image, refusing to believe in it. It went. But how long, he wondered, could he hold out against his own illusions? He looked desperately at McCoy.

"To my knowledge," Spock said softly, "I have seen nothing unreal since I arrived. And I have been on the planet longer than anyone who has remained unaffected."

Kirk and McCoy both looked at him. "You were unconscious most of that time," McCoy said.

"True, Doctor."

"Bones," Kirk asked, crouching down beside the Vulcan, "could it be that his mind is unaffected because it's different from ours?"

"Well, it's possible," McCoy admitted, also looking anxiously into the Vulcan's face. "It may also be that he takes longer to be affected, because of his natural resistance. Or, again, he may be having illusions all along, and simply not be aware of it."

Spock bristled. "Doctor, I am not in the habit of imagining—"

"How do you know?" McCoy grated. "How do you know that Jim and I are real? That we're not just figments of your fevered imagination? You wanted to be rescued. Whatever it is that's doing all this might just be providing Jim and me to do the rescuing."

"You are real, Doctor," Spock said.

"I know that! But how do you know it?"

"I can see you, I can touch you . . ." Spock stopped. It was an impasse. If one's senses could not be trusted, how could one prove what was true and what was false? He looked from McCoy to Kirk. His hand locked onto Kirk's arm, or he thought it did. It seemed solid.

"What do we do?" he asked.

"We have to take a chance—all of us. McCoy and I will have to risk that you're not affected and that you see what is real. You'll have to believe that we're not just your imagination."

"I don't know if he's well enough," cautioned McCoy, eyeing the Vulcan's pale, drawn face.

Kirk got to his feet. "He'll have to be," he said bluntly. "We've got to get out of here before whatever this thing is makes us lose our will to return to the ship completely . . . or makes us think we have already returned."

"Just a minute." McCoy produced a hypo, loaded it, and shot the contents into Spock's arm. "It'll help," he said.

Spock nodded. Already he could feel the benefit of the drug in his veins, releasing fresh energy from his inner reserve. When it was spent, he would be exhausted, but that didn't matter now. Kirk helped him onto his feet. Spock fixed his gaze on the direction in which they had been going and set off. Kirk and McCoy followed, keeping close to him. Reluctantly, McCoy passed the shuttle he saw. He reached out a hand and touched the cool, hard metal. He could feel the faint lines of the machining, the texture of the paint. Kirk caught his arm and forced McCoy to follow the Vulcan, refusing himself to acknowledge the ship he half-saw.

Spock saw the glitter of water ahead. He stopped and studied it suspiciously. McCoy and Kirk were following him like blind men now, their arms locked tightly about each other, staggering. Kirk had one hand on Spock's arm, gripping it hard, forming them into a chain that could not be broken.

Spock led them through their illusions, but whether he himself was traveling through an illusion of his own, he had no way of knowing.

He stopped again at the edge of the trees. The shuttle was there, silhouetted darkly against the bright starlit water. It seemed a sinister shape in the dark.

"Do you see it, Jim?" he asked.

Kirk looked beyond him, dazed. "I don't know. I think so." Spock looked at McCoy. The doctor was beyond offering an opinion. He was fighting, struggling desperately with Kirk's arm, trying to gain his freedom.

"It would seem," Spock observed out loud, "that whatever is causing these illusions is unwilling to let its victims escape."

He began walking again; this time, it was up a slight slope to the shuttle. The lights glowed welcomingly from the open hatch. Spock maneuvered Kirk and McCoy ahead of him across the ramp. Once inside, he carefully closed and locked the hatch, wondering as he did so whether the shielding would make any difference to the illusions of the humans. It seemed to, or else the influence lessened of its own accord. For a time they sat slumped together in their seats; then Kirk stirred and looked at him.

"Is this real?" he asked.

Spock nodded once, assured. "This is real, Captain."

Kirk looked at him, curious. "How do you know?"

"I know."

Kirk understood. Spock knew his own mind better than most men. His Vulcan abilities made it possible for him sometimes to see truth and reason through falsehood. Now that his mind was working on the problem, that indeed was the case. So far, he was unaffected by the lies in which the humans were being made to believe so completely. Kirk trusted his judgment. He could see, too, that the Vulcan was tired almost to the point of collapse. He got up and went over to him unsteadily.

"Are you all right?"

Spock nodded. "I am."

Kirk glanced at McCoy, who was now sitting up and looking at them wearily.

"We'd better get out of here, back to the ship as fast as we can." He reached forward to the control console and threw a switch. The central window shield drew upward into the hull. Beyond the lead-crystal port, Kirk could see a whole city: slim buildings in the starlight; wide, paved walks; hovering air cars. He sank back into the command seat.

"I can't," he said. "It's still working on me. I'd kill us all."

Spock looked out at the trees and the still lake. "I'll do it," he said, and slipped into the navigator's seat.

Kirk felt the shuttle begin to tremble as the drives warmed into life. Spock lifted the ship, and it seemed to Kirk that they rose up through the city. A white-tiled wall tilted disastrously close. The nose of the shuttle rose. A slender silver tower centered itself in the port, grew larger, nearer, until Kirk could see every nut and bolt, every rivet, until he felt that he had to snatch the controls from the Vulcan's hands. They'd never get up, they'd never get away! They were all going to die! He reached for the controls in front of him. McCoy's hands clamped on his wrists.

"It's not real, Jim," McCoy rasped in his ear. "It's not real. You have to believe that! Let Spock fly the shuttle. Just concentrate on not believing! Don't believe any of it!"

Kirk gripped the sides of his seat. He could see the sky through the spidery framework of the tower. He could see the lights in the windows of the turret at the top. No! No, it was not real! It could not be real!

The shuttle soared upward, triumphing over gravity, gaining height in the dawn-brightening sky. The sky blazed with the red-gold of the rising sun, and then darkened once more into violet and indigo, until it changed finally to the star-studded blackness of space. Kirk sat back in his seat and tried to relax. Surely the influence that dwelt on the planet could not reach them here, beyond atmosphere and gravity.

Spock locked the controls of the shuttle as soon as they attained orbit, and leaning back in his chair, closed his eyes. McCoy bent over him, concern in his eyes.

"He has to rest. That bang on the head has taken more out of him than he'll admit. I should really give him a sedative and put him to sleep for a while."

Spock rolled his head against the chair, once, back and forth. "Not necessary, Doctor," he said, without opening his eyes. "I'll rest."

McCoy straightened, satisfied with his promise.

"Come aft, then, and I'll make you more comfortable."

Spock got up and went with him wearily. Kirk studied the instruments. They had an hour of orbiting before they would catch up with the starship. An hour during which they would go on gaining height, drawing away from the planet that was so treacherously beautiful. He looked at it through the port, a blue-and-gold crescent, the greenness of its pastures splotched with shimmering seas and a single vast ocean.

McCoy, having settled Spock comfortably and covered him with a blanket, came back and sat down in the navigation seat.

"That planet looks so beautiful," Kirk said, without taking his eyes from it. "How can it do such ugly things to a man's mind?"

McCoy didn't answer. He had no answers to give.

"At least we're safe here," Kirk went on. "It can't touch us here. Once we're back on board the *Enterprise,* we'll devise . . . some way to get the crew back."

"I think it's more powerful than you're giving it credit for," McCoy said quietly. "I think it was able to reach out and kill Durban on the *Enterprise.*"

Kirk took his eyes off the planet and stared at him. "How?"

"I can't say exactly. But, most likely, with his own imagination. It made him live out some experience in which he died. And it was so real that he did die!"

Kirk felt his mouth go dry. He returned his attention to the spinning world beyond the port, not wanting the doctor to see the look of fear in his eyes: if the influence could reach the ship, they could never be sure that anything was real.

But McCoy read his thoughts anyway. "If we're made to think that we've docked, we could open that hatch and find ourselves breathing space."

Kirk looked over his shoulder, back to where the Vulcan lay half-upright in a seat, head to one side, as he breathed evenly—to all intents, asleep. Again McCoy knew what he was thinking.

"We can't go on relying on his mind, Jim," he said,

"He's being pressured. Whatever it is, it will get to him eventually. At what stage do we stop trusting him? And then, whom do we trust?"

"We've got to get to the ship—to work something out before we all break down completely. Let's hope Scotty has those Transporters fixed."

"There may not have even been anything wrong with those Transporters. Perhaps we were just made to think there was—another mass hallucination."

A large silver star appeared through the port now, beyond the tip of the crescent. The star took on a familiar, comforting shape. Kirk looked at it doubtfully and studied the instruments. The sensor configuration was right, and so was the ETA. But could he trust them?

"You'll have to get Spock up here," he said.

McCoy glared at him. "Is that an order, Captain?"

Kirk stared at him in surprise. "Doctor?"

"The man's sick, Jim. I consider him medically unfit for duty."

"And what about the rest of us?" Kirk asked levelly. "How do we know if that's the Enterprise, or some image of an illusion? How do I know what these instruments tell me is right?"

"You're the captain," McCoy said flatly. "Your command can't depend on one sick man."

Kirk dithered. He didn't know what to do, but a decision had to be made, and he was the one who had to make it. He reached down to the radio.

"Kirk to Enterprise."

"Enterprise here, sir," Scott replied at once.

"Prepare to receive shuttlecraft, Mr. Scott. We're approaching the ship from above the stern."

"Aye, sir. Hangar deck evacuating and preparing to receive shuttle. We missed hearin' from you, sir. Did you find Mr. Spock?"

"I had too many things on my mind to call the ship, Scotty," Kirk said with an attempt at lightness. "Yes, we have Spock. He's had a bad bang on the head."

"I'll have a medical team stand by. Did you find out what's been happening to our crew?"

"We have some theories, Scotty. Has anything odd happened on board since we've been gone?"

"No, sir. Repairs to the Transporter are nearing completion."

"Good." Kirk exchanged dubious glances with McCoy.

"Opening the hangar doors for you now, sir."

A bright vertical slit appeared in the tail of the starship and slowly widened as the recessed doors slid apart. The vast chamber beyond glowed beneath the vivid lighting—landing flares marking out patterns on the floor, glide lanes, and the landing circle. Kirk lowered the shuttle's nose and lined it up with the first pair of lights.

"Coming in for final approach, Scotty," he said into the radio.

Static crackled back at him. Kirk frowned, but his concentration was focused on berthing the shuttle. As they approached from above and behind, the *Enterprise* lay spread-eagled beneath them, a silver-pyloned city with wings held high and neck proudly raised. In spite of his problems, Kirk felt his heart lift at the sight of her. She was beautiful. Her nose lifted as she leaned slightly in orbit, her belly toward the planet. Kirk adored the smooth sharp lines of her and the demanding female personality that emanated from every angle.

He looked down on her with fondness, but as he looked, a subtle change came over the starship. Her hull lost its silver hue and began to glow dull gold. Kirk watched in horror, his mouth frozen open, his hands locked rigidly on the controls. The golden gleam grew brighter. An energy discharge danced luridly over the plates, a lingering corposant glow. The ship appeared consumed with flameless fire, an inferno of vivid cold light—and the shuttle was sailing straight down to destruction in the chill bright furnace.

McCoy was also witness to the horrifying transformation of the starship. "Jim!" he yelled after a moment of frozen speechlessness. "For God's sake, get us out of here, you'll kill us all!"

Kirk said nothing. His mouth was now a hard line, his eyes glaring from beneath lowered brows at the landing platform, still visible. He studiously ignored the gleaming gold hull; he braced himself against the vibrant tremble that was coming through the superstructure of the shuttle, and pretended it did not exist.

One part of his mind was screaming. The *Enterprise* was burning from within, consumed by radiation. To set the shuttle down was madness, suicide! Both he and his two friends would perish!

McCoy leaped at him, adding his vocal objections to the reasoning of Kirk's own mind.

"Jim! That ship's death! Get us away!"

"I won't let it win!" Kirk grated harshly. "It's an illusion, and I won't let it win!"

"How can it be an illusion?" McCoy screamed. "We can both see it happening!" He leaned over Kirk, reaching for the controls, intending to do something, anything, to bring the shuttle up, to make her overshoot the bay, somehow to avoid collision with the ship itself. Kirk threw him roughly aside.

All there was in the port now was the rear of the ship—its open doors and the bright lights beyond, and the glow of the radiating hull. Kirk dismissed the impression. The *Enterprise* was as she had always been. Everything else was false. He knew that he had to believe it. The landing lights passed beneath the craft. They were inside the ship. All he had to do was set the shuttle down. The circle was there, coming up underneath. Kirk set the controls. The blazing deck came up to meet him. There was a somewhat less than gentle thump, and then Kirk leaned forward onto his arms and closed his eyes.

Scott looked at him in concern. "Are you sure you're all right, sir?"

"I'm fine. What about Spock and McCoy?"

"Well, they've both had a bang on the head now, but they'll be all right. I must say, that was the roughest landing I've ever seen. For a moment I thought you'd flown right through the deck."

Kirk managed a grin. "So did I," he admitted. "Scotty, how many crew do we have left?"

"Fifty-two, sir," Scotty answered promptly. "And that includes you, Mr. Spock, and Dr. McCoy."

"If it's anything strenuous, you can count me out," McCoy said, coming through the Sickbay door and gently touching a sizable lump on his head. He was followed by Spock, who had regained at least some of his coloring.

"Bones," Kirk said, "the two women we brought back—what's their condition now?"

"Physically, they're fine, but they do have an urgent but fortunately nonviolent desire to return to the surface. They seem to feel that they left something behind there."

"They did," Kirk replied grimly. "The thing that mattered to them most—whatever it was." He turned away from his officers and walked toward the wall, not really seeing the charts that hung there. "As I see it, gentlemen," he went on, "we have only one course of action. We can't get our crew back; the influence won't let them return. All we can do is get back to a starbase. The specialists there might be able to devise some means of jamming the force, or at least a way of shielding us from it long enough to come back and get our men out."

"You can't go off and leave them there!" McCoy protested at once. "Jim, you just can't do it! Those men are prey to whatever they think up; if they think about death, they'll die!"

"And the same thing will happen to us if we stay here," Kirk said quietly.

"The moral aspect apart, Captain," Spock stated, "there are practical difficulties to be considered. To man the *Enterprise* in warp flight with a crew of a mere fifty would involve not only hardship, but a considerable degree of danger."

"Mr. Spock is understating the case, sir," Scott said boldly. "In my opinion, there'd be little chance of us ever reaching a starbase alive. The ship canna fly herself."

Kirk nodded wearily. "I know that, Scotty, but we have to do something. If we stay here, we'll all eventually come under the influence of whatever that is down there. And then we won't be able to help anyone. If we make the attempt . . ."

"I wonder what the devil it is," McCoy mused.

Spock looked at him. "I believe it has to do with the sailors," he said.

"The sailors? How?"

"I have noticed that they are always in the vicinity when the hallucinations begin."

"That's right," Kirk said. "Durban died in the lab, and there is a sailor in one of those sample cases. Is it possible that they could have some form of intelligence—that they could be reasoned with?"

Spock shook his head slowly. "Doubtful, Captain. Intelligence does require a certain level of cranial capacity. The size of the sailor's brain is well below the accepted norm."

"We have to try it," Kirk said, and started for the lab.

The sailor looked out at them through the glass mesh of its container with two bright amber eyes. It had a flat, furry face, a pliable sausage-shaped body, also covered with fur, and three-toed feet with a curved, gripping claw on each toe. Bending double, his face close to it, Kirk had to admit that he felt rather a fool extending grave diplomatic courtesies to the creature. His officers gathered around, listening with grave attention, as did the sailor—though he made no noticeable attempt to respond.

In the end, Kirk straightened and put a hand on a back that ached.

"It's no good," he said, disappointed. "I think you're right, Mr. Spock. It displays no signs of intelligence."

"Neither has it affected our minds since we've been here, although we have provided it with an ideal opportunity to take over the entire command personnel of the ship," Spock observed. "If you will permit me." He stepped forward and reached a hand into the cage. He grasped the back of the creature's head firmly, and for a moment his eyes became clouded, distant. Then he stepped back. Kirk looked at him expectantly. Spock merely shook his head.

"Very well," Kirk said, "the sooner we start away from here, the less affected we'll be and the more likely to survive the journey. Mr. Scott, you'll see to the engine room. Mr. Spock, go down to Auxiliary Control and channel everything through to the bridge. We'll handle it all from there. Dr. McCoy, I'm ordering a stimulant shot for everyone."

"Jim! I can't . . ." McCoy's objection went unheard. Kirk was already on his way to the bridge.

The bridge was peopled with a full command crew. For a moment, Kirk couldn't believe it. He stared around in amazement, and then the import hit him, and a great joy overwhelmed him: somehow the influence from the planetary surface had released the minds of his people. His talk with the sailor in the lab must have proved effective after all. The creature had contacted its kind, and his crew had returned, free. He ran down the steps to the helm.

"Mr. Burnhard, set course for Starbase Fifteen. Lieutenant Jones . . ."

"Captain?" Spock said querulously from the turbolift doors.

Kirk turned, beaming as he spread his arms. "It's all right, Mr. Spock, everything's all right. The crew are back!"

Spock ran down the steps to him, his face anxious. He looked around the bridge—nothing. "Jim,"—he took Kirk firmly by the arms—"you're imagining it. They're not here . . . they're really not here!"

The smile faded from Kirk's face. He looked around the bridge incredulously. He could see his crew. He could hear the murmur of their voices. Tina Jones was close to him. He could smell her perfume, reach out and touch the smooth softness of her hair. He looked back at Spock and shook his head.

"You're wrong, Mr. Spock. They are here. The sailors have let them go. Now we can stay and finish out the shore leave and—"

"Jim!" Spock shook him so hard that his teeth rattled. "It's an illusion! Just another illusion!"

Kirk looked at him and shook his head again. Not believing. Not wanting to believe.

Spock stared into his face. "Jim, have I ever lied to you? Believe me! Now, of all times, believe me!"

Kirk gazed into the dark alien eyes. The Vulcan seemed to see into him, into his very soul, and the bond between the two men asserted itself. Kirk believed. He relaxed and let Spock go. But for themselves, the bridge was empty. Kirk felt behind him for the support of the command seat. The turbo-lift doors opened, and McCoy stepped out onto the bridge, followed by Sulu and Uhura and a man from Scott's department who was to man the power boards.

McCoy looked from Kirk to Spock and back again, sensing that something of deep significance had been going on. "What's the matter?" he asked. "Jim, are you all right?"

"The captain is quite well, thank you, Doctor," Spock said formally. "It is his wish to leave this place with the utmost speed."

"I think we all wish that," McCoy retorted crisply. He went down the steps and looked into Kirk's face. "Jim, are you sure you're all right?"

Kirk sank down into the command seat and nodded. "Just give me that shot, Bones," he ordered.

Spock mounted the steps to the computer station, while McCoy obliged Kirk's wish.

"Mr. Spock," Kirk said wearily, "lay us a course for Starbase Fifteen. Maximum warp."

Spock reached for the computer, and then his hand hesitated. He turned in his seat and looked down at Kirk. In the depths of his eyes something was kindling. His face was intent with what was almost a dawning joy.

Kirk stared back at him with mild alarm. "Mr. Spock?"

"Jim," Spock said in a whisper, "why do we have to leave here? We can stay. Just you and I. We don't need those others."

"He's off his head." McCoy grunted. "He's finally cracked."

"No. The thing's finally got to him," Kirk said, climbing out of the command seat. "It's offering him the one thing . . ." He stopped abruptly, realizing that he was giving too much away. He ignored McCoy's startled look and went up to the Vulcan.

"Spock!"

"We can go down to the planet," Spock explained reasonably. "We can be together, always. . . ."

"Spock!" Kirk dragged him onto his feet and shook him.

"Jim, you don't have to hurt me."

"Snap out of it, or I will hurt you!" Kirk snarled into his face.

Spock shook his head, bewildered. Kirk hit him hard across the face—once, twice, three times. A small trickle of blood ran from the corner of the Vulcan's mouth. He lowered his eyes and very slightly shook his head. Kirk carefully let him go, and he put a hand against the computer console to steady himself.

"I'm sorry," he murmured, so low that only Kirk could hear. Kirk touched him on the arm and turned to meet the curious stares of the crew.

"We've got a job to do," he said. "Let's get back to it."

"Jim," McCoy said sharply. "Spock was talking about brain capacity. . . . What if it's a form of composite brain? All the separate units acting as one whole?"

"No, Bones." Kirk shook his head. "If there'd been any intelligence at all, Spock would have felt it when he mind-melded with the creature."

McCoy's hope turned to dejection. "Oh."

There was a silence.

"Captain . . ." Spock spoke quietly from behind him. "The doctor may be right."

Kirk turned. "How?"

"It may be a composite brain. Your planet has them—ants, bees . . . And so does mine. Creatures which, in themselves, are mindless and yet act with a mass intelligence for the good of the whole. It may be that we have been directing our thoughts toward the wrong species."

Kirk frowned. "If it's not the sailors, then what . . . ?"

"Such intelligences are confined entirely to insect populations," Spock said. "The sailor is a warm-blooded egg-layer."

"Insects?" Kirk stared at him. "But what insects . . . ?"

"Of course!" McCoy yelled. "The butterflies! They're everywhere down there!"

"Quite so," Spock agreed. "We have already observed that they live in communities, that they have individual markings, and they are present in such prolific numbers as to be, numerically at least, the dominant species on this planet."

Kirk looked at him and then at McCoy. "Well, let's go find out."

The strangled Durban had amassed a considerable number of the butterflies in his collection. Spock reached his hand into the case, and after a few moments one of the tiny creatures perched on his finger. He drew it out, and it remained there, flexing its scarlet wings. Spock held his hand close to him, and with the forefinger of his other hand he touched the head end very gently. He remained quite still for several seconds, and then his eyes closed.

"They intended us no harm," he told Kirk some time later as they watched the ship gradually refill with the errant crewmen. "What we experienced was merely the overlap, the stray brain waves of their own communal thought. They exist merely for living their dreams."

"Butterflies," McCoy said with undisguised disgust. "Who'd have thought that butterflies would have been the dominant species anywhere?"

"It may not always be so, Doctor," Spock replied. "They are not a particularly resourceful species, and there are several promising types on the planet which may one day evolve to take their place—just as the dinosaurs were once replaced by other species on Earth."

"Any change would be an improvement on butter-flies," McCoy said grumpily.

Spock raised an eyebrow at this remark. "I wonder if the dinosaurs would agree with you, Doctor," he said softly.

McCoy glared at him.

Scott stuck his head around the door of the Trans-porter room. "Everyone's aboard, sir. Shall I close the Transporter down?"

"I think Mr. Spock has something to beam down," Kirk said.

Spock bent down and picked up the case containing the butterflies and carried them into the Transporter room. McCoy watched him go, scowling.

"Dinosaurs indeed!" he grunted. "Jim, what was he saying about you and him on the bridge a while back?"

Kirk didn't look at him as he started for the turbo-lift. "As I think you remarked, Bones, he was off his head."

Introduction to The Mind-Sifter

by *William Shatner*

These are the new voyages of the Starship *Enterprise*—its continuing mission: to seek out new life, new civilizations, strange new worlds. . . .

It is odd to realize that nearly a decade has passed since the *Enterprise* began its "five-year mission," and both sobering and heartening to realize that the strangest new world of all is old—and is home.

But what else can be said of a planet where those first voyages are still watched by more people every day than ever saw them when they were new—watched in nearly every country and every language of the world of their birth?

What else can be said of a world where thousands of people dream new voyages for the *Enterprise?* Where hundreds of thousands, even millions, continue to read of the old voyages and press for new ones to be recorded in books and on film?

Strange?

Yes.

But perhaps not so strange on the world where man has already taken the first step onto a strange world. Captain James T. Kirk would understand "one small step for a man, one giant step for mankind." The sum of such small steps will finally add up to a world that will be like his—strange, new, and still a home for mankind.

The small steps, not only into space but also into the inner worlds of better understanding of self and others, are necessary—and sometimes painful. If they can be helped and guided at all by something like the vision of the world of the *Enterprise,* that is a beautiful thing and an enormous bonus for everyone involved.

I am always astonished and sometimes shaken to realize the feeling so many people have for that vision. I have often felt at a loss to explain that feeling, and perhaps the only true explanation is in each of those people individually. Yet it is clear from the magnitude of their efforts—writing, reading, studying, thinking, dreaming, talking, getting together by thousands and tens of thousands, welcoming new people warmly into their ranks—that they are responding to something in common, and to something they consider terribly important.

Each of us who sailed on the *Enterprise* can only be grateful for that, and when she sails again—and she will, in these stories and others, and again on the screen—it will be because of those people's efforts.

A "thank you" is in order—and is hereby ordered.

On a more personal level, I am touched and moved by the interest in the character of Kirk—an interest that, for some strange reason, I happen to share.

Seriously, I have been asked how I would play Kirk now after these years and in new voyages. I have given that considerable thought, and it strikes me that I have learned and grown in a number of directions in those years, and I believe that Kirk would have, too. One key aspect is that I believe even more firmly in the importance of openness, willingness to communicate real emotions, willingness to be even more revealing of self— to have the courage to communicate: this is how I *am*, this is how I am angry, this is how I love, this is how I cry.

That can be a difficult thing to do, but it is terribly important. It was something that Kirk had partly learned, and something that people evidently responded to in him. I believe that he would have learned more.

How would he be now? How would I see him now?

Perhaps very much as Shirley Maiewski has in this story.

It asks the question: What remains of a man when nothing is left to him—nothing but his most basic self?

If the answer it gives for Kirk is true, and this is some of what people saw in Kirk and in his world, then perhaps that is part of the answer to why people in our world still care.

And perhaps that caring is not so strange, after all. I would like to think so.

Mind-Sifter

by *Shirley S. Maiewski*

He seemed to be climbing a long, steep incline. Up
ahead, he could see a dim light. Not really—only a
lessening of the darkness that now surrounded him.
He stumbled. What was he walking on—a road, a
walkway, a deck? It appeared to be smooth, hard. It
leveled off. He put out his hand, touched a smooth surface—cool, smooth, yes, but also rough. Paint, flaking
paint. He felt some come away and brushed his hand
against his leg. Felt cloth—loose, rough. He kept going; the light brightened. A corner, sharp—not curved?

A voice. It stopped him—short of the corner. Careful . . . careful. Danger!

Voice hard, rough: "He's gotta come out sometime."
Another: "Yeah, he'll get hungry."

Hungry . . . food . . . yes . . . that was it . . . but . . .
Danger. Danger.

He pressed against the wall, fear, overpowering, awful fear, striking him. His legs began to tremble, a whimper grew; his hands covered his mouth. Quiet. Be quiet.
Danger!

The footsteps—going away; the fear subsided, his
hands dropped, he moved to the corner—careful . . .
go slow. Slip around . . . empty hall. The light brighter,
coming from an exposed globe, hanging from a wire,
revealing brown, dirty walls, cracked paint, brown,
dirty floor, a door.

Careful—trap? Round handle; he reached out,
touched, pulled back. He stepped back. The door
stayed open. Shouldn't it close? No. He gave it a slight
push; it swung easily . . . slammed!

Noise. Danger.

His knees began to tremble again; he backed quickly around the corner, the whimper building in his
throat. He crammed his fist into his mouth to silence it,
but still a whine of fear escaped. His knees gave way;
he sank to the floor, curled into a ball, his knees pulled

179

up against his chest, one arm clasped tightly against his legs, trying to make himself as small as possible.

Then . . . footsteps. Coming toward him. . . . Hide. Hide! He curled tighter, arms over his head now. The whimper grew into a cry, crawled up his throat. . . . "Help me. Please!"

A voice. Different. "I'm coming . . . wait there!"

The footsteps came around the corner, stopped beside him. A hand . . . was it? Fear! Something touched his arm gently; then the voice again—soft, full of compassion. "Oh, Jimmy . . . I was so worried. Why did you run away?"

The fear subsided. Slowly he relaxed, uncurled a little, looked up and up, along smooth legs, to white dress, to arms reaching down, hair, swinging around a face— a smiling face. Danger? Unreal? A trap? Another whimper.

"No . . . no, Jimmy, don't cry. It's all right. I'm Jan. You remember Jan, don't you? Come, take my hand."

Jan? Jan was . . . nice . . . gentle . . . yes, she . . . she would help. Slowly he put up his hand and took hold of hers.

"That's right, Jimmy . . . you remember. Come, now, get up. You must be so hungry."

Hungry? Yes. When had he eaten last? What? No memory came. Wait. A tray? Bright colors? No . . . a bowl . . . dull, but food.

He began to uncurl more, her hand encouraging him. He got his feet under him, pushed up—against the wall—his hand still holding tightly to hers.

"Good for you! That's fine, Jimmy. Come, let's go and find you something to eat." She tugged gently at his hand, toward the corner . . . toward danger.

He stiffened, pulled back; his pull drew her toward him, off balance. She tripped, fell. He grabbed at her, held her by the shoulders. Soft. Nice. A girl; no, a woman. He looked down into her face—turned up to his now, eyes widening, meeting his. Slight frown. . . .

"Jimmy? Let me go now, Jimmy."

"No! I . . . I want to . . . to . . ."

"What, Jimmy? You want to what?"

"I . . . want . . ." He stopped, what did he want?

Her shoulders were soft, yet firm; they felt good in his hands—deep within him, something familiar . . . a warmness . . . a . . .

"Hey! What's he doing?" Shout. Harsh, rough hands reaching, pulling. "Get away from her, you nut!" A slap, a blow against his head, danger. Danger.

"Stop! Oh, stop! Frank, don't. Please!"

"Why? Crazy nut . . . whadya think you were doin'? Why'd ya let him get so close?" Big harsh hands yanked him off balance, threw him around the corner.

"Hey, Fred! Here's our Superman. Caught him fooling around with Miss Hamlin."

Another set of hands—hard, coarse—caught him, slammed him against a wall.

"Don't, please—leave him alone. He didn't mean anything."

Something was thrown around him; his arms jerked and pulled—forced into sleeves, twisted. He was spun around, shoved again, against the wall. His face scraped over the rough, peeling paint. He jerked back from the pain, only to receive a crashing blow on the side of his head. Blackness reaching. . . .

"Stand still! We'll teach you to keep your dirty paws off our nurses."

"Frank! He didn't mean anything. I tripped—he helped me. Kept me from falling. Oh, don't—don't put that thing on him. Please!"

"Trying to tell me my job, Miss Hamlin? I've seen you with this guy before—you're kinda soft on him, ain't ya?" the voice snarled. "Hey, Fred, pull those straps tighter—wanta lose him again?"

The yanking grew rougher; his arms were pulled around to his sides, binding; he struggled; the wail grew to a scream of sheer terror.

"Aw, shut up. Damnit, ya'll start all the loonies in the place howling. Shut up!"

"I'll report you, Frank! Dr. Wright will hear about—"

"Oh, no, sweetie—no ya won't. I'll tell him I saw you snuggling up to this . . . this Superman. He don't look so pretty now, does he? Face all scraped like that. Aw, gee—ain't that a shame? He fell down and bumped his pretty face. Nah, you tell Wright, and next time, I won't be so gentle with him. C'mon, Fred, let's get him back where he belongs."

As though from a great distance he could feel himself being hauled up and dragged along by the straps of the jacket binding him . . . saw a door pushed open . . . bright light blinding him . . . felt himself pushed, staggering. He fell full-length, his hands instinctively struggling to break the fall, but they were tied to his sides. He crashed to the floor, his head hitting hard . . . darkness again. . . . Pain. Awful pain. Another cry. "Help me! Help me, Sp . . . Spock? Help me!"

Silence—dead, ear-aching silence. He blinked . . . looked again, avoiding the light . . . saw a bed beside him. Low . . . gray mattress, rumpled sheet, but better than the floor. He raised himself, got his knees under him, pushed against the wall. Up . . . staggered to the bed . . . collapsed again, on the bed this time.

"Water . . . please . . . water! Spock?" His voice echoed. Silence again. . . . "Help . . . help me? Spock?" No, not Spock . . . Jan! She said she'd help. . . . "Jan!" he cried. "Where are you?" His throat was sore; it ached from thirst and his screams.

A noise. A clanking. The rough ones again? Danger. Hide, hide!

"Jimmy?" The soft one. "Jimmy? Here I am. . . ." A swirl of white, a figure rushing toward him. He opened his mouth to scream. "No, no, Jimmy. I won't hurt you—shh—it's Jan." Soft hands on his face, stroking, pushing back his hair. "Jimmy—they hurt you. I'm so sorry." Face close to his, eyes—blue eyes— peering anxiously at him; eyes wet with tears. A soft, cool wetness on his cheek. Water? A cloth, soft and wet. . . .

Pain! Sharp. "Hurts."

"Shh, Jimmy, let me clean up your cheek; it's scraped and bleeding. Now, now, Jan won't hurt you—shh." The soothing voice crooned, the pain became less, was gone. Gone with it some . . . most of the fear.

In place of the fear, a thought growing. . . .

"Jan?"

"Yes, I'm here, Jimmy. Come, sit up so I can undo these straps."

"Where, Jan. Where?"

She looked at him, realizing that he was looking at her with a different expression. Was that a glimmer of intelligence in his eyes?

" 'Where' what, Jimmy?" she asked gently. For the first time in the six months that he'd been there, she thought she saw a change in him.

"Where am I?"

"This is . . . a hospital, Jimmy. You've been very sick. I am a nurse. I am taking care of you." She spoke each word very slowly and distinctly.

He frowned, shook his head as though to clear it, and then looked into her eyes again. "Sick? How . . . how am I sick?"

"In your mind, Jimmy," she said gently.

"No—no—no!" He started to get up. Couldn't; with his hands still confined, he was off balance, helpless. He sank back on the bed, thrashing his head from side to side, tears pressing out from between his tightly closed eyelids. "No! Not that!" he cried.

"Jimmy, don't, please. I'm sorry. Hush, now." Jan Hamlin caught his rolling head between her hands and held tightly, meanwhile murmuring quietly to him. At last he stopped fighting her hold and lay still, sobbing softly, like a broken-hearted child.

Jan's mind was racing—he knew what she meant! So far as she knew, this was the first time that an idea had registered in his mind. He knew the implications of a sick mind.

"Jimmy, come, let me get this awful jacket off you. Sit up, please?" she coaxed, smiling.

He looked up at her, at her smile, drew a shuddering breath, and struggled to sit up. She helped, and soon he was sitting on the edge of the bed. She quickly unfastened the buckles and straps of the heavy canvas straitjacket that held him. Pulling it away from him, she tossed it disgustedly to the floor. He sat looking at her, rubbing his hands together. The sobbing stopped. Once more he shook his head, then rubbed one hand over his face and eyes as if to clear away cobwebs. Again he looked at her, a tiny smile crooking one corner of his mouth.

"Thank you," he said.

Jan felt a thrill of hope. Yes! There was a change. She was strangely attracted to this man. Many times she'd tried to work with him, but never before had he shown any sign of coming out of the black pit of horror that seemed to enfold him.

She thought back to the day he'd been brought in —six months before. She'd been in the admissions office when two policemen had come in supporting, almost carrying, a man who fought and screamed and sobbed in absolute terror. Orderlies had come running with a jacket and shortly had him bound securely. A doctor had come and administered a heavy sedative, and soon he'd been slumped in a chair.

"Who is he?" the police had been asked.

"We don't know. We found him staggering along a back road, near the city limits."

"What's that costume he's wearing?"

"Never saw anything like it—that yellow shirt, the insignia, looks like some kind of team shirt or something. Strange material. He was covered with dirt— musta fallen a lot—but it brushed right off."

"Any identification?"

"Nothing. Not even any pockets in that outfit. We'll inform Missing Persons. Somebody will probably claim him. . . ." The police left shortly afterward.

The man was admitted, his strange clothes marked and packed away, the doctors examined him—a well-built, physically healthy man in his mid-thirties, as far as they could judge.

He was listed as "John Doe"—the few words he'd mumbled or screamed were English—American English—and he was started on a series of tests and treatments.

No one came looking for him; his fingerprints weren't on file anywhere.

She was glad when the strange man was assigned to her wing of the giant hospital. Something about him appealed to her. When he wasn't in one of his periods of violence, he at times would stand quietly looking up at the sky through the barred windows.

One day, when he was standing so, she'd stopped beside him and had spoken to him, calling him "John." He'd turned, looked at her, and said very clearly, "James."

Then, almost as if the name had been a signal, he'd become violent. Since then, except for only a few unconnected moments, he'd dropped back into the well of horror that seemed to engulf him. At times he was like a small child, whimpering and sobbing. She'd found that calling him "Jimmy," as one would a child, sometimes brought response. Other times he would rage and fight and need restraints. He'd been given all the tests; one doctor swore he was a schizophrenic, another a manic-depressive, but it all added up to a big zero. They really didn't know. They changed his name to "James Doe," after Jan had told of his response, but beyond that—nothing. Except for periodic treatment, medication to calm him when he was violent, nothing could be done. He became just one more poor unfortunate, forgotten patient in a large, overcrowded, understaffed state institution. No one cared, except Jan Hamlin. With the limited time allotted to her, she did her best to see that he was cared for.

When she'd come on duty this day, she'd been told that her "pet" had escaped into the hospital's basement. She had been teased before for bothering with the "Superman," as the orderlies who attended him called him, partly from his strength and partly from the strange clothes he'd been wearing when brought in.

The rough treatment he'd received wasn't unusual. But the special care Jan Hamlin gave him was. The pay for orderlies was low. As a rule, only people who couldn't find other jobs applied here. Jan often felt sickened by what she saw: the sadism of the orderlies, the laxness of nursing care, the indifference of many doctors. She often wanted to quit, but she couldn't. She just couldn't walk away, so, to the limit of her strength, she did what she could to help the unfortunate beings in her care. She tried not to favor any, but in James's case, she couldn't help it. Something about him kept drawing her back.

Now, finally, after all this time, a sign of comprehension—a few words—two words: "Thank you."

Jan's smile lit her face. "You are welcome, Jimmy," she said happily.

"Jim," he said, glancing at her sharply.

Her mind flashed back to the other time, and she caught her breath.

He frowned. "Jim," he repeated. "Yes, Jim—not Jimmy. . . ." He smiled again.

"Jim what?" she urged.

"Jim . . . I . . . I . . . don't . . . Just Jim," he said, looking worriedly at her; she saw tears forming and hastened to say, "That's all right, Jim. It doesn't matter. Come, now, let me get you down to the dining room— there's still time for supper." She took his hand and urged him to his feet.

At the dining-room door he stopped, looking around a little wildly. The clash and rattle of dishes startled him. Jan remembered when, another time that she'd tried to bring him in, he'd broken and run frantically back up the hall. This time, however, he just gripped her hand tighter—hurting her, although she'd have endured much more if he would only keep improving.

"Everything's all right, Jim," she said. "Come, I'll get you your supper."

As always, she was revolted by the quality of the food the patients were given—coarse, unappetizing, often greasy, colorless, unrecognizable food. She knew it was probably nourishing; the patients didn't starve, but why couldn't the food be made to look attractive? She sighed and picked up the battered spoon.

"No," Jim said.

" 'No' what?"

"I . . . I can."

She sat back and watched while he took the spoon from her. Dipping it into the grayish mess that was some kind of starchy casserole, he began to eat. She sat quietly beside him, hope building. She couldn't believe the change in him. He was awkward with the spoon; it was hard for him; a fork would have been better, but forks are sharp. He spilled the first couple of spoonfuls, but gradually he did better, and soon was eating easily. He drank thirstily from the cup of cold coffee, made a face.

"Cold! I never liked cold coffee," he said clearly, as casually as though they had been talking for hours. He glanced at Jan. "Please—I want some hot coffee."

"And you shall have it," she said, standing up quickly and starting for the serving counter.

"Jan, no. Don't leave me!" He jumped up frantically, shoving back his chair. Jan turned back quickly and caught hold of his arms. He was as tense as a bowstring, ready to panic.

"Jim. Jim, I'm here. I won't leave you."

"Jan?" He whimpered, and her heart sank. Was he regressing again? She'd been a fool to move so quickly.

"Yes, I'm here, Jim. Come—you come and help me get the coffee." She took his hand, and he followed her. This time she moved more slowly. She kept talking to Jim, and he quieted, the fear slowly leaving his eyes.

Taking a clean cup, she drew some fresh coffee from the urn and carried it back to the table.

"Now, Jim, be careful, the coffee is hot," she warned.

He picked up the cup and carefully tasted the steaming liquid. A smile lit his face. "Good," he said. "That's how I like it. You programmed the selector just right, Jan."

"I . . . what, Jim?"

"I said, you programmed the selector just the way I like my coffee." And again he drank from the cup, deeply this time.

"Oh. Yes . . . ." She was puzzled. Programmed? Selector? Just what kind of strange ideas were these? He seemed so sure of what he'd said, as though it were perfectly natural. Programmed—that was something you did with a computer. But . . . a selector?

"Jim, what is a . . . ?" Suddenly a bell sounded in the hall, a loud, clanging bell, signaling the end of visiting hours. Jan hated the bells; they always startled her, and she'd seen many patients react in fear at the sudden onslaught of sound. This time was no exception; all over the room, bodies stiffened, cries of fear were heard.

There was a violent crash beside her. Jan looked around, to see Jim standing beside his overturned chair. He was looking around, his lips moving. "Red Alert!" He started for the door, not running, but moving fast.

Jan hurried after him, caught up just outside the door. He was looking up and down the hall. "Where is it?" he asked when she came up to him.

"Where is what?" She'd expected to find him frantic with fright, but he seemed almost calm, just business-like.

"The turbo lift. Which way?" He snapped out the question.

"Jim, there's no . . . turbo lift here," she said.

"There must be!" He started down the hall, striding rapidly along, not shuffling or running—striding! She had to run to keep up with him.

"I've got to get there. It's a Red Alert! They need me."

Almost as he said it, the bell stopped its clamor. He took a few more steps, then slowed to a halt, turning slowly to Jan. "It's stopped. What happened? Why did the . . . ?" He frowned, trying to remember. "Jan? Where . . . where is . . . is . . . ?" She saw helpless confusion growing in his eyes, saw him raise his fist to his mouth, heard an all-too-familiar whimper start to build in his throat. Her heart sank; she reached out her hand, and he took it, like a lost child. Tears formed in his eyes. "Jan? It's gone. I almost . . ." He started to sob quietly.

"Sh-shh, Jim. Come, I'll take you back to your room. It's late. Come," she urged, drawing him down the hall. Once in the room, he quieted, and the sobbing died away.

Finally she said, "Jim, I must go now. The orderly is coming; he'll help you get to bed. Will you let him help you?" She knew that he sometimes fought the attendants, who would just go away and lock the door, letting him sleep on the floor if he wanted to.

He didn't move even when she said good night and went out the door.

He was alone. He lay on his back, staring at the window at the foot of the bed—a window covered with a heavy webbing of bars. The night sky was awash with brilliant stars. While he lay there looking at them, something moved—a late plane at a great height, only a pinpoint of light. He watched it, only his eyes moving, until it was gone. A sob grew in him; a line of tears formed and ran down the side of his face. His lips moved silently; then words formed: "Spock? Spock?" It was only a whisper. "Help me? Please . . . help me?" Finally he slept.

Spock looked up from the journal he'd been studying. The buzzer at his door had sounded. "Come," he called, and the door swished open.

Dr. Leonard McCoy, chief medical officer of the Starship *Enterprise,* stood in the doorway. "May I come in?" he asked formally.

"If you wish, Dr. McCoy." Spock switched off his viewer and indicated a chair across the desk. His voice was cold. It sounded as though he didn't care if McCoy came in or sat down or stayed away.

McCoy moved slowly to the chair and sat down. He didn't speak for a moment, just stared at a rack of Vulcan bells on the wall as though he'd forgotten what he'd come for.

"Well?" Spock prompted finally.

McCoy roused with a start, turned to Spock. "Do you know what the date is?"

"Shall I repeat the exact hour and minute for you, Doctor?"

"Yes—you'd know to the minute, wouldn't you? Is that all? Just numbers? D-don't you know what day this is, Spock?" McCoy snapped out the name distastefully.

"If you mean that this is the anniversary of the day that Captain Kirk disappeared, yes, I know what day it is. Why do you ask?" Spock had leaned back in his chair and had steepled his fingers before him, light gleaming from the gold braid on his arms, two bands of gold, with short dashes between—captain's stripes.

"Aren't you going to do anything to commemorate the day?" McCoy asked. "Wouldn't a memorial service be in order?"

"To serve what purpose, Doctor? A memorial service is to honor someone who is dead. We do not know that James Kirk is dead."

"Of course he's dead, Spock! Otherwise he'd have come back. Jim Kirk would come back from hell if he could. If he were alive, he'd have shown up somewhere, somehow! He's dead."

"Can you prove it, Doctor? Can you show me a body, a phaser burn—anything?"

McCoy flared. "Damn you, Spock! Maybe you have what you wanted—you are captain of the *Enterprise* now."

"Doctor, I did not wish—"

"Don't give me that old spiel 'I do not wish to command'! You took it fast enough when Jim disappeared."

Spock sighed. "I took command in order to keep an efficient crew together. I have explained this to you before, Dr. McCoy. Very well. Since you feel so strongly that some observance of the date should be made, you have my permission. However"—firmly—"I will not attend."

"Why not? Guilty conscience?" McCoy rose from his chair and started for the door without a backward glance.

"Dr. McCoy! You will not use that tone with me." Spock stood also, and his face darkened.

McCoy whirled on him. "Why, Spock, did I finally hit on the truth? You're willing to admit you're glad Jim's gone? Okay, put me on report! I don't care anymore. I'm thinking of leaving the *Enterprise* soon anyway." McCoy was breathing hard, glaring at Spock.

"Doctor. I am captain of the *Enterprise*. I command here. I do what I think is best for this ship, and I do not have to explain my actions to you. There are reasons why I cannot believe that James Kirk is dead, but I will not go into them with you. I understand how you feel about him, so I will overlook your outburst.

However, you cannot leave this ship unless I approve. Since I do not approve, you will stay."

"Why you . . . !" Fists tightly balled, McCoy took one step toward Spock, stopped. "Oh, what's the use?" he said, turned, and stamped out the door, which closed behind him.

Spock stood looking at the closed door. At last he sighed, sat down at his desk, and again switched on the viewer.

However, although the words on the screen came and went at his usual reading speed, he didn't see them. Instead, in his mind's eye he again was seeing the face of the man he'd called his friend—a young, vibrant ship's captain, James Kirk. A man who'd been closer to him than any other being. Spock thought again of that day, one Earth-year before, when Kirk had come bounding into his quarters.

"Spock!" He could hear the voice ringing in his mind again. "Spock, how about coming on shore leave with me? Scotty says he's going to pass it up this time. He'll take charge here. Come on, Spock, there's a place here I just have to show you! You'll never believe it." Kirk had grinned widely at him, excitement showing in his face and in his manner.

As if viewing a tape, Spock seemed to see himself answering his friend: "No . . . no, Jim, I have a new science journal with a report I must study. You go ahead. I do not wish to take leave now."

Kirk's face had fallen a little, but soon regained most of its former animation. He winked broadly at Spock, leaned over and said, "You'll be sorry!" waved his hand, turned, and hurried out the door.

Spock hadn't seen him since.

Kirk had beamed down to the R & R station. And vanished.

The *Enterprise* had remained in orbit while the planet was searched from end to end for sign or trace of James Kirk.

Nothing.

Ships leaving the planet had been searched—but there'd been time before that for him to have left. Or been taken. Klingon ships and others had left.

It was an Open Planet—one of several near the edge of the Federation's sphere of influence, not far from the Klingon Empire. It was used by Humans and aliens alike. Klingons were often seen there, as well as other non-Human races. It served as a kind of clearing-house for contacts, official and unofficial, between various races and cultures.

On the third day of the search, Lieutenant-Commander Scott returned to the *Enterprise* under guard. He had obviously been in a fight; he had a black eye, and his uniform was torn. He stood stiffly at attention in the Transporter room before Commander Spock.

"What happened, Mr. Scott?" Spock asked.

"I . . . have nothing to say, sir," Scott replied.

"Mr. Scott. You will tell me what happened." Spock's voice cracked at him. "Why were you sent back here in this condition?"

"Sir, I . . . well, I just couldna stand there and listen to what they were a-sayin' about Captain Kirk . . . sir." Scott's voice revealed his anger.

"And what was it 'they' said, Mr. Scott?"

"Sir, they . . . they said the captain has sold out to the Klingons! Sir!"

"I see. Who are 'they,' Mr. Scott?"

"A bunch of heathens from the *Lexington,* sir. They say the captain must have been paid off. . . ."

"That is enough, Mr. Scott. I quite understand your impetuous reaction. You are excused." Spock turned away from Scott for a moment, then looked back at him. "However, you will remain on board this ship un-til I give you permission to leave."

"Aye, sir." And Scott didn't leave the *Enterprise* again while they were in orbit around that planet. However, the story grew; others began to wonder, even while the search for Kirk continued.

On the sixth day, Spock received a message from Star Fleet Command: "Commander Spock. We regret that we can no longer allow the *Enterprise* to remain out of service. The search for Captain Kirk will be con-tinued by the civilian authorities. . . . You are hereby appointed acting commander of the *Enterprise* and will return the *Enterprise* to Starbase Eleven for reassignment."

The message had been heard by the bridge crew. There were expressions of shock and surprise when it ended and Spock ordered Chekov to lay in a course for Starbase Eleven.

"You mean you're gonna leave here without finding out what happened to Jim?" McCoy had railed at Spock.

"Doctor, I have my orders."

"So what? You can't do this, Spock."

"Dr. McCoy, there is nothing further we can do here. Star Fleet has already given us several extra days in which to search. They can no longer have this ship out of action."

"But . . . Spock!"

"That will be all, Dr. McCoy," Spock said. He turned his back on McCoy and stepped to the command chair. For one short second he paused, looking at it. Then the cold Vulcan mask closed over his features—never to change in the days that followed. He settled down into the chair. "You will lay in the course for Starbase Eleven, Mr. Chekov."

"Yes, sair," Chekov replied. "Laid in," he said sharply, not raising his eyes from his board.

"Take us out of orbit, Mr. Sulu," Spock ordered. "Warp two."

Sulu hesitated.

"But . . . Mr. Spock," he said, looking back at the Vulcan behind him. Sulu had never, to anyone's recollection, questioned a direct order from Spock before. Uhura gasped; she could feel the tension on the bridge. All heads turned toward the two figures, whose eyes were locked, the alien Vulcan and the Old Earth Oriental—races that had been set apart in their own times.

"Lieutenant Sulu. If you do not comply with my order immediately, I will have you relieved of duty," Spock said.

Sulu flushed; a smear of red flooded his cheeks. He turned back to his controls—"Aye, aye, sir"—savagely snapping the switches controlling the great starship.

Spock turned his attention to Engineer Scott, who

was standing near his bridge control board. Another red-shirted crewman was seated there. "Mr. Scott, I believe the lieutenant can handle the required engineering duties here. I also believe your duties can be better handled from your office in the main Engineering section. I shall notify you when your presence is required on the bridge. Dismissed."

Scott's mouth opened in surprise and shock. Then it snapped shut, opening only long enough for: "Yes, sir!" as Scott whirled and stalked to the turbo lift.

"And you, Dr. McCoy, will find work to occupy you in your Sickbay," Spock said, without looking at the doctor standing behind him.

McCoy took a step toward Spock, stopped, glanced at Uhura, whose face registered her shock and disbelief. His eyes swept on around the bridge, taking in the rigid figures seated at their stations. Finally he looked at Spock. He could see only one pointed ear, the sharp profile, as Spock stared straight ahead.

"Yes, Commander," McCoy said through stiff lips. "I shall not bother you with my presence here again— unless ordered." He joined Scotty at the door of the lift, and the two disappeared from view. From that day on, Montgomery Scott and Leonard McCoy had appeared on the bridge of the *Enterprise* only when ordered. They did what was required of them, most efficiently, but no more.

The *Enterprise* was no longer a "happy" ship.

When the *Enterprise* reached Starbase Eleven, Spock had been ordered to report to Commodore Méndez' office. Méndez was waiting at his door when Spock arrived. "Come in, Mr. Spock."

"Yes, sir," Spock said. The two moved into the office, and the door closed behind them.

No one aboard the *Enterprise* learned exactly what happened behind that closed door. All they knew was that several hours after he beamed down, Spock returned to the *Enterprise*. Lieutenant Kyle was alone in the Transporter room when Spock materialized. He, therefore, was the first one aboard to see the result of the meeting. He'd glanced up from his controls casually when the materialization had concluded, gasped in surprise, and then had snapped to attention.

"Ah . . . welcome aboard, sir—ah—Captain Spock, sir!"

The familiar blue shirt Spock had worn for so many years was gone. He now wore command gold, and two and one-half rows of gold braid designating his rank as captain gleamed at his wrists.

"Thank you, Mr. Kyle," said Spock, stepping down from the pad. He walked quietly from the room, leaving Kyle staring dumbfoundedly after him. Spock went immediately to the bridge, stepped down to the command chair, and seated himself.

"Lieutenant Uhura, open the all-ship speakers, please," he ordered.

"Ye-yes, sir—uh—Captain," Uhura stammered. The unflappable communications officer finally blew her cool and hit the wrong button, creating a squealing feedback for two agonizing seconds.

Spock shot a dark glance at her, then spoke: "This is . . . Captain Spock. I have been ordered to take full command of the *Enterprise*. As soon as the ship has been resupplied, we will continue our regular mission. There will be no shore leave granted at this time. Spock out."

A stunned silence, broken only by the click and hum of automatic equipment, swept the giant ship. Then, throughout the ship, a hum of voices began. Groups of crewmen formed, separated, reformed.

"Did you hear that?" "Yeah! I can't believe it!" "What about the captain?" "He's the captain!" "Did you hear?"

Nurse Chapel stood rigidly in the center of Sickbay, staring at the speaker of the intercom—unable to comprehend what she'd heard.

"Well, Nurse Chapel, he finally did it," McCoy said grimly.

"Sir?"

"Ever since I've known Spock, he's said he didn't wish to be captain. Now, Jim has been missing for less than two weeks, and Spock has taken over. That blasted Vulcan!"

"But, Dr. McCoy, someone has to be . . . captain of the *Enterprise* until . . . until . . ." She couldn't bring herself to finish.

"Until Jim comes back?" McCoy finished for her. The good doctor couldn't as yet bring himself to believe James Kirk was dead. Many of the crew members were beginning to say it, but he couldn't. Not yet. The thought was too painful, too awful to accept.

"Um . . . yes, Doctor," Christine said hesitantly. She, even more than the others, had been shocked and confused by Spock's sudden change. She hadn't spoken to him since the day McCoy had stormed into Sickbay after Spock had ordered him from the bridge. He'd told her, "Your beloved Mr. Spock has reverted to his true Vulcan colors, and I'll be damned if I'll ever set foot on that bridge again without a direct order!"

Now McCoy went on: "They didn't have to make him captain; he could have commanded as first officer for now." But in his heart he knew the *Enterprise* had to have a captain. He turned away from Christine Chapel, entered his office, and closed the door.

The *Enterprise* stayed at Starbase Eleven only three days, then moved away.

They went to the planet of the Guardian of Forever, shocking McCoy and the others who had been there and decided that it must remain their secret. One report, most secret, recommended that it was too dangerous even to garrison or guard, since it held the power of changing all history. Spock beamed down alone and returned without a word. McCoy couldn't ask. Wouldn't. Routine seemed to resume.

The ship spent a lot of time near the Klingon Empire. Often they encountered Klingon ships and personnel. But the peace imposed by the Organians held. And Spock held his peace, but did not look peaceful.

A year passed.

Leonard McCoy couldn't know that, on the night that James Kirk had disappeared, Spock had awakened in his quarters, shaking with horror—his mind a whirling torrent of pain and fear. In the midst of it all, he'd seemed to hear James Kirk screaming to him for help. The feelings and sensations were identical with those he'd experienced long ago on the neutral planet of Organia, when he'd been subjected to the agony of the Klingon Mind-Sifter. That time his powerful Vulcan mind had been able to withstand the torment, and he'd suffered no permanent damage from the experience, except for the memories.

However, if James Kirk or any other Human had been subjected to even the limited amount of exposure he'd endured, the consequences would have been devastating. And on that night Spock seemed to see the same savagely urbane, smiling face of Kor, the Klingon commander they had faced there. Almost regretful at the destruction of his valiant enemy, but pursuing the war.

The sensation had faded quickly. Anyone other than Spock would have said it was a nightmare, but Spock knew better. He knew James Kirk had been taken by the Klingon, knew he'd drained Jim's mind—but not killed him.

Spock would have known that—then or later, days later, when that which would let him know had been cut off in a burst of agony, but not in death. A burst of agony and another call for help, and the old agony that had flared in the Mind-Sifter—Edith Keeler dead and lost back in time, through the Guardian, get to her, help me, Spock.

Nightmare. But not unreal. Not to be proved to Humans. But if Kor knew of the Guardian, all history lay in his hands. And in Spock's.

Jim Kirk, also. Lost, Spock believed, somewhere in time. His mind lost even further.

Spock knew that he could not think about that too closely. His friend had cried out to him for help in his agony, and he hadn't been able to respond. But help there must be.

He locked away in his mind the realization that his friend, his only real friend, James Kirk, could be to all intents and purposes a mindless vegetable—if he was still alive. Spock did what he thought was best—for himself, for Jim, and for Star Fleet: took Jim's place as commander of the *Enterprise*.

As one of the terms under which he took the cap-

taincy, he'd requested that the *Enterprise* be assigned
to the quadrant of the galaxy nearest the Klingon Empire. And he spent his time off the bridge searching
ancient archives through the library computer. The
Guardian could not or would not answer questions now.
Hopeless to try to find one man lost in all of time and
space. But one Vulcan must try.

There had been times when Spock had been tempted
to tell McCoy what he knew. However, he could never
bring himself to do so. McCoy would not have believed
him, perhaps. But if he had, how could the Human live
with the knowledge, and with the agony of hope, where
there was, in logic, no hope? How could any of the
Humans live with that?

McCoy knew nothing of this, so he went ahead, as-
sisted by Lieutenant Uhura, Mr. Sulu, and Engineer
Scott, to hold the memorial service for Captain James
Kirk. It was an emotional experience for all of them.
The service was piped to all decks.

Captain Spock had appeared on the bridge just before the time for the service and had taken over the
command chair, thus allowing Ensign Chekov to attend the ceremony. Chekov had been surprised when
Spock had told him he could go; it was the first "human" thing Spock had done since becoming captain.

The service was heard on the bridge. Several crewmen stole furtive glances at Spock during it. The only
thing they could report afterward was that when Lieutenant Uhura had broken down while singing one of
Captain Kirk's favorite songs, a twinge of something—
they couldn't say what—had flashed across the cold
Vulcan face and then was gone. Nothing more.

Jan Hamlin stopped outside the locked door leading
into Jim Doe's room. She'd looked through the small
pane set in the heavy panel and had seen him standing
by the window gazing out. As always, he was looking at
the sky.

Jan had just gone off duty; she wanted to go home,
she was tired. But the lonely figure standing motionless
drew her in. She unlocked the door and walked quietly
inside. "Jim?" she said softly, hoping not to startle him.

"It's Jan." She walked around and stood where he could see her face.

Slowly he lowered his head, and his eyes shortened their focus. A slight smile formed. "Hello, Jan." He had recognized her at once this time—quicker than usual.

She smiled brightly back. "How do you feel today, Jim?"

"I'm fine. I . . . feel . . ." He paused, as if in thought, then continued, "I think I feel well, Jan, I just can't . . . remember."

"That's all right, Jim—don't worry about it," Jan broke in hastily. "How would you like to go outside and walk under the trees?"

"Out . . . outside?" He seemed confused, and a frown formed on his face.

"Yes, Jim, I'll take you. But you must promise that you'll stay close to me and not try to run away."

"I . . . won't . . . I will not run," he said slowly.

"It's cool, Jim, get your sweater."

He moved to the bureau, took out a sweater, and shrugged himself into it. Lately he'd been doing more for himself. There had been a long period of regression following the day he'd escaped into the cellar of the hospital. For some weeks he'd been completely withdrawn. Then, one day, he'd again seemed to know her, called her Jan, and responded to the name of Jim. Since then there'd been a slow but definite improvement. He was like a child in some ways, learning how to eat by himself, how to dress and care for himself. Only once or twice had he been overcome by the wild fears that had consumed him earlier. He'd recovered more quickly each time, and Jan had again begun to hope that he might, in time, truly recover.

"Come, now, take my hand, Jim," she said, opening the door.

"No."

"What?" she said in surprise. He'd always taken her hand willingly before.

"No . . . not your . . . hand. A . . . a man . . . no . . . a woman takes a man's . . . arm when they . . . walk together," he said slowly. He bent his arm and offered it to her.

"Yes! That's right, Jim," Jan said happily, and she placed her hand through the bend of his arm as they walked slowly toward the doorway. She had to remove her hand to unlock the outer door, but once through it, she again placed her hand on his arm, and they stepped out into the brilliant sunshine.

"Out. Outside," Jim said. He smiled slightly and took a deep breath of the clear, cool air. "It's nice, Jan, a nice day." He smiled again, looking down at her.

"Yes, Jim. Come, let's go over there under the trees and walk on the grass."

"I like to walk on grass when I'm on shore leave," he said casually.

" 'Shore leave'?" Jan thought. She'd learned not to question him when he made statements like that; it seemed to confuse and frighten him when she didn't know what he meant. But "shore leave" was a military term. Navy—that was it! Her brother had been in the Navy; she'd heard him tell about going ashore on leave before ... before he'd been lost off Korea. ... He, too, had said once how good it was to walk on grass after the hard decks of ships; she was going to take a chance. "Yes, I suppose the decks do get hard, don't they, Jim?"

"Yes; of course, the floor coverings in my quarters are softer, and those in the rec rooms, but the corridors and the . . . ." He stopped and frowned again.

"Well," she said brightly, not appearing to notice, "here we are; isn't this nice? Come, Jim, let's sit here in the sun. You can lean against that big tree and rest." Soon Jim sat beside her. He put his head back and looked up into the branches above him, where the blue sky could be seen in patches through the leaves.

"Beautiful," he murmured. "Just like the sky on Omicron Ceti Three. Too bad we can't ever go back there." He smiled to himself.

"Yes, isn't it too bad we can't go back?" Jan wondered what he was talking about; it seemed so real to him.

"Well, you know, if we did, the Berthold Rays would . . . ." He stopped suddenly and looked at her. "You . . . you weren't there, Jan!" A crafty look came into his face; his voice hardened. "Why did you say that?" He took hold of her wrist and started to squeeze.

"Jim, please, let go of my wrist," Jan said quietly. Her heart was racing; he'd never tried to hurt her before. Was this some new phase? "You're hurting me, Jim." She spoke in the same quiet tone.

He looked down at her hand, which was starting to redden. He released it quickly and looked up into her eyes. "I'm . . . I'm . . . sorry . . . I wouldn't . . . hurt you, Jan." His eyes started to swim with tears.

"It's all right, Jim, I'm not hurt. Please don't cry." His emotions were always very close to the surface.

"I . . . I . . . didn't mean . . . to hurt you," he said. "Jan . . . you are . . . nice. I like you . . . Jan."

"And I like you too, Jim," she said with a laugh. Then she realized that she did in fact "like" him—that she was beginning to feel more than just a professional interest in this man. Realized, with a pang of regret, that she must not, as all the textbooks said—as all her experience in nursing had taught her—"get emotionally involved." But he was smiling at her now, and with a tiny catch in her breath she thought what a fine-looking man he was. His eyes were hazel, and he had a nice smile—when he used it. The old green sweater happened to fit him. Usually the clothes issued to the patients were shapeless and ill-fitting, but this one fit him well. She made a mental note to see if she could find something of her brother's that she could bring for him. They were about the same size. . . . "Oh, oh!" she thought. "Be careful!" Oh, well, giving him something decent to wear wouldn't be getting involved. Nobody else cared.

That was true; nobody did. No one had come forward asking about him. It wasn't fair—here he was getting better, at least a little, and she was the only one who noticed. She decided that she was going to do something about that. "Jim . . ." She took a deep breath; this might be dangerous. "Do you remember anything about the time before you came here?"

He looked startled, then puzzled. He frowned and seemed to be concentrating very hard. "Before? Before? Was I somewhere . . . somewhere else?"

"Yes, Jim, somewhere else where there was a turbo lift, where food was programmed. Can you remember?"

"Turbo . . . turbo . . . Yes! The turbo lift—it took me to . . . the bridge. Yes! The bridge." He leaped suddenly to his feet, and she scrambled up after him. "I must . . . I must get there. They . . . they need . . ." He looked quickly around. "No. I am on shore leave! Trees . . . grass. I'll have to . . . to beam up. . . ."

She saw him reach around under his sweater to a point over his right hip and fumble around at his belt. "It's gone! My communicator. It's gone!" He whirled around to her and grasped her arms. "Jan! I must find it. Help me look." He dropped to his knees beside the tree and started brushing his hands through the fallen leaves and grass. "Help me, Jan, help me!"

She sank to her knees beside him and put her arm around his shoulders. "Jim, don't—you won't find it here. It isn't here, Jim. You don't have a"—a what?—"com-communicator." Was that it? "Come, let me take you back now."

He stopped rummaging around in the grass and sank back on his knees, sitting on his heels. The motion brought him against her, and for a moment he was still. She kept her arm around him and held him tightly. She could feel him trembling and expected to see him break into tears again, as he usually did when he'd been "remembering." This time, however, he didn't. He seemed to draw comfort from her touch, and for a time the two of them knelt there quietly. At last he drew a long breath, turned his head to look into her face, and said, "It's gone again, Jan."

"What is, Jim?"

"I don't know. At times I think . . . I seem to be right on the edge of . . . remembering?" He said it as a question. "Is that it, Jan? I can't remember?"

"Yes, Jim, that's it. If only you could remember." She realized he was talking very rationally. There was an improvement—if only he didn't slip back again.

She stood up, and he followed her. For a moment he stood looking down at her. Then he raised his hands and took hold of her shoulders. She thought of the time before, in the dim passageway in the basement. "Jim," she said, wondering what was in his mind, "what is it?"

"You are a lovely woman, Jan," came the surprising answer, as he smiled gently at her.

"Thank you. It's nice of you to say that." And she realized she was blushing.

"No . . . no. It's true. You are." He smiled again and broke into a little chuckle. "And you're blushing, too." At that he laughed out loud and threw his arms about her—held her tightly to him for a couple of seconds. Then, before she realized what was happening, he kissed her, softly, gently. It seemed so natural that for a second she responded; then, remembering, she pushed away from him with a little self-conscious laugh.

"Jim! It's getting late. I must be going home." Her mind was whirling. What was she doing? She must not . . . This was wrong! But it hadn't seemed wrong, not while she'd been in his arms. It had seemed so right. He seemed so relaxed, as he stood there smiling at her.

"Really, Jim, I must go now," she said, returning his smile.

"Okay, then," he said, laughing again, "come on. I'll walk you to the door." He started moving quickly, surely toward the entrance.

The next morning, Jan Hamlin made an appointment with the hospital director. When she was admitted to his office, she set about telling him what she thought she'd learned about James Doe. That he'd been in the military, probably the Navy; that he'd traveled a lot—no, she didn't know where, the places he'd named were unfamiliar.

"He must be known somewhere," she finally burst out. "Dr. Wright, somebody must know him!"

"Miss Hamlin, we've tried. We've already checked with the military services—Army, Navy, Marines—they have no record of him. The FBI has no record of his fingerprints. Missing Persons has no record of anyone meeting his description. What more can we do?"

"Couldn't we publish his picture in the papers?"

"Miss Hamlin, what good would it do? If anyone was looking for him—"

"But maybe they think he's dead, Dr. Wright," she insisted urgently. "They may have given up looking for him."

"Well, yes—I suppose that could be the case," Wright said thoughtfully. "Tell you what, I'll call the papers and see if they will do it. I'm sure nothing will come of it. Every now and then someone's picture appears, and nothing results. Just one more forgotten patient in a mental hospital. . . . All right, I'll try."

Presently she had a thought—the clothes he was in when they brought him. Wright agreed and said that a news team would be over soon. She collected the bundle, greeted Jim, explained. He seemed to understand.

She started to help him.

"No . . . no, I can . . . I can do it."

Jan stood back. He slowly took off the shirt he had on and picked up the yellow one from the bed. He stood holding it in his hands for a moment. He traced the insignia with one finger and seemed to be lost in thought. He shook his head slightly, then, with a sudden, quick motion, thrust his arms into the sleeves and pulled the shirt over his head. His hands moved quickly to the collar and closed the opening. She hadn't noticed a zipper and wondered how he'd done it. But before she could ask, Jim had picked up the pants; then he looked up at her with a slight smile. "Turn around, Jan."

"Oh, Jim, I'm a nurse!" She laughed.

"No! I won't put them on unless . . ."

"Oh, all right." Jan turned and looked out the window. She heard a rustling behind her and smiled to herself. He must be feeling better if he were becoming modest.

Finally she heard him say "All right," and she turned back. He was sitting on the edge of the bed, pulling on the long boots. They tucked up under the legs of the pants. Again, his fingers seemed to know how to fasten them.

"There," he said, standing up. "Is that right?"

She caught her breath. He looked like a different person. He stood easily, lightly balancing on the balls of his feet. His fists were planted on his hips, and he looked . . . he looked as though this were the way he'd always dressed. Only his hair was disarranged. Jan reached into her uniform pocket and took out a comb.

"Here, Jim, comb your hair," she said, smiling at him.

"Sure." And he quickly drew it through his hair. She'd often helped him before and now stood watching him as he easily did it himself. Soon his hair was smooth, except for one stray lock that fell over his forehead as though it had a mind of its own. She'd tried before and had found that no amount of combing would make it stay in place.

"You look fine, Jim," she said happily. It was going to work. Surely someone would recognize him now. "Come along, we'll go over to Dr. Wright's office, and the photographer will take your picture."

In the office Jim became uneasy again at the reporter's talk, but finally stood quietly. The photographer raised his camera and flash and snapped the picture. Jim started at the light but didn't cringe. "Okay, one more."

"Stand still, Jim," Jan called. "He's going to take another one."

Again the flash. This time Jim didn't move.

"Good. Very good." Dr. Wright moved around his desk and spoke to Jim. "That's all for now, Jim. You may go back to your room now with Miss Hamlin. Maybe we can talk sometime."

Jim looked at the gentle-faced man. His eyebrows drew together in concentration. "Who . . . are you?" he asked.

"I'm Dr. Wright, Dr. Leonard Wright, chief of staff here."

"Dr. . . . Dr.," Jim said slowly. Then his voice rose sharply. "Dr. Leonard . . . Bones? Dr. Leonard McCoy. McCoy? No! You're not McCoy—where is he?"

"Jim." Jan hastened to his side and took his arm. "Come, let's go back. . . ."

"No!" He pulled away from her grasp and backed

away from her—from all of them. "I want to know. Where is Bones? What have you done with him? He's my chief medical officer—not you, Dr. Wright." He seemed to be completely rational; he didn't shout or cry, he just snapped out the words as though he expected an answer.

"Jim, what are you talking about?" Wright asked. If he could keep the patient talking, maybe they'd learn something important.

"If Dr. McCoy isn't here, then where's Nurse Chapel? Or Dr. M'Benga? One of them must be here."

"No, Jim," Jan said quietly. "That was the other place, remember? We talked about it yesterday." An idea struck her—he was remembering so well—maybe now was the time to ask: "What is your name? James . . . ?"

"I'm Captain James T. Kirk of the . . ." He stopped. An expression of absolute and total horror came over his face. He clutched at his head with both hands, and with a scream of pain sank to his knees. "Spock! Spock! Help me! Help me-e-e-e!"

The twentieth-century doctor, nurse, and newspapermen had no way of knowing that Captain James T. Kirk was reacting to a form of posthypnotic suggestion implanted in his mind by one of a band of aliens, extremely savage examples of a race known in the twenty-third century as Klingons. The trigger was his name and rank. The Klingons hadn't known of the diminutive "Jimmy"; Jan's use of that name had, in a way, healed part of his tortured brain—had taken him back to his childhood and had rebuilt the broken cells and nerve patterns. She'd helped, more than she'd ever know.

But now, the full force of the agony caused by the Klingon Mind-Sifter struck him again. The trigger words had set off visions of unspeakable horrors and fears that no mind could withstand, along with impressions of excruciating pain. The result was devastating. Kirk became violent; orderlies rushed into the office at Wright's call, wrestled the screaming man to the floor and into a straitjacket. He was dragged, helplessly tethered, back to his room. Nurse Hamlin, tears streaming from her eyes, was excused, and Dr. Wright escorted the newspaper people to the main entrance.

"This'll make a great story, Doe," Reporter Blair gloated. The photographer had snapped one more picture, one of the strange man who called himself "Captain James T. Kirk," struggling on the floor with three orderlies holding him down.

"I'd rather you didn't use that final picture," Wright said as the men turned to leave.

"And spoil the story?" Blair laughed. "No chance!"

The next day there was a feature article on the front page of the local paper. A headline screamed: WHO IS THIS MAN? Under it were two pictures: one full-length of a good-looking man, dressed in an odd costume. The other showed the same man thrashing around on the floor, his face drawn into a grimace of pain and horror, being forced into a straitjacket by hospital orderlies. The story accompanying the pictures played up the oddness of the man's behavior—how he called himself Captain James T. Kirk; how he'd asked for a Dr. Leonard McCoy whom he'd said was "his chief medical officer." It finished with the request that anyone knowing who this man might be should contact the hospital.

The story was picked up by the press associations and given rather wide coverage. Other reporters who tried weren't allowed to see James Kirk. He was in restraints and under sedation. His condition was as bad as when he'd first been admitted.

Several days went by—a week. No one came forward. There were the usual crank calls, but nothing that was of any value. The excitement died away. One or two news magazines carried the story then; as old news always is, the story was forgotten.

Jim Doe's name was changed to James T. Kirk in the hospital records, and his strange clothes were returned to the storage room. Everything was as it had been before.

The *Enterprise* continued her mission. Things didn't get better, but they didn't get worse, either. The crew became accustomed to its new captain, and duties were performed efficiently.

McCoy and Scott spent much of their free time together, sometimes over Scotch and brandy, mostly, as today, in a rec room over coffee, talking softly, not to be heard by the Vulcan, who was bent over a library-computer outlet in a far corner, as he always seemed to be in odd moments, even when eating. McCoy looked back from Spock and met the engineer's eyes. "Scotty, I just realized, I haven't thought about Jim Kirk in . . . in almost a week."

"Aye, Doctor, I find meself doin' that too—forgettin'. The memorial service last month seemed to put an end to my hope of ever findin' him, or hearin' of him again."

"I guess that was it," McCoy agreed moodily, staring down into his cup. He heaved a sigh. "If only we knew what'd happened. Then we could accept it."

"Aye." Scotty sipped his coffee, lost in thought.

Suddenly Spock seemed to stiffen over the computer. McCoy saw him shudder.

After a long moment Spock rose with the pose of Vulcan control and came to them. "I have just confirmed that Jim is trapped in the past," he said. "I have believed it since he vanished. A telepathic impression, not suitable for evidence. The Klingons took him and . . . used the Mind-Sifter. Learned the secret of the Guardian. I believed Jim had escaped Kor there and tried to reach Edith. I searched, beginning with periods near the 1930's. He is in the 1950's, and he is insane."

Spock closed his eyes, opened them, and stared unblinkingly at McCoy. "I have known part of this ever since the night Jim disappeared. Doctor, I heard him crying to me—for help—in my mind. I could do nothing to help him."

McCoy flared, "Why didn't you tell me?"

Spock winced ever so slightly. "You would not have believed me, Doctor."

McCoy's mouth, which had been open to shout at him again, closed. A look of sadness, of understanding compassion, crossed his craggy features. "No," he said softly. "No, I wouldn't have."

Then Spock showed them the pictures.

Much later, the door of McCoy's quarters swished open to reveal Captain Spock.

"May I talk to you, Doctor?"

"Of course, Spock. Come in," McCoy said gently.

"I regret to disturb you, Doctor. I know you need to be rested and ready for the events ahead. However, I wish to . . . to explain. . . ."

"Spock, you don't have to explain anything to me. I understand. You did what you thought best. I've told you that repeatedly."

"But still, I wish . . . I must be sure you know why I acted as I did," Spock insisted.

McCoy smiled. "Spock, we've known each other a long time. Don't you know by now that I know some things about you? Once I realized what you'd learned about Jim, when I finally got through my thick skull what it was you were living with, don't you think I understood? My God, Spock! What I can't understand is why you didn't break. I would have—I couldn't have gone on as you did. I should've known something was wrong, but I was too pigheaded to see it. Now I know you were making us all hate you so that we wouldn't think about Jim so much. I'm the one who should've come to you. I'm the one who should say 'I'm sorry.' "

"That is not necessary, Doctor. You acted as would any Human who has suffered a great loss. I knew that, I only regret that I . . ."

"Look, Spock, let's forget it. We have a big job ahead of us. Let's concentrate on that now," McCoy broke in.

"Agreed. One thing more, though . . . Bones. He may yet be dead. He might be better off if he were dead. I have told you what the Mind-Sifter can do. He has been living in primitive conditions for over a year. He could not have received proper care. I have checked and have found that the care given mental patients in those times was most limited. There is a very great chance that he has not received any care at all. If he is alive, you must prepare yourself for this: he will not be the Jim Kirk you and I once knew."

"I know that, Spock. I've known it ever since you told us those Klingons used the Mind-Sifter on him. I can face it—now. I just have to know, to know whether he is alive or dead. If he's alive, we'll bring him back and he'll receive the best care our technology can give him. If he is . . . dead, and we can prove it, we'll know it's so and can learn to accept the fact." McCoy sat quietly for a moment, lost in his thoughts; then he looked up at Spock and smiled. "Spock," he said, "I'm glad you came. I've wanted to tell you—to thank you—for not letting me transfer off the *Enterprise*. I hope we can forget this past year. I'm trying to. It's foolish for us to dwell on it."

"I agree, Doctor. It would be . . . illogical." A small smile quirked the corner of Spock's mouth.

"I thought you'd say that, Mr. Spock!" And Leonard McCoy laughed, the first time he'd done so in over a year.

The sound of the Transporter beam faded, and two figures had appeared on a quiet city street. At three A.M., the street was completely deserted.

Dr. Leonard McCoy and Ensign Pavel Chekov moved off down the dark street. The *Enterprise* was in synchronous orbit far above them. Implanted in their arms were the Subcutaneous Transponder devices that would enable them to be located and beamed back aboard without having to carry open communicators. They each had a communicator—McCoy had two— one in a secret compartment in his "doctor's bag," an antique, according to him, that had been duplicated in the *Enterprise*'s shops. A doctor of the 1950's, however, would've been quite puzzled by the contents.

They would have to contact such a doctor, go through regular channels to get Kirk out, not leave a mystery in the past. They had all the forged identity, clothes, and other odds and ends they would need. The Vulcan was thorough.

He had not even risked coming himself. The ears could scarcely be explained with the "mechanical-rice-picker" story this time. Hadn't worked too well before, either.

McCoy smiled to himself. There was just a chance that he and Jim would laugh over that one again someday.

Jan Hamlin came back from her month's vacation feeling rested, but restless.

As her duties took her through the wards and floors of the institution, she gradually became reaccustomed to the gaunt, pale faces she saw. Most of the patients couldn't eat properly and tended to be underweight. They seldom went outside during the winter months; thus many looked pale and ill.

She had almost not gone, and now went straight to the room she'd almost dreaded to return to—the room where the man who'd called himself James T. Kirk was confined. She hesitated to go in. She'd wept night after night over what had happened the day the reporters had come. She blamed herself for the whole thing. If only she hadn't asked him his name. He'd improved so much, until the awful moment when he'd said, "I am Captain James T. Kirk" and had fallen into whatever horrible nightmare those words had invoked.

She'd looked in on him once or twice before she had left, but he hadn't known her, nor responded to anything she'd said. He'd been fastened securely in a heavy straitjacket, and she hadn't been allowed to remove it. The doctors had insisted he would injure himself or someone else if he weren't restrained. In the end, she couldn't stand it, and went.

Now she drew a deep breath to steady herself and entered his room. Someone else was there with Jim—Frank Thomas; the orderly must have been transferred from another ward. If she had known . . . How could she have left?

Thomas was an ignorant, heartless sadist. Jan knew this, and she'd reported him several times for mistreating patients, but she never could prove it. He knew of her efforts and only laughed at her.

When she entered the room, Thomas was tormenting Jim, offering him water, then pulling it away.

"Frank!" Jan exclaimed. He jumped guiltily, managing to spill the water all over Jim.

"Oh, hell, Miss Hamlin! Look what you made me do," he said, all innocence.

"I saw what you were doing, Frank. Is that how you're taking care of Jim—by torturing him?"

"Miss Hamlin, what a thing to say! Why, I wouldn't harm a hair on your Superman's pretty head." He leered at her.

"Get out of here, Frank," she said in disgust.

"Why? So's you can cuddle him?" he insinuated.

She whirled on him. "Get out!"

He saw her face, and got out.

Jan didn't waste any time looking after him. She turned to Jim, who was cowering in a far corner of the room. "Jim? Jimmy? Don't be afraid. It's Jan," she said quietly, putting out her hand toward him. Her heart sank; he just stared wildly at her. She looked closely at him and gasped.

He looked terrible. When he'd been admitted, he'd weighed about one hundred and eighty pounds. He'd been tan and in generally good physical condition, in spite of his mental state.

Tears flooded Jan's eyes. Even the day the reporters had come, Jim had been looking so well. He'd been eating properly, and although he was thin, at least he wasn't too far below the norm for his height. Now Jan realized that he couldn't weigh more than 130. He was deathly pale, his face gaunt and drawn. His hair was a wild tangle, and he hadn't been shaved in days. Jan knew something had to be done or he'd be so weak that even a slight cold might prove fatal. She wondered why the doctors hadn't put him in the infirmary. Probably Thomas hadn't reported his condition.

While these thoughts flashed through her mind, she moved slowly toward Jim. He pressed ever closer into the corner, the old familiar whimper growing, panic starting to build within him. She stopped. "Jimmy, I won't hurt you. Please. Let me help." She held out her hand—palm up.

He stopped pressing into the corner. His eyes seemed to come into focus. He looked at her, at her hand, took one faltering step toward her.

"J-Jan?"

"Yes, Jimmy. Jan."

He knew her! She put out her other hand, opening her arms to him.

"Jan . . . you . . . you came back!" He took another halting step toward her. She could see a dawning of intellect in his eyes. He started moving faster. Just as he almost reached her outstretched hands, his foot, clad in its worn old slipper, skidded and slipped on the water Thomas had spilled. Jim stumbled, lost his balance, couldn't compensate because of his bound arms, and fell crashing to his knees at Jan's feet.

"Jim!" she cried, sinking down beside him, throwing her arms about him, and she cradled him to her.

"Jan?" he whimpered. "Help me?" He laid his head against her shoulder.

"Yes, Jim, yes," she crooned, rocking him slightly in her arms. He was sobbing softly, like a child, and kept saying over and over, "You came back. You came back." She didn't hear the door behind her open. She was murmuring to Jim, smoothing his hair and holding him close.

"Miss Hamlin!" a loud voice exclaimed right behind her, making her jump. Her sudden motion, and the voice, startled Jim, who cringed back in fear.

Before Jan Hamlin could turn her head, she heard another voice: "Oh, my God!"

Twisting her head around, Jan saw two men standing behind her. One was Dr. Wright, who'd spoken first. Another man, fairly tall, with dark hair beginning to turn gray and with a kindly, craggy face, was staring at her—no, at Jim! His eyes showed his shock and perhaps deeper emotion; even as she looked, a mist formed in them, dulling their blueness.

For an instant no one moved. She continued to kneel, clinging tightly to Jim, who once again was whimpering with fear. Jan began murmuring to him, "Sh-sh, Jim —they won't hurt you—I won't let them hurt you."

"Miss Hamlin," Wright said again, moving to take her arm.

"Wait just a minute, Doctor," the other man said, and came quietly to kneel down beside Jan. "Miss Hamlin," he said softly. "Please, let me speak to him."

Something in his voice, in his manner, told Jan that he meant no harm to the frightened man trembling in her arms. There was a gentle sadness in his voice, as well as a ring of authority that made her trust him. Sinking back on her heels, she released Jim, who immediately started to shrink away.

The man beside Jan reached out and put both his hands on Jim's shoulders, gripped them tightly, and said in a soft voice, "Jim. Look at me, Jim. It's Bones. I've come to take you home, Jim. I'm here—Bones. I'm here. You're safe now."

Jim's head came up slowly; he seemed to be listening; his eyes tried to focus. "Bones? Bones? Where . . . ?"

"Here, Jim. I'm right here beside you. Look at me, Jim," he said sternly, shaking him a little.

Jan drew in her breath sharply. Had she been wrong to trust this man? She put out her hand and touched his arm. "Who are you?" she asked.

He looked over his shoulder at her. "I'm his friend, Miss Hamlin, an old friend. My name is Leonard McCoy, Dr. Leonard McCoy."

She remembered something Jim had said in Wright's office. At that time, he'd confused Dr. Leonard Wright with a Dr. Leonard McCoy. He'd called out for "Bones"—just before she'd asked his name. . . . "You are Bones?"

"Yes, he calls me that."

Jan turned back to Jim, who was still trying to focus. There was a look of bewilderment on his face. His lips kept forming the word "Bones." She leaned closer to him and said, "Jim, he's here. Bones is here, Jim. Look." She put her hands on either side of his face and turned it gently toward McCoy. "Speak to him again, Doctor," she urged softly.

"Jim!"

"Bones? Bones?" Jim looked into McCoy's eyes, and recognition slowly dawned. "Bones!"

"Yes, yes, Jim. Bones. I'm here!" A huge grin lit McCoy's face.

"Oh, God," Jim breathed.

"No, not God, just me. . . ." McCoy's voice broke, his tears—of joy—clearly visible now.

"Help me, Bones," Jim said, trying to get up.

McCoy and Jan stood. Between them they assisted Jim Kirk to his feet. McCoy gasped. "What is this barbarous thing you have on him, nurse?"

"Why, it's . . . it's an ordinary straitjacket, Doctor," she said, surprised that he didn't recognize it. "But," she hurried on, "I wanted to take it off, and they wouldn't let me. . . ."

"Get it off him—now!" McCoy ordered.

Wright stepped up. "Ah—now, just a minute, Dr. McCoy. Do you really think she should?" He protested. "He's violent—he'll hurt someone."

"He'll hurt anyone?" McCoy snorted. "In his condition? Look at him—what have you been doing to him?" he flared, letting his temper get the best of him.

Wright bristled. "We've been doing the best we can —Doctor!" His voice also rose in anger.

Jim cringed, shrinking away from the anger in their voices. McCoy noticed, turned to Wright, and said, "We're frightening him. I'm sorry. I shouldn't have criticized. Please, may I have some time with him alone? Would you leave, please?"

Wright hesitated a moment, but he was a good man, though an overworked, frustrated one. He understood and bit back the retort he might have given. "All right, I'll be outside the door if you need me."

"Thank you, Doctor. Oh, will you send in Mr. Chekov, please?"

"Certainly. Coming, Miss Hamlin?"

Jan nodded and started after the administrator.

"No," cried Jim. "Jan! Don't go—don't go."

She stopped and looked at McCoy. "Please, Dr. McCoy, he seems to like having me. . . ."

"By all means, then, stay, Miss Hamlin. You can show me how to get this . . . this thing off of him." McCoy fumed.

"Certainly, Doctor," Jan said briskly, the good efficient nurse. She immediately began to undo the buckles and straps, as she'd wanted to do ever since coming into the room. She had the ugly thing off almost before Wright left the room and had turned to put it on the bed, when the door opened again to admit a young man. He looked around, a frown creasing his face; then his eyes fell on Jim, who was standing in the middle of the room rubbing his arms.

"Captain! Captain Kirk!" Chekov exclaimed.

James Kirk screamed, turned, and flung himself into the farthest corner of the room, where he tried desperately to hide, cowering down into the corner, curling his arms over his head.

Chekov stood dumbfounded, unable to move, while Jan and McCoy rushed to Jim's side.

"Nurse," McCoy cried, "what happened?"

"The young man called him 'Captain—Captain Kirk'. This always happens when he says or hears that name or the word 'Captain,'" she explained quickly.

McCoy dropped to his knees beside Jim, fumbling with the unfamiliar latch on the bag he carried. Once he had it open, he quickly snatched out an instrument, adjusted something on it, and pressed it against Jim's arm. There was a hiss, and almost immediately Jim quieted, relaxed, slumped against the wall. The suddenness of his reaction was a shock to Jan. "What did you do, Doctor?" she asked in astonishment.

"I just gave him an ordinary tranquilizer, Nurse," McCoy said, not even looking at her.

"An 'ordinary' . . . Doctor, I've never seen anything work that fast!"

McCoy looked up quickly then: he'd made a mistake! "Oh. . . . Well, yes, I guess . . . it isn't an ordinary drug, it's something I've been experimenting with, that I've had good results from," he stammered. She was still staring at him, at the hypo-spray in his hand.

"And that?" she persisted. "You injected him right through his shirt."

"Not 'injected,' Nurse. 'Pressured in'—also an experimental technique. It should be standard equipment shortly. Look,"—he changed the subject hastily, before he did any more harm—"let's get him up out of this filthy corner. Help me, please," he ordered, taking Jim's arm and helping him to his feet.

Jim Kirk was quiet now, didn't resist as they led him to the bed and sat him down on the edge.

All this time, Pavel Chekov had stood rooted just inside the door. The captain's violent reaction to his greeting had shocked him terribly. Even though he knew Kirk had been subjected to the Klingon Mind-Sifter, he had no idea he would be like this.

"Pavel, speak to Jim," McCoy ordered. "Don't use his full name, just speak quietly to him," McCoy instructed.

Chekov looked down at the man sitting there. For a moment he couldn't speak, couldn't trust his voice.

"Ah . . . yes . . . hello . . . Jim, how are you?" That's all he could think of, not much, but it served. James Kirk's head came up. He looked at Chekov's face, squinted a little to see better; then: "Mr. . . . Mr. Chekov?"

"Yessir, it's me." Pavel didn't dare say more, but he was thrilled to see a slow smile spread over the captain's face.

"Are you going to navigate us back to the *Enterprise*—back home, Chekov?"

Pavel shot a look at McCoy, who nodded.

"Yessir, I'll lay in the course—as soon as Dr. McCoy says you are ready," he said with a happy grin.

"Good . . . good," Kirk said. "Stand by, Ensign."

"Aye, aye, sir."

Jan Hamlin was looking back and forth from one man to the other. Of course, she had no idea what they were talking about, hadn't heard McCoy telling Wright about the patient's "obsession with the Navy." McCoy saw her confusion and explained in a few brief words.

"Oh," she said, "I see. That explains . . ."

"Yes, I thought it would," McCoy replied.

Kirk was sitting quietly between them on the edge of the bed, smiling to himself, completely relaxed. McCoy's shot had done more for him than all the treatments he'd received since he'd been brought to the hospital.

Now McCoy said to Jan, "I'd like to examine him, Nurse." He paused, looking down at the bed for the first time. "Nurse! Look at this bed. It . . . it's filthy!"

His gentle face showed his outrage. "So this is how you've been taking care of him?"

"Doctor . . . please. I've been away. I entered this room only about five minutes before you did. I was shocked, too. The orderly who was on duty here isn't very conscientious. I'm having him removed from this floor. He . . . he isn't a very good worker, Doctor. . . ."

"Yes, so I see. Look at his clothes—is this how patients are dressed here?"

"Yes, Doctor." Jan's face started to redden. Obviously this man came from a new or private hospital where good help could be hired, clean new clothing provided.

"Barbarous!" McCoy snapped. "Can you get me a clean cover for this bed, and clean clothes for him?"

"Of course, Doctor." Jan started away, then paused. "Are you planning to take him away with you?"

"Just as soon as I can."

"Do you want the things he was wearing when he came here? He was wearing strange clothes. . . ."

"Ah, yes—that would be a gold shirt, black pants, and black boots?"

"Yes."

"Well . . . yes." McCoy knew that Kirk's uniform was out of place, out of time here. "That would be fine. He would want to take them with him."

Jan Hamlin hurried away. As she left, Dr. Wright stepped into the room. "Everything all right, Doctor?" he asked.

"I've seen cleaner hospital rooms—Doctor!" McCoy snapped. But he relented a little, seeing the man's weary knowledge of the shortcomings. Good man. Tough spot.

They discussed arrangements for taking the patient to a private clinic. Wright offered to expedite the paperwork and took Chekov with him.

Jan came back as McCoy finished with the scanner and another hypo-spray shot, but he didn't think she had seen the scanner. Nor could she know what was in the shot—more relaxant, several drugs that Jan Hamlin would never hear of, vitamin concentrates and tissue rejuvenators that wouldn't be invented for years to come. The relaxant made Jim drowsy, but he rallied enough to make her turn her back while McCoy helped him with the clothes. Then he dozed, looking small in the captain's clothes.

"We'll let him rest for a while, Nurse," McCoy said.

Jan stood looking down at Jim. Everything had happened so quickly. Now it suddenly struck her: he would be gone soon. This doctor would take him away. She was glad Jim would finally be cared for properly, but . . . she wouldn't see him again, and . . . it hurt. She turned to McCoy. "Dr. McCoy, please, can I go with you and help take care of him? I have nothing to keep me here, no family, no . . . nothing. You'll need someone on the journey."

McCoy was smiling but shaking his head. "No. Thank you, Nurse, but, no. Mr. Chekov and I will manage nicely. There's no need—"

"But, Doctor! At least tell me where you're going. He likes me—I could come to see him. . . . I . . . I think I've helped him. . . . Please." Her voice broke a little, and her eyes filled with tears.

McCoy looked closely at her and said, a bit brusquely, "Nurse Hamlin—you're not being very professional about this."

Jan sank down on her knees beside the bed and gently took Jim's hand in hers. She looked up at McCoy. "I don't feel very professional, Doctor. I'm sorry. I didn't mean . . . I didn't intend to . . . to . . ." She started to cry softly.

McCoy understood. "Miss Hamlin, you love him, don't you?" he asked gently.

"Yes—oh, yes." Jan sobbed, his sympathy destroying all her reserve. "Please, please, Dr. McCoy. Let me go with you!"

"I only wish I could," McCoy said honestly, "but . . ."

"I'll go anywhere, travel any distance. Please!" Her voice was rising; she seemed to be getting a little hysterical.

McCoy stood and moved over to sit on the edge of the bed. Jim moved restlessly. "Miss Hamlin, you could never travel far enough to get where we're going. I'm sorry, it's impossible." His voice, too, had risen; he had to reach her over her sobs.

Jim began to moan, to stir restlessly. McCoy put his hand on Jim's shoulder to quiet him, but he began to murmur, to mutter. At first, the words were unintelligible, just sounds. Suddenly and very clearly: "Spock! Help me, Spock! The Klingons . . . they . . . they want . . . Spock! They'll take . . . take over Earth! I can't—I must not tell them . . . It . . . it hurts—they'll change history, Spock! The pain! Oh, God! I can't—I can't stand . . . Spock! Help me!" He started up, struggling against McCoy's restraining hand, as his voice began to rise toward a scream. McCoy reached into his bag, snatched out his scanner and ran it over Jim's body, took a fast reading, then quickly used the hypo-spray again. Jim fell back limply, and again seemed to be in a deep sleep.

"Damn those Klingon monsters!" McCoy muttered. "As soon as we get back in space, I'll . . ." He broke off, suddenly aware of what he was saying, wishing he could choke the words back. But it was too late. Jan Hamlin was staring wide-eyed at him, at the scanner and hypo-spray in his hands, at Jim.

She stood up and moved away from the bed, fear and panic growing in her expression. "I know—I know!" she blurted.

"What do you know?" McCoy challenged.

"You . . . he—both of you—and that other man. Jim wasn't talking about our Navy. . . . You aren't a real doctor. Those things you're using—there's nothing like that around here, maybe not on all of Earth! I've read about those . . . those UFO's everybody's been seeing. Either I'm going insane, or else . . . or else you're . . ." Her eyes were becoming wild; she looked as though she were going to scream.

McCoy cursed himself silently. If he'd kept silent, hadn't used his scanner, he could have said Jim was delirious. But, no, he himself had also talked about Klingons, space, and spaceships. He had to do something; the nurse was moving toward the door. He moved quickly after her, took her arm, even as she shrank away from him.

"Miss Hamlin, please, don't be afraid. Listen to me!" Again, the ring of authority in his voice reached her. She stopped, turned to look at him.

"I'll tell you. . . . Only, please try to understand. We're not here to hurt you. You're right. Jim, Pavel, and I aren't from here, from . . . now. We're from your future." He paused, giving her a chance to comprehend what he was saying.

"From . . . from the . . . future? What . . . ? How . . . ?"

"Jan, I can't explain it to you, you couldn't understand, but does that make us monsters in your eyes? Look at me. Am I so different from other men you know? Look at Jim. You said before that you love him. Does it matter when he was born? I know you're frightened. I don't blame you, but think, Jan. What is there to be frightened of?" McCoy continued to smile gently. She seemed calmed, was listening to him, looking from him to Jim and back again.

"No . . . no—I guess. But I don't understand. How . . . ?"

"Of course you don't, Jan." McCoy chuckled. "It's hard for me to understand, and I'm supposed to know how we did it. Pavel and I—and others—have been looking for James Kirk for a long time. I can't tell you the details, you couldn't comprehend, but know this much: Jim is a very important man, so important that hundreds of lives were risked by our coming back through time to find him. Now, we have to take him back, back to his own time, to his own life. He will be cured. In his time—our time—there is only a tiny handful of people who can't be cured, and even they are helped and cared for by the finest doctors in the galaxy."

" 'The galaxy'?" she asked, her eyes widening.

"Yes, Jan, the galaxy. Man has reached the stars in James Kirk's time, in my time." Now he'd really done it! But at least she was listening to him and not running screaming down the halls. He continued. "I shouldn't tell you these things, Jan. I shouldn't take the risk of changing history by telling you. You say you love Jim Kirk?"

She hesitated. He knew she was weighing her love

against this new, awesome knowledge. She moved slowly back to the side of James Kirk's bed and stood looking down at him. Could she love a man who was alien to her, to all she knew? He hadn't changed. He was still the helpless, sick man she'd had to care for so long. His arm was hanging down over the side of the bed. She stooped and took his hand, gently lifting it back onto the blanket. "Yes," she said deliberately. "I still love him. What you've told me makes no difference."

"Then you must promise me that you will never tell anyone what I've told you today. For his sake, you must let him go, and protect our secret," McCoy said sternly.

She turned to look at him, a light of hope in her eyes. "Take me with you! You say you'll take him back. Take me, too. Dr. McCoy, please! I'll go . . . anywhere, do anything, just to be with him."

"No. I doubt if you could ever adjust to our time; just as he couldn't adjust to yours. Jim has his own life to lead, Miss Hamlin."

"Is . . . is he married? Is there someone else?"

McCoy smiled ruefully. "No, he isn't married, and there isn't anyone—no woman. He has another . . . interest, you could say, a love—his career, his . . ." He stopped. He'd said too much, far too much, already.

Jan began to cry softly. She knelt down beside Jim, took up his hand, and pressed it to her cheek.

McCoy sighed. He'd done all he could. He would have to talk to Spock.

They had wakened Jim, rounded up Chekov, told Wright a car would call for them, led a quiet, bemused Jim out across the grounds to a grove of trees.

Jan had held up, but now she burst very quietly into tears. She tried to stifle her sobs. She turned away and seemed about to leave. Jim held tightly to her arm. "Don't go, Jan. Please. You can't leave me. What will I do without you?"

McCoy stepped forward. "Jim, listen to me. Jan shouldn't come with us. Think, Jim!"

"No! I won't go away and leave Jan. Why can't she come with us?"

McCoy realized that Kirk probably didn't realize they were "back in time." He knew that if he tried to explain it to Jim now, he would become more confused than he already was.

"Wait a minute, Jim," the doctor said softly. "Let's talk to Spock. He'll know what to do."

"Spock—of course! But . . . where is he, Bones?" Kirk looked around. "Spock isn't here. . . ."

"He's on the *Enterprise*, Jim. I'll call him; you stand right there with Jan. Miss Hamlin, please, take his hand. I don't know what will happen when he hears Spock's voice," he said quickly, drawing out his communicator.

"Who . . . who is Spock?" Jan asked. "And . . . what is that?" indicating the communicator.

"Spock is . . . a friend, and this is a . . . kind of radio," he explained, flipping up the grid. "McCoy to *Enterprise*. Come in, Spock."

"Spock here, Doctor. Have you found . . . ?"

"We have. He's right here beside me."

"Are you prepared to beam up, Doctor?"

"Ah, well, almost, Spock, but we have a problem here. I don't really know how to solve it. There's a young woman—a nurse. . . . Through my stupidity, she's discovered who and what we are. She's standing right here with us; she loves him, and Jim won't leave her!"

"I am coming down. . . ."

"Spock! Do you think that's wise?"

"Necessary, Doctor. Are you out of sight?"

"Yes," McCoy conceded morosely. He tried not to let the worry he felt creep into his voice—worry about what Spock's arrival would do to Kirk. He'd find that out soon enough—the sound of the Transporter beam was beginning to build. . . .

Jan swung around at the sound, in time to see the sparkle of materialization begin. She stood transfixed, watching a figure grow, build, and solidify into a man —dressed in the same type of clothing that she'd seen on James Kirk. She felt Jim's hand tighten on hers; it began to hurt.

For a moment his eyes widened, as if in astonished greeting of a familiar shape, then narrowed, as if in some unreadable agony.

"Jim . . . Jim! Please, you're hurting me." She tried to pull her hand away, but he wouldn't let go. She looked up at his face. It was twisted into an expression of anger—of rage! "Jim! What is it?"

"My shirt!" Kirk growled, starting toward Spock and McCoy, dragging Jan along with him.

"Dr. McCoy!" Jan cried.

McCoy and Spock looked up and saw James Kirk rushing at them, uncontrollable fury written in every move.

"Jim, stop!" McCoy shouted.

"Why is he wearing my shirt?" Kirk cried. Letting go of Jan, he threw himself bodily at Spock, pounding at him and tearing at Spock's gold uniform shirt.

Spock easily warded off the blows, caught Kirk's hands, and held them. "Jim, stop it," he said softly.

"Why are you wearing my shirt?" Kirk shouted. "You . . . gave me up. I'm not dead. I'm . . . I'm the captain!" The agony hit him again. Kirk screamed and sank to his knees, the old familiar look of unbearable horror on his face.

Spock bent. Placing his long fingers on Kirk's shoulder, he pressed the one spot known only to Vulcans. James Kirk slumped. Spock caught him, took him bodily in his arms, and lifted him up—holding him as one would a child.

Jan Hamlin stood staring for a moment, then, looking up at Spock, gasped, "What did you do to him?"

Spock turned to look at her, and it was then that she noticed, saw the "difference," knew that this . . . person who stood before her was different, was alien to her understanding. She gasped again and turned pale.

McCoy quickly stepped to her side and slipped one arm around her, steadying her. "Don't faint on us, Miss Hamlin. Jim's all right; he isn't hurt. Spock just . . . well, put him to sleep. He'll come out of it in a few minutes." He spoke quietly while Jan regained her composure. She looked up at Spock again, in time to see an expression of profound sadness cross the face of the tall, thin, odd-looking man holding Jim easily in his arms—an expression that quickly vanished, to be replaced by a mask of nonemotion when he saw her looking at him.

McCoy stripped off his overcoat and spread it on the ground. Spock laid Kirk down on the coat, and Pavel used his own to cover the silent figure. Spock then straightened up and turned toward Jan Hamlin, who shrank a little from his intense gaze.

"Miss Hamlin," he said quietly, "Dr. McCoy has told me that you love James Kirk. Is that correct?"

"Yes . . . yes. I do," she said firmly, her chin raised in defiance—of him and of her fear.

"I believe you do, Miss Hamlin. I also understand that you know about us—where and when we are from?" His eyes seemed to be boring into her, as though this strange being was seeing behind the mask of her face, reading her inner self.

Jan was frightened, but her love for Jim gave her strength to stand her ground—though all she wanted to do was run, far away from whatever, or whoever, this calm, quiet, but relentless being was.

His quiet, deep voice continued. "Miss Hamlin. Please do not be frightened. James Kirk is my friend. I can understand what he means to you; it is regrettable that you and he are from different times. In his own time, he is a lonely man. He needs . . . love, needs someone who cares, but his position as a captain in the Federation Star Fleet denies him the right to give himself fully to any woman."

Spock paused, and Leonard McCoy shot a wondering look at him. He'd never heard Spock talk like this before. But he remained silent; he was sure Spock had a reason for talking like this, for telling Jan Hamlin even more about the future than what she'd already learned.

"Then, if he's so lonely, take me with you! I could . . ." She stopped when he shook his head.

"No. We cannot, for several reasons. It is highly unlikely that you would be happy in our time. You would be . . . out of place. . . ."

"I could learn! Oh, please!"

"Yes, but . . ." Spock shook his head again. "Our reason is that taking you could change our future. Even he might cease to exist. But you, also, must have a reason. Miss Hamlin, has it occurred to you that Jim probably does not love you?"

She winced. That had hurt!

"He . . . he likes me. He says he doesn't want me to leave him."

"That is not James T. Kirk talking, Miss Hamlin. That is a voice from a man with a sick mind—an incredibly hurt and tortured mind. You have been kind to him; you have tended and cared for him. From what I understand, you are unusual in that you care for your patients. This is to your credit. If James Kirk recovers—and I have reason to believe that he will—he will be ever grateful to you, but . . . would gratitude be enough? He might come to resent you, for he would be responsible for you—a woman out of touch with her own reality. Do you understand? If you really love him, you must give him up. You must forget James Kirk and all that you have learned about him, about us, and about the future."

"How can I? I can't forget him, or you, or Dr. McCoy, or that other man—all I've seen and heard today!" she cried.

"I can help you . . . forget," Spock said quietly, reluctantly, almost as though the words had been forced from his lips.

"Wh-what do you mean?" She was frightened again; did he mean to kill her? She drew away from him.

"Miss Hamlin. I will not hurt you. Dr. McCoy, would you please assure her that the mind-meld could not possibly injure her?" Spock said, turning to McCoy.

The doctor smiled gently at Jan Hamlin and took her hand in his. "Jan, I know you're frightened. I would be, too, in your position. Please believe me when I tell you that Mr. Spock is the least violent, most gentle person I know, in spite of his strange appearance—and even I can't get used to that!" His eyes sparkled with what to Jan seemed an inner glee, a private joke. "Trust him; trust us. I'm sure you know what Jim means to us; we've both told you he's our friend. We certainly wouldn't harm someone to whom we owe so much—someone who has cared for our friend.

"What Mr. Spock proposes is called a mind-meld. I've experienced it several times. So has Jim. It's saved our sanity and our lives many times. Let Spock help you. It won't hurt. All he'll do is place his hand on your forehead. That's all—believe me."

His quiet words had been reassuring to Jan. She turned back to Spock. "Do you really think this will help Jim?"

"Yes, Miss Hamlin. It will, and you as well." The deep, quiet voice was reassurance in itself.

"Well . . ." Jan turned and looked down at Jim, who lay, as if in sleep, on the ground at their feet. She felt a rush of love for the helpless man; then a thought crept unbidden into her mind: was it "love"? Or was it . . . pity? A type of love a mother would have for a child that depended upon her? Could that be it? No . . . no! She remembered again the time in the fall, when he'd held her for a fleeting moment as a man held a woman he loved, his kiss—that had been real love she'd felt then, whether he did or not.

She bent down and drew the coat more tightly over him, touched his cheek gently with her fingers. Then, drawing a deep breath, she stood again and said, "What do I have to do, Mr. Spock?"

"Nothing, Miss Hamlin. I shall do it all. Just let your mind go as blank as you can. Relax. Do not fear me. However, I have one question: Do you wish to remember your feelings for James Kirk, your experiences with him as a patient? Or do you want all of that removed from your memory, along with the knowledge that you have received of the future?"

"Can you do that?"

"Yes, I believe so."

"Then, please, let me remember him."

"As you wish. Do not fear me now. I am going to place my hand on your forehead. Please relax; do not be afraid. . . ." He could feel her tremble as his long fingers pressed gently against her. He closed his eyes.

Jan Hamlin felt very little. A calmness seemed to flow over her mind; the tension and strain of the day ebbed from her. She felt a relief. Something—something that had bothered her—was drawn away. She could stop worrying about Jim now; he would be fine. That kind Dr. McCoy would care for him; he'd be all right.

Jan walked slowly back into the hospital. She'd miss Jim; maybe she'd be able to look in on him at that clinic. . . . She entered the big doors of the hospital and went back to helping people. She didn't hear the hum that sounded briefly behind the great old trees on the hospital lawn. . . .

Commander Scott had the con. He was beginning to think that he had been born in the command chair and would get old there.

His engines were feeling neglected, and he was happy. Irritated but happy. All this charging around at Warp seven and eight, and he didn't really know what was happening. Slingshot effect back through time, then to Starbase Eleven, then the Guardian planet, and back to Starbase Eleven.

Scott still shuddered at the memory of the pitifully thin, almost unrecognizable form he'd seen cradled in Spock's arms when the landing party had materialized. Scott had cleared the halls leading to Sickbay. He'd told no one what he'd seen; neither had McCoy or Chekov.

Only McCoy and Spock had seen Kirk after they whisked him into seclusion.

Spock kept his thoughts to himself. Scott knew that he'd spent most of the time the *Enterprise* was traveling to the Starbase at Kirk's side, but that was all he knew. McCoy had put a little meat on Kirk's bones before they beamed him to the Base hospital. He looked more peaceful, but extremely withdrawn, still permitting Spock to carry him through the cleared halls.

McCoy had come back from the Starbase with Spock, and Scott could hardly credit that either had

been pried away from Jim. But they had beamed to the Guardian planet together, and returned with the look of dubious satisfaction of men concluding that half a loaf is better than none.

McCoy had been as closemouthed as Spock, and Scott had finally given up on him.

Plainly the two would not rest until the captain was well, if he ever was. But the mood of the ship had lightened. He was alive. Impossible to believe that anything could keep James Kirk down for long.

And now Spock had beamed down, an hour ago, to Méndez's office and the Base hospital.

Likely the Vulcan would come back only with the report that they must go on about their business, wait, and hope. Likely the captain couldn't even have visitors.

Scott sighed. A man could hope.

Suddenly Uhura spoke.

"Mr. Scott. I'm receiving a message from Commodore Méndez. He orders you to prepare to receive the captain aboard." Her eyes widened. "Mr. Scott! He requests that you have an honor guard present and that you, Dr. McCoy, and . . . Mr. Sulu, Mr. Chekov, and I attend!"

Scott felt his own eyes widening with a wild guess. "It couldna be . . ." But he caught himself beaming from ear to ear. "Well, then—what are we waitin' for?" He pulled up long enough to say, "Mr. Riley, see to it. You have the con." Then he cheerfully gathered up Uhura and raced for the turbo-lift.

Minutes later the Transporter hummed, and two figures started to solidify in the beams. Lieutenant Josephs, head of the honor guard, sounded his boatswain's pipe, piping the captain aboard, but the piping ended in a sudden squawk when Josephs' eyes focused on the men standing before him—Captain James T. Kirk, and beside him, dressed in his old familiar blue science uniform, Commander Spock!

For a couple of seconds no one moved, no one spoke. Then, a broad grin spreading over his face, James Kirk stepped down from the Transporter and said, "Isn't anybody going to say 'Welcome aboard'?"

There was a very undignified welcoming-aboard ceremony. Backs were pounded, hands were clasped; Uhura gave and received kisses; tears, cheers, and shouts of welcome echoed throughout the Transporter room, leaked out into the quiet corridors; heads turned, bodies followed. Word spread like lightning throughout the great ship: "Captain Kirk is back!"

Many hours later, James Kirk, Leonard McCoy, and Mr. Spock sat relaxed in Kirk's quarters, a bottle of Saurian brandy on the desk. Even Spock had taken a small glass in honor of the occasion.

Kirk had toured the entire ship, greeting everyone he knew and meeting those he didn't—replacements who'd come aboard while Spock was captain. One or two of these wondered what all the shouting was about. After the new—to them—captain moved on, they were told in long and careful detail by the old hands.

It had been a very emotional day for Kirk. Now he was exhausted. He lay back in his chair and luxuriated in the quiet and familiarity of his quarters. "Well, Bones, Spock," he said. "It's been a long time. I never thought I'd ever see this place again."

"Jim," McCoy said, "you don't have to answer if you'd rather not, but I've been wondering. . . . How much of what happened do you remember?"

"Some of it, Bones. Funny thing—I remember very clearly how it all began. It's been—what?—almost two years? God!" He paused, then continued. "I remember that girl, a pretty little thing. Somehow, I found myself taking her to dinner; we danced—I remember I'd had a couple of drinks. I remember getting into a cab. Must have passed out in that cab. . . ."

"Probably drugged."

"Yes, could be. Anyway, the next thing I knew, I woke up on a Klingon ship—Kor said it could still be a glorious war. Sort of . . . a private war. Tried to question me. When I refused, he got rough. Gave me a choice: tell, or he'd use the Mind-Sifter. I didn't tell." Kirk took a long drink from his glass and sat looking at it for a while.

"After that, well . . . I remember snatches of things. Beaming down with him to the Guardian. Thinking of

Edith, Spock, you. Breaking away from him and jumping. Looked like about the right time. Then, very little.
I remember a big building, I remember someone who
helped me—a girl . . . woman, I guess, who was gentle
and kind."

"That was the nurse we met, Nurse Hamlin," McCoy
informed him.

"Yes. I remember . . . Jan. Hamlin? Was that her
name? Funny, I don't remember that. Guess I never
knew it," he mused. "She was . . . good to me. I wish I
could have thanked her. I think I could have . . ." He
sighed. "But now it's too late." He stopped speaking
and seemed lost in thought.

McCoy glanced at Spock and moved restlessly in
his chair. He cleared his throat noisily and said, "I'm
sorry, Jim. I didn't mean to bring it all back to you."

Kirk smiled quietly at him. "That's all right, Bones.
Most of this is in my medical records. You'll get copies of them. The doctors went over and over it with me.
They said it was better for me to remember what I
could, otherwise more than a year of my life would be
gone." He refilled his glass, offered more to Spock, who
shook his head, gave McCoy a refill, and once again
leaned back in his chair. "Spock, you think it will be
all right about the Guardian . . . Kor?"

"I achieved a certain rapport with the Guardian,"
Spock said, "and the doctor helped in talking to it.
When it understood what had been done to you, it
understood that some beings are not like its makers. It
will not permit itself to be properly garrisoned and
guarded against the Klingons. But it will permit a small
scientific party dedicated to historical research. I believe that, in a curious way, it wants . . . company."

Kirk smiled gently. "Loneliness is not exclusively a
Human emotion."

"No," Spock said very quietly. His face set again.
"We may pay for the Guardian's loneliness with acci-
dents that could change history. Nor do I care to have
Kor running loose. However, he seems to be acting on
his own. A protest to the Empire and the Organians
may be of use."

McCoy decided to change the subject. Kirk was becoming a little too quiet. And Spock might say too much. He turned to Spock. "You could've knocked me over with a feather when I saw you standing there beside Jim in your blue science uniform, Spock," he said, awaiting the inevitable response.

"Why should I attempt to strike you down with the horny epidermal outgrowth of a bird, Dr. McCoy?" Spock asked calmly, an eyebrow climbing into his hair.

"Why, you pointy-eared computer!" McCoy flared. "You know what I meant!"

"Then why did you not say what you meant, Doctor?"

"I *did* say what I meant!" McCoy sputtered.

James Kirk lay back in his chair and howled. He choked and sputtered and laughed until the tears came into his eyes. McCoy and Spock turned to him.

"Ah . . . Jim," McCoy said; then, louder, "Jim! What's wrong?"

"Oh . . . ha . . . oh, my . . . ho, oh, Bones! Spock!" Kirk sat up and wiped his eyes. "Now I know I'm home. You two idiots!" He went off into another spasm of laughter.

McCoy grinned, turned to Spock, and winked. A slight quirk lifted the corner of Spock's mouth—for him, a broad grin. It was the first time since James Kirk had disappeared that the two of them had entered into one of their famous "arguments."

McCoy turned back to Kirk and said simply, "We're home, too, Jim." Then, to Spock, "Would you tell me, Spock? I heard you announce to the crew that Jim was in command again, but why were you . . . ah . . . well, demoted?"

"I was not demoted, Doctor, because I was never really promoted."

"But . . . but, you were the captain. You wore the stripes; the title was yours."

"In name only, Doctor. That was the understanding under which I took over command of the *Enterprise* —until the day that Jim came back."

"You mean they didn't even offer . . . ?" Surprise silenced him effectively.

"Yes, but I have told you many times, I do not . . ."

" '. . . wish to command.' I know. But lord! Spock, you've been in command for almost two years!"

"If I were a Human, I would say that I 'disliked' it for two years, Doctor. No. I am quite . . . content to be what I am, science officer and second-in-command to Captain James Kirk."

"Yes, but . . . Look, Spock, why didn't . . . ?"

The intercom on the desk bleeped, and Kirk leaned over to activate it. "Kirk here."

"Captain, this is Nurse Chapel. Is Dr. McCoy with you?"

"Right here, Miss Chapel. Bones?"

"What is it, Nurse?"

"Doctor, Ensign Thomas of Engineering slipped on a ladder. . . . They think his leg is broken."

"I'll be right there." McCoy snapped off the speaker and got up to leave. "No rest for the weary. Thanks for the brandy, Captain." He walked to the door, then looked back. "Glad you're back with us, Jim." He smiled, then left.

Spock stood up. "I, too, must leave, Captain. I have some things—"

"Spock, stay a minute more, please," Kirk said. "Sit down."

"Yes, sir." Spock reseated himself.

"This is the first minute we've had alone. I want to thank you," Kirk said simply.

"Captain, you do not owe me any thanks. I did what was necessary."

"No, Spock. You did much more. Commodore Méndez told me how you . . . you practically begged him for the permissions to search for me, to go to the Guardian, the Klingons—to bring the *Enterprise* back in time. Told him you'd resign—or pull another stunt like Talos IV. Now, for God's sake! Don't get embarrassed." A slow tinge of green had started to spread across Spock's face.

"Sir! Embarrassment is a Human emotion."

"Sure, I know. So why are you turning green?" Kirk chuckled softly and continued. "Look, my friend, it's time you and I stopped fooling ourselves. I know you have emotions, you know I know, so why not admit it? At least, in here"—Kirk smiled—"I promise not to tell McCoy."

Spock didn't speak for a moment. He seemed to be struggling with himself; then he looked into Kirk's eyes and smiled ever so slightly as he said, "Captain . . . Jim. I am what I am. I cannot change."

Kirk didn't insist. Even this much was a great concession. "I know, Spock. I hope you don't change—too much." He paused for a minute; then: "When sanity began to filter back to me, finally, in that place I was in, I remember thinking of you, Spock. It was one of the first realities I remember. Somewhere there was a . . . a friend I called 'Spock.' Where, I didn't know, but somewhere. Then, when you did come, I acted so . . ." Kirk stopped, his turn to be embarrassed.

"Jim, that was not you—that was the Mind-Sifter," Spock said gently.

"Yeah, I suppose so." Kirk finished his drink and pushed the glass aside. "But why did you not give up? Why throw the book at Méndez on an impossible chance?"

"I knew Kor had you, but Méndez, at first, would not—"

"You *knew?*" Kirk broke in.

"Yes, Jim. I . . . heard you cry out to me when the Mind-Sifter's force hit you."

"I . . . I didn't know," Kirk said. "I . . . tried not to weaken, but . . ."

"Jim, I have also been subjected to the agony of the Mind-Sifter. I know what it can do. You could not help yourself," Spock said, compassion for what James Kirk had endured showing clearly in his eyes.

For a time, silence fell between them, as each remembered his separate hell; then Kirk drew a shuddering breath. "I am thankful you heard me, although I couldn't hope you would."

"I tried to tell Méndez," Spock explained. "He did not believe me. He thought you were dead, Jim. He offered me command of the *Enterprise*—as captain. I considered resigning, but I needed the ship, and he finally gambled with me. Said he'd seen me go off on my own before. It would be safer. I took the command, under the conditions you heard me explain to Dr. McCoy." He sighed. "I told McCoy and Scott when I had evidence. Interesting—they believed me before they saw it."

Kirk leaned back in his chair and smiled, "Well, as long as you found me!" A thought struck him. "Spock, this idea that you could read my mind over a vast distance—what does it mean?"

"Does the thought disturb you, Jim?"

"I . . . don't know. . . . Do you . . . ? Can you 'read' me all the time?"

"No, Jim. Very seldom. Not unless I am in physical contact with you, as in the mind-meld. Nor would I if I could, for it would be an invasion of . . . No, it must have been the intense agony of the Mind-Sifter, your great need. . . ." Spock hesitated.

"My great need for your help, my friend," Kirk added quietly. "It seems I always turn to you when I need help."

"As I have turned to you, Jim. It is because we . . . we need each other that our minds are drawn together."

"Well, let's hope the occasion doesn't arise too often," Kirk said. "Anyway, I appreciate your staking your career to search for me."

"Captain, it was only my wish that Star Fleet would not lose the services of a fine officer."

"Shut up, Spock! I don't believe you." Kirk grinned at him.

"Sir?"

"Never mind. I'm grateful. From what Méndez told me, everyone else gave up—even McCoy."

"But only after all searching had failed, Jim," Spock broke in quickly. "McCoy was the last to lose hope." Kirk realized that Spock was actually defending the doctor.

"Yes, I'm sure of that. Well, I don't feel any resentment. I probably would have given up, too. Still . . . thank you."

Spock nodded slightly, accepting what Kirk had said. "Just one more thing, Spock." Kirk straightened in his chair. "The doctors told me what you did after you brought me back, how you used the mind-meld to erase the fears my name triggered in my mind, how you took that into your own mind and conquered it. I can never repay—"

"Jim, please. Do not say more. I did what was necessary. I know how to overcome the effects of the Mind-Sifter. You did not, you *could* not." He stood then, and Kirk did too, stretching languidly. He was tired, but it felt good. He'd rested so darn much in the hospital, regaining his strength and health; they'd never let him get tired.

"I understand we will resume our mission now, Captain?" Spock asked.

"Just as soon as we're refueled and restocked, Spock. Then, it's back to the old grind."

" 'Back to' . . . ?"

"Just one of my old Human expressions." Kirk laughed. "By now, you should know I'm full of them."

"Yes, Captain, you do seem to have one to fit every occasion. There is one, however, that I believe fits this occasion," Spock said solemnly.

"And what is that?"

" 'Welcome home,' Jim. Welcome home!"

Sonnet from the Vulcan: Omicron Ceti Three

by *Shirley Meech*

I thought the memory of you was gone—
I thought it buried underneath the years.
But now it rises, bright as Vulcan dawn,
And I remember you, and Earth, and tears.

Your tears were falling like the rains of Earth;
You were the storms and roses of Earth's spring.
You could not know that, almost from my birth
The rites of Vulcan bound me to T'Pring.

I could not break those ties; I had no choice—
Returned to space, left you and Earth behind.
But still I heard the echo of your voice,
Found rain and wind and roses in my mind.

You told me that you loved me, and you cried.
I said I had no feelings. And I lied.

ABOUT THE EDITORS

SONDRA MARSHAK and MYRNA CULBREATH are a new writing and editing "team" whose efforts in the past year and a half have centered around "Star Trek." Sondra Marshak is one of the co-authors of *Star Trek Lives!*, a recent collection of notes and anecdotes concerning the creators, actors, fans, conventions, and writers of "Star Trek." She and Myrna Culbreath, founder of the Culbreath Schools in Colorado and editor of *The Fire Bringer*, have produced two television specials on "Star Trek," and have begun work on forthcoming books with Gene Roddenberry, William Shatner, and Nichelle Nichols. Sondra and Myrna have been in great demand as guest speakers at various "Star Trek" conventions, and have spent a lot of time working with both professional and aspiring writers on their "Star Trek" and other fiction. Sondra and Myrna were brought together by an article of Myrna's, "The Spock Premise." Myrna moved from Colorado Springs to Baton Rouge, Louisiana, where Sondra lives with her husband, Alan, a professor of electrical engineering at Louisiana State University; their young son, Jerry; and her mother, Mrs. Anna Hassan. Sondra's background includes a B.A. and an M.A. in history, while Myrna has a B.A. in philosophy and psychology.